'Featuring wine in coffee mugs, dinner parties with ulterior motives, and Naomi and Oliver being (almost) caught with their pants down, this is perfect for readers who love the dishy women's fiction

'Layn...reminde... and sweet....ant

By Lauren Layne

Marriage on Madison Avenue

LAUREN LAYNE

HEADLINE
ETERNAL

Published by arrangement with Gallery Books,
An Imprint of Simon & Schuster, Inc.

First published in Great Britain in 2020
by HEADLINE ETERNAL
An imprint of HEADLINE PUBLISHING GROUP

1

Cataloguing in Publication Data is available from the British Library

ISBN 978 1 4722 6512 8

Offset in 9.98/14.95 pt Fairfield LT Std by Jouve (UK), Milton Keynes

Printed and bound in Great Britain by Clays Ltd, Elcograf S.p.A.

Headline's policy is to use papers that are natural, renewable and recyclable
products and made from wood grown in well-managed forests and other
controlled sources. The logging and manufacturing processes are expected
to conform to the environmental regulations of the country of origin.

HEADLINE PUBLISHING GROUP
An Hachette UK Company
Carmelite House
50 Victoria Embankment
London EC4Y 0DZ

www.headlineeternal.com
www.headline.co.uk
www.hachette.co.uk

Marriage on Madison Avenue

Prologue

*A*udrey Tate had dreamed about this moment dozens of times. Maybe hundreds.

Standing outside a church? *Check*.

A little breathless? *Definitely*.

A bit shaky? *Yup*.

Her heart pounding as she prepared to walk up the steps and down the aisle toward the man who'd determinedly swept her off her feet and stolen her heart? *Absolutely*.

But in her dreams, she'd been wearing white. In her dreams, the man she was walking toward hadn't been someone else's husband.

In her dreams, he hadn't been *dead*.

Audrey felt someone give her arm a comforting squeeze as they passed, and another kissed her cheek. She forced an absent smile, even though she didn't bother to look at the well-wishers. She was too busy trying to do what *they* were all doing: walking up those steps to say a final farewell to Brayden Hayes.

Audrey took a deep breath and ordered her right foot to move.

And it did. But not in the way she intended. Before Audrey could think through the consequences, she started walking, not *into* the church, but away from it. Away from him. Away from his wife.

Away from her dreams.

She barely noticed when she reached Central Park, and when she veered mindlessly to the left, she didn't register that her four-inch Louboutins were hardly suited for the dirt path.

She angrily wiped away her tears. She'd always been a crier, but this was a whole new level. Her eyes had been in a chronic state of *leaking* ever since she'd gotten the news.

Brayden was dead. Brayden was married.

Had been married.

Audrey was so focused on trying to get a grip on the warring grief and anger that she didn't realize what she was inadvertently walking toward. She halted in her tracks, blinking rapidly as she waited for her imagination to get a *freaking* grip. But no matter how long and hard she stared, the women sitting on the bench were *real*.

And one was the very woman who'd haunted Audrey's every waking hour since she'd learned that her boyfriend had drunkenly fallen off his sailboat and drowned.

She blinked again, but there was no doubt about it. Audrey was staring directly at Brayden Hayes's widow. The other woman, a stunning redhead, was a stranger—maybe vaguely familiar, but Audrey lacked the mental or emotional energy to sort out how or if she knew her.

What do I do?

Audrey's self-preservation instincts instructed her to run,

even as her conscience demanded she do what needed to be done and walk forward. In the end, it wasn't her decision. As Audrey stood there debating her next move, Claire Hayes turned her head, and though she wore sunglasses, Audrey could feel her gaze boring into her.

"Audrey."

She felt her eyes widen. "You know who I am?"

The blond woman gave a short nod. "You're Audrey Tate. I did a little digging after you called the house that night." There was a lengthy pause before she spoke again, her voice soft. "I know you were sleeping with my husband."

The redhead whipped her head toward her companion, then looked back at Audrey. She too was wearing sunglasses, but Audrey sensed she was just as shocked by Claire's pronouncement.

Brayden's wife *knew*.

Audrey let out a hiccupping sob and walked to the bench, sitting down, mainly because she wasn't sure her shaky legs would support her much longer. She looked at Claire Hayes, and then the words started tumbling out. "I didn't know," Audrey pleaded. "I didn't know until you picked up the phone that night that he was married. I swear to you, he told me his wife had left him, that he was separated . . . I *never* would have— You have to believe me. I didn't know—"

"Oh, honey," the red-haired woman interrupted, sounding horrified by Audrey's verbal diarrhea. "You've got to get it together."

Irritation wriggled its way through Audrey's misery, and she glared at the interloper. "Respectfully, you don't know the first thing about what's going on here."

"Well now, that's the thing," the redhead said, looking down at her manicure. "I sort of do."

Claire jolted in surprise, looking as shocked as Audrey felt. These two women didn't know each other, Audrey realized. Whatever she'd walked in on, it hadn't been one friend comforting another, but two strangers.

Claire's next words confirmed it. "Who are you?" she asked the redhead.

Instead of answering Claire, the redhead studied Audrey, and though she wasn't usually so bold, this time, she studied her right back. Even with the oversize sunglasses, she could tell the other woman was gorgeous, and not just because of the vibrant red hair. The woman *herself* was vibrant—seemingly crackling with an energy and confidence that was perfectly suited to the designer dress, flawless makeup, and not-so-tiny diamond studs in her ears that Audrey would bet her favorite Chanel bag on were real. Again, she was struck with the sense that there was something familiar about her . . .

The redhead pushed her sunglasses on top of her head, her gaze steady on Claire. "I'm Naomi Powell. The *other* other woman."

Audrey felt her mouth drop open in surprise, both at the woman's identity and her bombshell. Brayden Hayes hadn't *just* been cheating on his wife with Audrey. He'd also, apparently, been sleeping with one of New York's most well-known female entrepreneurs. The ultimate girl boss.

Audrey had never been introduced to Naomi Powell personally, but anyone who was anyone in Manhattan recognized the name of the Bronx-born up-and-comer who'd built a wildly successful jewelry empire.

Claire, on the other hand, didn't seem to have the same recognition. That, or she was too stunned that her husband had been sleeping with *two* women. Who were now sitting with her on a park bench. On the day of his funeral.

Audrey resisted the urge to giggle at the absurdity of it.

Claire continued to stare at Naomi. "What?"

The redhead sighed. "Your husband was putting his pickle into one too many sandwiches. Well, two too many if you count her." She jerked her chin toward Audrey.

Audrey did giggle this time, lifting a hand to her forehead, trying to sort out her thoughts. "Did you just compare . . . pickle . . . oh my God, *sandwiches*."

Claire's head dropped forward, her chin resting on her chest, and Audrey's laughter faded, replaced by shame. What kind of woman *laughed* when a funeral was happening just a few blocks away from where she sat beside the widow? Instinctively, she started to reach for Claire's hand, but she stopped when she realized that Audrey was probably the last person Claire wanted to comfort her.

Well, it was a tie, perhaps, Audrey thought with a quick glance at Naomi. There were, after all, two other women.

Naomi looked as alarmed as Audrey felt when she realized Claire's shoulders were shaking, not with silent sobs, but amusement. Claire's head fell back, tilting her face to the sky as she let out an audible laugh.

Good. *Good*. Not broken then. Just a little cracked.

"I hate to be the one to tell you this," Audrey told Claire, "but I don't think he's up there."

Naomi let out a startled chuckle, and they exchanged a tentative smile. This had to be one of the weirdest moments of Audrey's life. Of anyone's life. And yet somehow it didn't feel nearly as odd as it should have.

"Shouldn't we be at the funeral?" Claire asked quietly, still looking at the sky.

"Nah," Naomi said, waving her hand. "I mostly showed up

to tell God not to allow that one through the pearly gates, and as Audrey pointed out, I think He probably already figured that one out."

"I never thought I'd be here," Claire said, sounding exhausted. Audrey wondered if Claire's nights had been as sleepless as her own. The way Claire's fingers lifted to her temples confirmed that she was definitely suffering the same grief-induced headaches as Audrey.

Or perhaps they were anger-induced headaches. Truth be told, Audrey was still trying to figure out how she felt. She grieved. Obviously. A man had died. A man she loved had died, and far too young.

And yet. If she were really honest with herself, she was mad, too. At Brayden, for the lies, obviously. But also at herself. *So angry at herself.*

"You mean sitting on a park bench with your husband's mistresses while his funeral goes down just a couple blocks over?" Naomi asked.

Claire laughed, oblivious to Audrey's turmoil beside her. "Yes. That. I just keep thinking I know I should be sad, but instead all I can think about is how stupid I was, and that's *before* I knew there were two of you. How did I not see it?"

"We were just as stupid," Audrey said, giving in to the urge to comfort this time and setting a hand on Claire's arm. "He was my boyfriend for a year. I just thought he traveled a lot."

"Three months," Naomi said, flicking a manicured finger toward her chest. "He told me most of his business dealings were in Hong Kong and that he had to work most nights. I totally bought it."

There was a long moment of silence, and Audrey realized that for the first time in a week, something besides anger and guilt was creeping in around the aching numbness. *Relief*. Relief that she wasn't totally alone in the jumble of complicated feelings.

There was a strange camaraderie here. She didn't know how, exactly, but she felt it as purely as she did the New York sunshine beating on the top of her head.

Naomi straightened and turned toward them. "I have a confession."

Claire's eyebrows winged up. "Worse than the fact that you were having adult sleepovers with my husband?"

"Who I didn't know was your husband," Naomi said, with a correcting finger waggle. "But no, my confession is that while I'm really mad at Brayden, I'm even angrier at myself. For letting him fool me."

Audrey's flicker of relief roared to a flame—someone else understood. "Same. I mean, it's a little more self-loathing than anger, I guess, but . . . I just can't stop thinking about how I didn't see it. And if I didn't see *him* being a snake, how will I ever spot another man being a snake?"

Claire glanced down at her lap, staring at her hands. "I'm not worried about it. After all this, I'm pretty dead set on turning into the old lonely lady with cats."

"*Nope*," Naomi said, shaking her head. "We are not going to let him do that to us. I'm not really a long-term relationship girl, but I do like a male companion, and I have no intention of letting Brayden sour me on . . ."

"Pickles?" Audrey suggested.

"I was going to say sex, but yeah. That, too."

Audrey forced a smile, but her heart squeezed, and she couldn't hold back her smile as she spoke the truth. "But I *am* the long-term relationship girl. I want the ring and the babies and the—"

"Please don't say white picket fence."

"Oh God no," Audrey said, her head snapping back. She pointed down at her stilettos. "These red soles are meant for Fifth Ave., not the burbs. But I still want the fairy tale, and I just . . ." She swallowed. "It's harder to believe these days."

"So let me get this straight," Naomi said, looking first at Claire. "You're going to turn into a cat lady, and you're giving up your Disney princess dreams," she said, turning toward Audrey. "All because of a *guy*."

Put that way, it did sound . . . ridiculous. She flicked a glance at Claire, who was watching her, the same look of contemplation on her face.

Naomi pressed on. "Ladies, I know we just met, but let's face it, we have the same shoes and we were screwed over by the same guy, so as far as I'm concerned, we leapfrogged a few steps in the female-bonding process."

"Perfect, I'll invite you over for a slumber party," Claire said in a cutting tone. She stood, apparently deciding she'd had enough of this. Whatever *this* was.

"Hold up," Naomi said, reaching out to stop her. "I'm not suggesting we get matching tattoos, just that we can help each other."

Audrey was skeptical, but intrigued, and Claire seemed to be as well, because she sat back down. "You want me to help my husband's mistresses—do *what*, exactly?"

"We watch each other's blind spots as it relates to men. Left to our own devices, obviously we're no good at seeing a guy for who—and what—he really is. But what if we combined forces? Help each other spot another Brayden."

Audrey pulled her bottom lip between her teeth, running a hand over her hair as she considered the proposition with undisguised skepticism. "Respectfully, I don't even know you. I get your point, but why would I have two strangers do a gut check on a guy I like instead of my friends?"

Even as she said it, she saw the flaw in her own logic. She had plenty of friends. But none of them had protected her from Brayden. Not even Clarke West, her best friend since childhood, had been able to stop the hurt, and she knew he'd do anything for her. Audrey winced, belatedly realizing that poor Clarke was waiting for her in the church, probably worried about where the hell she was.

Naomi was still pushing her plan. "Because who knows better how to spot another woman getting scammed than three women who just experienced it?"

Damn. It was a good point. A *really* good point. And the truth was, Audrey didn't know if she could survive the past week for a second time. She bit her lip and looked at Claire. "You know, I don't hate this plan?"

Claire wasn't as sure. Audrey could see it in the way her eyes remained wary, the way she fiddled with her watch as though biding her time until she could politely excuse herself from the situation.

Naomi's gaze was also locked on Claire's watch. "Cartier."

Audrey hadn't been paying much attention to the watch itself, but she jolted at that. She wasn't in the accessory business like Naomi, but she knew a Cartier watch.

She knew because she had one at home. Her gaze dropped to the watch. She knew what she'd find, but her heart twisted all the same. They didn't just both have Cartier watches. They had the *same* Cartier watch.

Claire looked up at Naomi, her confused gaze indicating she was a step behind Audrey's realization. Or perhaps, deeper in denial. "Yes. How'd you know?"

Naomi didn't look away from Claire. "I know designers. I *also* know that I have the exact same watch at home."

Claire sucked in a startled breath. "Brayden . . . ?"

Naomi nodded.

"Me, too," Audrey said, almost inaudibly.

Claire stared down at the watch on her left wrist, and Audrey could feel her caving—understanding what Audrey and Naomi already understood. They *needed* each other.

Naomi extended her hand. "Hands in, girls, we're making a pact, high school–style. May neither of you ever fall victim to a cheating bastard again. Not on my watch."

Audrey didn't even hesitate in placing her palm on top of Naomi's hand. "*And* to helping each other find the right man. That's on my watch."

And she meant it. She might not be worthy of a happily ever after, but she was determined that these women would find it. It was the least she could do.

Claire hesitated for a moment longer before slowly resting her hand atop Audrey's. "Oh, what the hell. I'm in. To no more assholes."

Audrey felt something click in that moment, feeling a connection that went beyond friendship, a sense that this was a pivotal point of her life. Not Brayden's death, but what came after.

As they slowly pulled their hands back, Audrey let out a long sigh before glancing across the park in the general direction of the church they'd all ditched. "I guess we should make an appearance, huh?"

Naomi let out a derisive snort and, standing, flicked her sunglasses back onto her nose with a finger. "Screw it. Let's go shopping."

"I'm in," Claire said, also standing. "Let's stop by Sugarfina on the way and get some ridiculously priced but fabulous gummy candies. Brayden *hated* gummy candies."

"Did he?" Naomi said. "I didn't know that, but hell, let's buy the whole shop."

Audrey stood as well, but slower. *She'd* known. She'd known Brayden hadn't liked gummy candies. Just like she'd known they'd both loved chocolate. And she knew his smile had been higher on the right than the left and that he didn't really like black pepper but always asked servers to add it to his food anyway, as though saying no would be an affront to his manhood. She knew his favorite cocktail was a Tito's martini with a blue cheese olive and that he liked to sleep on the right side of the bed.

She knew everything a wife would know. But she would never be his wife. Or anyone else's. Not because she'd turned cynical. Audrey still believed in happy endings. She believed in them *with her whole heart*. She believed that a man and a woman could get married and live happily ever after so long as someone else didn't come along and ruin that happiness.

Which was exactly what Audrey had done.

She'd thought she'd been living her own fairy tale, but really she'd been the villain in Claire's. In her quest to find her own Price Charming, she'd been borrowing someone else's. Maybe even *two* someone else's, she realized, with a glance at Naomi.

Audrey silently made another pact, this time with herself. She'd help these other women find a second chance at happiness. She still believed in love. Just not for herself. She wasn't at all sure she deserved it.

Chapter One

*N*aomi Powell looked at the glass of brownish-green sludge in front of her face, then glanced up at Audrey. "Why is this happening to me?"

Audrey gave the glass a little waggle. "You haven't even tried it."

Reluctantly, Naomi took the glass and sniffed. "It smells like farts and dirt."

"That's the brussels sprouts and kale," Audrey said, handing a second glass to Claire, who took it with almost as much reluctance.

"Cheers!" Audrey said, lifting her own glass and taking a sip of the smoothie.

Naomi took the tiniest of sips, following it with an immediate gagging noise, and Claire merely shook her head without trying it, setting the glass back on the table with a firm *nope*.

"Yeah, all right," Audrey acknowledged, giving the glass a swirl, noting that the thick sludge barely moved. "It's not great."

"Why do you even have that gunk?" Naomi asked, setting the glass as far away from her as her arm would reach.

"Why is that stuff even in *existence*?" Claire added.

Audrey walked back into her kitchen and held up the powdered mix. "Super Fuel. It's got approximately nine million vitamins and antioxidants and like a year's worth of fiber. I told them I'd try it and, if it was any good, mention it to my followers."

Such was the life of an *influencer*. It wasn't a traditional job. Heck, as far as most people were concerned, it probably wasn't a job at all. Getting free stuff, evaluating it, and then sharing the good parts with her massive Instagram following wasn't exactly a hardship. But it *was* hard work. Whenever Audrey encountered a derisive snort after the requisite *what do you do* introductions, she merely smiled. Yes, she got free stuff. Yes, she made a rather staggering amount of money from endorsements and partnerships. Yes, from the outside her job looked as simple as taking a picture of herself with the newest *it* shade of matte lipstick.

But what people didn't see were the hours she spent managing her email, her Instagram DMs, and her Facebook messages. They didn't see the hundreds of queries she received in a single day. They didn't see the time she spent updating her blog, setting up her tripod, editing her photos, speaking at panels, staying active in her Facebook groups, monitoring comments, deleting spam and trolls, etc.

Audrey loved her job, but it *was* a job—a full-time one.

Naomi was wrinkling her nose. "Unless you hate your followers, put that down the garbage disposal and never speak of it again."

"No, don't!" Claire protested. "That stuff will probably turn into a brick and destroy the garbage disposal and this gorgeous kitchen."

"Oh, sweetie," Naomi said, patting Claire's hand. "Garbage disposals? You're *such* a contractor's wife."

Claire's smile was adorable and smug at the same time. "I am, aren't I?"

Audrey gave a smile of her own as she dumped the unappealing smoothie down the sink. Few things brought her more joy in life than seeing her friends happy, and Claire was *definitely* happy. Newly married to the gruff, flannel-wearing, bighearted Scott Turner, Claire's in-love glow was rivaled only by Naomi's, whose live-in boyfriend, Oliver Cunningham, was everything Brayden Hayes had not been. Loyal, loving, and *good*.

At the fridge, Audrey pulled out a carafe of orange juice and champagne.

"*Yes!*" Naomi said, in eager agreement, leaping out of her chair. "Where are the champagne flutes? I *knew* you didn't invite us over here just for dirt smoothies."

"Hmm." Audrey scanned the cupboards of the kitchen she was not yet familiar with. "No idea on the champagne flutes. You'll have to hunt."

"On it." Naomi set out opening and closing cupboards until she discovered where the movers Audrey hired had unpacked the stemware.

"I love the new place," Claire said as Audrey set the OJ and champagne on the table before cleaning away the abandoned smoothies.

"Me, too," Audrey said, glancing around and admiring her new kitchen.

"Do you miss the palace?" Naomi asked, returning to the

table with three of Audrey's personal-favorite champagne flutes in hand. An Anthropologie find, the gold-rimmed and rose-tinted glasses had been featured in one of Audrey's most popular posts to date.

Audrey rolled her eyes at Naomi's reference to the family home where she had lived until just a couple of weeks ago. Though, to be fair . . . the primary Tate residence *was* sort of a palace, albeit a Manhattan version of one. A towering penthouse with marble floors, a staggering view of the entire city, and more space than Audrey had known what to do with once her parents had moved to California to be near her sister and her sister's family.

"Creeping up on the big 3-0 while still living in my parents' house started to feel a little lame," Audrey admitted as Claire poured the mimosas. "Even though they didn't live there anymore, I was hyperaware of the pampered-princess vibe while living in the, as you put it, palace."

"As opposed to this hovel," Naomi said sarcastically, gesturing at the spacious, sparkling brownstone just down the street from her family's Madison Avenue penthouse.

"Yes, but I bought this place on my own," Audrey said a little tartly. "Big difference."

"*Big* difference," Naomi agreed, lifting her glass in a toast. "To fresh starts."

The three of them clinked glasses, and Claire smiled. "Did you know . . . I just realized that in the year and a half since we met in the park, we've all had a new home? Naomi moved into the Park Ave. place and then again to Tribeca. And mine wasn't *technically* a move, but the renovation made it feel like a new place. And now Audrey."

"And," Naomi chimed in, "shortly after moving, I found

Oliver. You found Scott with your renovation. Which means . . ." She darted her eyes over to Audrey.

"Mmmmm, yes," Audrey said, taking a sip of her drink. "*Clearly* you must be referring to my romantic success with Randy."

"In our defense," Claire said, "we *did* tell you not to date a guy named Randy."

"And you were right," Audrey said with a wince, horrified that she had to date Randy Weaver for nearly three weeks before realizing what a creep he was. Granted that was three weeks longer than she'd dated anyone else since Brayden, but that was also three weeks too long, considering.

"At least you found out about the video cameras before you actually starred in one of his, um, films," Claire said.

"Yeah, well, the cameras were sort of hard to miss, what with the bedroom being made of wall-to-wall-to-ceiling mirrors and all."

Naomi started cracking up. "It's seriously too good. To know that guys like that actually exist."

Audrey gave her a mock glare, but she couldn't stop her own grin. In hindsight, it *was* funny. Things had been going well enough with Randy up until that point. He hadn't exactly swept her off her feet, and there hadn't been any butterflies. But he had been kind. Considerate. A gentleman. Audrey had decided he was as good a guy as any to break her dry spell.

And then, she'd walked into his bedroom, which really and truly *had* been made of mirror, walls *and* ceiling. As if that weren't unnerving enough, then she'd seen the cameras. Plural. Along with a hidden big-screen TV built into one of the mirrors.

Not only did Randy only make love for the cameras, he enjoyed watching himself in past performances while in the midst of the *current* performance. He'd assured her it would be a turn-on if she'd give it a chance. She'd assured *him* he should lose her phone number forever.

Audrey sighed and decided it was time to get to the real reason she'd invited her friends over and was plying them with boozy beverages at 11 a.m.

"I need to tell you girls something."

Seeing she had their attention, she got right to it. "So, I told Randy about Brayden. Not everything, but . . . enough. I told him I dated Brayden knowing he was married but believing him when he said he was separated and the divorce was nearly final. I told him about the shock of learning upon his death that the 'separation' was news to his wife. I told him about both of you," she said, with an apologetic look at her friends.

"Okay . . . ?" Claire prompted, frowning a little in confusion.

"I trusted him," Audrey said quietly, reaching for her phone. "And . . . it turns out that trust was misplaced."

Knowing it would be clearer to show them, rather than tell them, Audrey pulled up Instagram and slid the phone between them.

Claire's head tilted down next to Naomi's red one as they read the Instagram post together.

"Who's Scandal Boy?" Claire asked.

"Knockoff of *Gossip Girl*," Naomi answered for Audrey, still scanning the phone. "Some little anonymous bitch who gets his jollies spreading rumors about the Manhattan elite. I've been mentioned at least a dozen times, none of it good, most of it untrue."

"Me, too," Audrey said. "The guy's always seemed to hate me, but it's never been *this* bad."

She nibbled nervously at the nail of her ring finger until her friends looked up. Her heart sank when she saw the furious expression on both of their faces. "I am *so* sorry, I had no idea Randy would betray me and tell the world about Brayden, or that Scandal Boy would hear about it."

"Can't you sue?" Claire demanded. "For slander, or something?"

"Slander only applies if it's untrue," Naomi said as she picked up the phone and read an excerpt from Scandal Boy's post. "'Everyone's favorite Upper East Side princess has a dirty little secret. The rumor mill's long been buzzing about Audrey Tate's involvement with the late Brayden Hayes, but this Boy's just learned that the Madison Avenue princess was no victim—she knew her prince was married the entire time and bagged him anyway.'"

Naomi lowered the phone with a disgusted look. "'Bagged'? Who *is* this guy?"

"A little twerp, that's who," Claire said, pulling the iPhone out of Naomi's hand, locking the screen, and setting it facedown in front of Audrey. "Forget about him. He doesn't deserve a second more of your time."

"Hear, hear," Naomi said in agreement.

Audrey looked between the two of them. "Wait. That's it? Aren't you mad?"

"Oh, *furious*," Claire said. "If I knew who he was, I'd put his nuts in a vise—"

"No, mad at *me*," Audrey clarified in exasperation.

They stared at her. "Why would we be mad at you?"

"For telling Randy about our . . . history."

"I told Oliver," Naomi pointed out.

Claire nodded. "And I told Scott. Well, granted, he already knew from Oliver and Naomi. But I never made any effort to hide it."

"Yeah, but those are *good* guys," Audrey said. "They can be trusted."

Naomi gave her a coy smile. "Yes, darling. And your guy was *not* one of the good ones. Now, if only we'd made a pact where the two of us could have told you that Randy was a shit . . . oh wait . . ."

"Naomi," Claire said in warning. "Do you *really* want us to bring up Dylan?"

"*Oof,*" Naomi said, blowing out a breath at the memory of the guy she'd flirted with briefly before realizing Oliver was the one. "Touché."

"Wait, you're really not mad?" Audrey asked her friends, still baffled.

"No, but we will be if you don't quit acting like this," Naomi said. "Look, it sucks. Neither of us likes knowing that this ass-hole's talking about you like this. But in terms of how it affects us?" She shrugged. "I'm good."

"Me, too," Claire said. "It's been a long time."

A year and a half. It had been a year and a half since Brayden had died, and her friends had moved on.

That was the crucial difference, Audrey realized. They didn't care about this dirt with Brayden coming to the surface because it couldn't hurt them anymore. They had new men, new loves. And Audrey was . . .

Fine. She was just fine.

Naomi had turned her attention to her own phone, and now her mimosa was frozen halfway to her mouth and she suddenly looked far more horrified at whatever she was reading on her own phone than what she'd read on Audrey's. "Um. Audrey."

"Hmm?" she asked, adding a bit more champagne to her glass.

Naomi's blue eyes met hers. "You've been paying attention to the Internet besides the Scandal Boy thing, right?"

Audrey gave an indelicate grunt. "Not really. I've been mostly offline since his shady post. I needed a break from the fake pity and the nosy questions. I figure tomorrow's soon enough to deal with it all."

"*Yeeeeah*, I think you have something new to deal with. Something . . . bigger."

She handed Audrey the phone. "Read Deena's message, then click the link."

Audrey skimmed the text from Naomi's assistant.

OMG, is it true?! Squee!

Audrey's thumb tapped the URL below the message, her gaze only needing to take in the headline to understand Naomi's concern.

Socialite Audrey Tate engaged to longtime companion Clarke West.

"Oh hell," Audrey muttered with a sigh, handing the phone back to Naomi. "Not this again."

Chapter Two

SUNDAY, JANUARY 5

Did you hear? A certain Madison Avenue diva's got
herself a new man, allegedly. How long he'll stick around
is the real question. Rumor has it our favorite girl's cursed
in love—she couldn't keep a man if he was chained to her
Bottega Veneta crocodile handbag.
—@ScandalBoyNYC

*C*larke's apartment was a ten-minute walk from Audrey's, which wasn't nearly enough time to walk off her anger. Not that she was mad at Clarke—she could handle him in her sleep.

No, Audrey was still pissed at the imbecilic @Scandal-BoyNYC, who, before she and the girls could even finish their mimosas, had taken yet *another* swing at Audrey on Instagram. The boy, man, woman, whatever, apparently had a well-connected source, which was more than a little annoying. Still, the guy should really be more careful about whom he spoke with.

Nobody in Audrey's acquaintance would have even *joked* about attaching a chain to a Bottega.

Petty and unfounded as they may be, the accusations still stung. Audrey was no stranger to social media trolling, but it was embarrassing to have her romantic life open to scrutiny. She didn't even tell her closest friends the innermost workings of her heart—to have strangers on the Internet assessing her single status was downright galling.

But she'd have to deal with that later. First, there was the not so little matter of her *fiancé*.

Like Audrey, Clarke West lived just off Madison Avenue, though a bit farther downtown. Ironically, Audrey noted with a smile as she turned onto Sixty-Fourth, right next to the Bottega Veneta store. Flipping the mental bird to Scandal Boy as she passed the high-end shop, she hopped up the stairs to Clarke's townhome.

She knocked and waited impatiently. When there was no answer, she pulled out her spare key and let herself in, fully intending to make herself at home and wait her best friend out. Opening the front door, Audrey was welcomed by the sound of Queen blaring from upstairs.

So he *was* home. Good. Audrey set her purse on the end table she'd helped him pick out and hung her coat by the front door the way she had hundreds of times over the years.

Clarke's house was gorgeous, and Audrey gave herself plenty of credit for that. Not for the prewar architecture, obviously. That had been somebody else's genius. But Audrey had refused to let such a gorgeous space be wasted with Clarke's barren man cave decorating sensibilities. With the help of one of Manhattan's top interior designers, Audrey had given the townhome a decidedly masculine, country-club vibe. The floors and staircase were a rich mahogany, the walls deep blues and greens. The furniture was an intentional mismatch of worn leather and offbeat plaids, the walls adorned with pictures of horses and hunting dogs that Clarke liked to fuss about but never bothered to take down. Audrey suspected that had far more to do with his mother hating the artwork than it did Clarke himself liking it.

She followed the sound of "We Will Rock You" up the stairs, already knowing she'd find him in the one room in the house that *hadn't* seen her touch—his home gym. She leaned against the side of the open doorway, not wanting to startle Clarke in the middle of bench-pressing. He'd outfitted one of the larger spare bedrooms with a treadmill, squat rack, free weights, and, as evidenced by the fact that he still hadn't heard her arrival, a top-of-the-line built-in sound system.

Dressed in gray sweatpants and a tight black workout shirt, Clarke pushed through the last of his reps and set the bar back on the rack. Swiping a towel off the ground, he levered up into a sitting position on the bench, freezing for a moment in surprise when he saw her standing there.

Grinning, he held up a finger. *Wait.* He reached for his phone and, with a swipe of his thumb, turned the music down.

"Hey, Dree!"

Dree. Not her favorite nickname, but he'd been using it since childhood, and there was no teaching this playboy new tricks. She crossed her arms, one shoulder against the doorjamb. "Anything you want to say to me?"

He smiled wider. "Your hair looks great today?"

Audrey lifted her eyebrows and waited.

Clarke wiped the towel over his forehead and merely grinned wider.

"You know that doesn't work on me."

"What?"

She waved a hand over him. "That grin. The perfect white teeth, the strategic amount of stubble, the Superman muscles."

His eyes narrowed slightly. With thick dark brown hair, classic good looks, a tall, broad-shouldered frame, and most damningly of all, the name Clarke, Superman references had followed him his entire life. He liked them about as much as she did the name Dree.

"Strategic amount of stubble," he repeated. "What, you think we men can train our facial hair to grow just so?"

"Well, gosh, I don't know," she mused. "Maybe I'll find out after we're *married*."

"Ah." He dragged the towel over his face. "That."

"Yeah. That. *Again?*"

"You say it like it happens all the time," he said, standing. "This is only the second time."

"Third. And that's three fake engagements too many. What was it this time, another debutante hoping that claiming her baby is yours will lure you down the aisle?"

It was one of her least favorite parts about being friends with a man of Clarke's considerable charms. He liked women, and they *really* liked him. In fact, Audrey wouldn't be surprised if there were entire book clubs and wine nights dedicated to figuring out how to get a ring on his finger. Mrs. Clarke West was a highly coveted position, and the more daring prospects had tried to trick him into it over the years.

Clarke's default escape plan was to announce he was already engaged. To Audrey.

"I don't date debutantes," he grumbled. "I'm not sure I even know what a debutante is."

"*Still* waiting for the explanation."

He sighed and faced her. "Elizabeth's back in town."

It took Audrey a moment to track. "As in your ex? Superstar lawyer who moved to DC?"

Clarke rolled his neck to loosen it. "Linda somehow talked me into meeting her for lunch on Friday. Except when I showed up at the restaurant, guess who was waiting at the table."

"I take it *not* your mother?"

He shrugged, looking for all the world like he didn't care that his mother had tricked him into a lunch with his ex-girlfriend. But Audrey knew him well. Knew from the tight line of his jaw that it bugged him. Everything about his mother bugged him. Hence why she was *Linda* and rarely *Mom*.

"I swear, sometimes I think Linda liked Elizabeth better than I did," he grumbled.

Audrey smiled. "Of course she did. Elizabeth is a mini *her*."

Clarke's mother had always been a bit of a mystery to Audrey. Somehow the woman managed to be a full-time interfering mother, a full-time controlling wife, *and* a full-time chief judge of something or other for the state of New York.

As for Clarke's ex, Elizabeth Milsap wasn't yet a wife or a mother, as far as Audrey knew, but she was a high-powered lawyer who'd left New York for DC a couple of years ago with political aspirations that hadn't involved Clarke. Audrey suspected that his mother had been more upset about the breakup than Clarke himself, and it didn't surprise Audrey in the least that Linda would try to maneuver Elizabeth and Clarke into getting back together.

Linda loved her son. She just had a manipulative way of showing it.

"Okay, but what does Elizabeth being back in the city have to do with the fact that the gossip section of the *Post* seems to think we're engaged?"

"Well." He draped the towel over the back of his neck and tugged on both ends. "After we had lunch—"

"Wait, you actually stayed and had lunch with Elizabeth?" Audrey was surprised. Clarke was a pretty easygoing guy, but not when it came to his mother's machinations. If Linda told him to turn right, he'd run left. When she'd suggested he wear a blue tie to prom, he'd worn red. When she'd told him to go to Yale, he'd chosen Dartmouth. When she'd told him to follow Elizabeth to DC, he'd bought a townhome in Manhattan.

The fact that he'd go along with anything arranged by his mother was unusual.

He grunted. "What was I supposed to do, just leave Elizabeth sitting there?"

"Would that have led to you and me not being engaged? Then, *yeah*."

"Nah, it wasn't lunch that did it. It was *after* lunch as I was leaving the restaurant. Tilda Covey was walking in as Elizabeth and I were walking out."

Audrey groaned. Tilda Covey was one of New York's most notorious busybodies, and one of Linda West's closest friends.

"Exactly," Clarke said in response. "She told me she heard congratulations would soon be in order, followed by humming that damn wedding stomp."

"It's the wedding *march*."

"Whatever." He tugged at the towel harder. "My mom obviously had told her Elizabeth and I were involved, and seeing us together all but confirmed it for Tilda."

"And your knee-jerk reaction was to say you're engaged to me?"

"Do you have a better idea?" he asked.

"The truth! Tell Tilda and your mother that it was one lunch and that you haven't seen Elizabeth in years." She paused and frowned. "Have you?"

"No," he said. "But you *know* Linda. I wouldn't be surprised if she had an engagement notice ready to send the papers in hopes of forcing me into it."

"She wouldn't do that," Audrey protested.

Clarke gave her a look.

"Okay, *maybe* she'd have done it. And *maybe* your reason for making us engaged was understandable. But now"—she lifted a finger in warning—"undo it. Today. Get us *un*-engaged."

"As soon as I'm done with my workout," he said with a grin, seeming relieved to be off the hook. "Have I told you you're the best friend in the whole world?"

"I already know."

He tossed the towel on the side of the treadmill and began to lower himself stomach-first to the floor. "Lay on my back."

"Pass," she said as he got into plank position.

"Come on. Like we used to do, when regular push-ups got too easy."

"First of all, nobody likes people who say things like 'regular push-ups got too easy.' Second of all, that was in high school."

He looked up. "I can wait all day, Dree. Just remember, the sooner I finish this workout, the sooner you don't have to marry me."

She pushed away from the door with a sigh. "You'll get me all sweaty."

"Good. If you ask me, it's been way too long since you've had contact with a man's sweat. Randy doesn't count."

"No, he doesn't," she agreed, since she and Randy had never gotten past the make-out stage before she'd seen his mirrored room of horror.

She kicked off her shoes and gingerly lowered herself so she and Clarke were back-to-back. "I don't remember this being so hard when I was fifteen," she said, putting her arms out for balance and laughing as she started to fall to the side when he lowered into a push-up.

"Yeah, you really have the hard part," he said with an exaggerated grunt. "Maybe we need to talk about your chocolate addiction."

She reached up and tugged his hair in reprimand. "A gentleman never comments on a lady's weight."

"Is that what this is? A *lady's* weight?"

She tugged his hair harder.

For all his complaining, his push-ups seemed effortless once she found her balance, and he did a couple dozen or so with both their body weights before collapsing to the ground. "You're right. It was easier in high school."

"Most things were," she said.

He turned his head slightly, propping his arms beneath his head, though making no effort to push her off. And she didn't make an effort to move. She'd forgotten the unique sort of comfort that came from physical contact with someone else, even if it was being sprawled platonically atop her best friend.

"What's up?" he asked.

She gave a little smile, appreciating that he knew her as well as she knew him. Appreciating that he knew, even from the most innocuous of statements, when something was bothering her.

She exhaled. "You know Scandal Boy?"

"I do not."

"Instagram influencer. But the mean, gossipy kind. Likes to dig up dirt and expose it."

"Ah. Society's vermin."

"Basically," she said. "Anyway, somehow Randy found him, or he found Randy. At least I *think* it was Randy. He's the only one other than you, my parents, and Naomi and Claire who know everything that went down with Brayden."

"Ah shit. *That's* out there?"

"Yup. Word on the street is I'm a home wrecker, who also can't keep a man, and oh yeah, I'm cursed."

"Well, that's bullshit," he said loyally.

"Is it?" She stared up at his ceiling. "I mean, I know I haven't exactly put myself out there on the romantic front since Brayden. I thought I wanted to be single, but . . . it's starting to get a little embarrassing. It's also not like guys have been banging down the door trying to woo me."

"Maybe it's because you use words like *woo*?"

"You're the worst fake husband ever."

"Our ill-fated love affair will end just as soon as you get off me."

"All right, all right." Audrey meant to move. But she didn't.

She felt an idea lurking.

Instead she turned her face slightly to the side, until her cheek rested lightly against his. "What if we didn't end it?"

"Hmm?" he asked, sounding half-asleep.

"What if we stayed engaged? Just a little bit longer. A couple days."

He laughed incredulously. "What?"

"What if we didn't correct the rumors just yet? What if we let people believe that it's true. That we really *have* done what basically everyone's assumed is inevitable—that we're super in love."

"I don't do super in love."

"But you could pretend to."

"I could," he said slowly. "But why would I?"

"To spite your mother? You know she's never liked me. It

would kill her to think that not only are you not marrying perfect, smart Elizabeth, but instead are marrying silly, flighty Audrey. She'd *die*."

"Tempting," he said darkly. "Very tempting. But I'm thirty-one. A little old to be playing the part of rebellious son."

"Says the guy who told the *Manhattan Post* he was engaged just to thwart his mother's plans."

"I merely planted the rumor to stay one step ahead of her. I wasn't *actually* going to pretend we're getting married."

"But we *could*."

He was silent for a moment. "What's really going on here?"

She rolled off him, lying on her side and propping her head on her elbow. He did the same, facing her.

"I know it's stupid," she admitted. "I know Scandal Boy is just a mean little troll, and I should be mature and take the high road. But it's all people are talking about in my Instagram comments. The conjecture about why none of my posts ever mention a man. Half of them think I'm a closeted lesbian, and I'm okay with that. But the other half are speculating I'm some sort of relationship pariah. One theorized that I had shark teeth for a vagina."

"Oh God," Clarke said, rolling onto his back and covering his ears. "What I wouldn't give to unhear that."

"And I *know* it's just Instagram," she pressed on, ignoring him. "And it's not real life, except it is for me. That's my job, and it's one I love."

He turned his head back toward her, searching her face. "And being 'engaged' will help?"

"Just for a little while," she said. "Social media has a ridiculously short shelf life. They'll be onto some other target in a few days, and we can break things off amicably, like we always do."

She poked his muscled shoulder with a finger. "Please? It's just a few days you'll have to keep it zipped up and pretend to be wildly in love with me, and then you can go back to sowing wild oats."

"What?"

"Sleeping with every woman in Manhattan," she clarified.

He pointed at his heart. "Wounded."

"I'm not judging. I have full respect for your bachelor brand. I just need your help. Just for a week or so? People think my vagina is made of *teeth*, Clarke."

Clarke continued to study her for a moment, his dark golden gaze thoughtful. Then he reached out and slapped her hip. "Get up."

When she didn't move fast enough, he jumped to his feet and hauled her up himself. "First, we need some ground rules. If we do this, the word *vagina* is officially banned."

She lit up. "Wait, you'll do it?"

"I'm going take a quick shower, then we'll head out."

"Head out to where?" she called after him as he sauntered toward the master bathroom.

He turned around and grinned as he walked backward down the hall. "Gotta go shop for a big-ass diamond ring for my wife-to-be."

Chapter Three

How many karats does it take to reverse a curse and hold
on to a man? A certain Madison Avenue influencer is
apparently trying to find out . . .
—@ScandalBoyNYC

I forgot how scary your parents' house is," Audrey muttered, leaning in to look at the door knocker on the West's 80th Street residence. "Is that a lion? With its mouth open?"

"Don't be ridiculous, Audrey," Clarke said, opening the door. "That's not a lion. It's *clearly* the spitting image of my mother."

A second later, they were greeted by the very mother in question, and Audrey was forced to acknowledge that Clarke's comparison of the lion wasn't far off. Not that Linda West resembled a lion, exactly. In fact, she very much resembled Clarke. She was broad shouldered for a woman, or perhaps it just looked that way because she favored vintage Chanel suits with boxy shoulders.

Linda's eyes were the same gold brown as her son's, and her hair was as dark as Clarke's—though at sixty, she probably had some salon help with that, Audrey was betting.

Personality-wise, though, Linda *definitely* had lion vibes. She managed to seem both graceful and fierce, and she was *definitely* at the top of her food chain.

"Clarke. Audrey. So glad you could clear time in your busy social schedule to join us for dinner," his mother said coolly as she greeted them both with an air-kiss.

"Thank you for having us," Audrey said as Clarke stepped behind her to help her out of her coat.

"Of course." Linda's smile was brief, and vaguely sly. "After all, you're going to be part of the family."

Audrey hesitated, but Clarke's palm pressed between her shoulder blades, reminding her of the game as he addressed his mother. "She absolutely is."

Linda's brown eyes flicked between them for a moment, then gave the slightest roll.

"Come on in. We'll have some champagne to celebrate," Clarke's mom said, heading toward the living room.

"She knows," Audrey said out of the corner of her mouth as Clarke ushered her forward. "She knows full well that we're not actually engaged."

"Of course she knows," he answered quietly. "It's her game. Hell, she's probably delighted we decided to play."

"Yes, but how does she possibly think she can *win?*"

Stepping into the formally stuffy living room a moment later, Audrey had her answer. Clarke's mother was opening a bottle of Dom Pérignon, and his father was preoccupied with his cell phone.

And sitting on the couch was Clarke's ex-girlfriend.

Audrey's eyes widened in surprise as Elizabeth stood to greet them. "I hope this isn't awkward," Elizabeth said with a smile, coming to hug them both.

"Of course it isn't awkward," Linda said as she removed the champagne cork with a pop. "Audrey knows that Elizabeth's an old friend of the family."

Uh-huh. If Linda had it her way, Elizabeth would be a *part* of the family.

Audrey accepted the hug even as her mind reeled. Clarke's mom was seriously ballsy. Elizabeth turned toward Clarke, and Audrey noticed Elizabeth's hug was as lingering as Clarke's was perfunctory.

"Liz," he said, his voice gruff.

Audrey gave him a sharp look. She'd assumed him indifferent to Elizabeth. After all, it had been years since they'd dated, and he'd hardly seemed the least bit fazed when they'd broken up. But Elizabeth didn't go by Liz, which meant it was a nickname—something she'd noticed Clarke was always careful to avoid with girlfriends. And there'd been something in his tone when he'd said it, something on his face right now . . .

Elizabeth held his gaze just a minute before slipping back into her congratulatory routine. "Linda had invited me over to join the family before we realized, well . . ." She reached for Audrey's left hand. "It's so nice to see you again. And I've been *dying* to see the ring!"

She gasped when she saw it. "Oh, Audrey. It's just gorgeous."

It *was* gorgeous. The Tiffany solitaire in a platinum setting was Audrey's dream ring, and hey, if you were going to have an engagement for show, why not make it perfect?

Clarke slid a hand around Audrey's waist, his palm resting against her hip, and she had to resist the urge to jump in surprise at the contact. They'd been playing *fiancés* all week. First with the Tiffany and Co. ring shopping, which he'd insisted she document in her Instagram Stories, in real time. Then fake-flirty dinner and a staged picture of her coffee table piled high with bridal magazines. Harmless, easily reversible stuff.

But this—the touching—this was new. Sure, she and Clarke had touched plenty in the past. Dances. Punches. Pinches. Pecks on the cheek. High fives. Hugs. But his hand on her hip was decidedly different. And posing as an engaged couple at his parents' house was a whole other level of *pretend*, one Audrey wasn't entirely comfortable with. She could stomach pretending for the sake of their public, but straight-up lying to friends and family didn't feel right.

Not that Audrey had lied to *her* friends and family. She'd called her parents in California immediately to let them know what was going on, and as expected, her fun-loving mother was delighted by the charade, and Audrey's father was affectionately tolerant. Naomi and Claire had also agreed to play along because it would mean getting Scandal Boy to back off.

But Clarke's relationship with his parents was a different beast—chilly on a good day, downright antagonistic on a bad one. His mother was cold and controlling, his father dispassionate about everything except the family business.

And Elizabeth was as beautiful as ever, Audrey realized. Not in a delicate, dainty way. Elizabeth was nearly as tall as Clarke in her heels, and she had the sort of striking bone structure that was almost masculine in its sharp edges. But it was softened by a full mouth and light brown hair she wore in soft waves around her shoulders.

Looks aside, Audrey had never *quite* seen what Clarke and Elizabeth saw in each other. Clarke was carefree and outgoing,

MARRIAGE ON MADISON AVENUE   39

where Elizabeth was uptight and reserved. They'd dated for
nearly a year—the longest romantic relationship of Clarke's life—
and yet, Audrey hadn't been surprised in the least when Elizabeth
had taken a job in DC and Clarke had opted to stay behind.

But seeing the way Elizabeth looked at Clarke just a little too
long, her assessment of Audrey just a bit too calculating, Audrey
was betting Elizabeth had plans for Clarke that did not involve
him walking down the aisle with Audrey.

"Yes, the ring is lovely," Linda said with a dismissive glance,
handing Clarke and Audrey champagne flutes. "And don't worry,
dear, I'm sure if you change your mind and want something different, you can get a full refund, am I right?"

"Ah—"

"Exchange," Clarke interrupted. "I think that's the word you
wanted. Not *refund*."

Audrey looked up at Clarke, unsurprised to see the tension
in his jaw as he engaged in a staring contest with is mother.

"Of course," Linda murmured. "Alton, grab those other champagne flutes. We need to toast your new daughter-in-law."

Clarke's father joined them, giving Audrey an absent peck on
the cheek that, while hardly affectionate, at least had less chill
than his wife's greeting.

Clarke didn't get along with his father much more than he
did his mother, but Audrey had never felt as wary of Alton as she
did Linda. The man was distant, to be sure, and he let his wife
order him around far more than Audrey would have expected for
a powerful CEO. She'd never quite been able to crack the man's
aloof surface, but she didn't think it was personal, merely a func-
tion of him inheriting an enormous company that had been
passed down in his family ever since the company's earliest days
as a railroad production. It had evolved into advertising for

railroads, then advertising for all things transportation, then *just* advertising, until it eventually became the ginormous media conglomerate it was today. In other words, the man had a lot on his plate and always seemed more distracted than vindictive. Unlike Linda, who never missed a single detail.

Audrey knew Linda's use of the word *refund* hadn't been a slip of the tongue at all.

Annoyingly, Linda was also dead right about Audrey's intentions with the ring. Audrey had made sure, before Clarke put his credit card down, that they *could*, in fact, get a full refund on the ring when they ended this next week.

Audrey had half planned on ending it *today*. But then Clarke's mom had invited them to dinner to "discuss the development," and Clarke had been just annoyed enough with his mother to rise to the bait and carry on the charade for one more night.

"Congratulations, son," Alton said, lifting his glass. "We're so happy you two kids finally decided to quit with that best friend nonsense."

Audrey pressed her lips together to keep from protesting that their friendship wasn't nonsense. That the fact that they'd been best friends since they were children showed that boys and girls *could* be friends.

And that men and women could be, too.

Clarke's fingers dug slightly into her hip, reminding her of the plan, and she played her part, winding an arm around his waist and beaming up at him. "Me, too. I don't know what took me so long to see that he's the one, but I'm glad I finally woke up."

The smoldering look Clarke gave her in return caused her breath to hitch just for a second and made her think the man had seriously missed his calling—that was some Oscar-level acting right there.

"So," Elizabeth asked, after the five of them had clinked glasses, "have you two set a date yet?"

"Oh, no, not yet," Audrey said, keeping the details vague, the way she had been all week. "We're just enjoying being engaged for a while."

"But of course, you'll be having an engagement party?" Linda pressed.

"Oh, we hadn't really—"

"Of course," Clarke interrupted.

This time it was Audrey who dug her nails into him. He shifted slightly beside her in discomfort but didn't back down.

"Well, I'd love to help with that," Linda said, the enthusiasm in her voice veiled ever so slightly with mockery. "In fact, I called Audrey's parents just this afternoon to see if they might be able to fly out next weekend for a party. My treat."

Audrey released Clarke to reach up and scratch behind her ear. *Damn*. The woman was good. She'd neatly and effectively called their bluff.

Ah, well. They'd had a good run. Time to concede gracefully.

She glanced up at Clarke to see how he wanted to handle the extraction from the mess they'd gotten themselves into. If he wasn't ready, she had a whole arsenal of ways she'd planned to get them out of their little game.

Actually, Clarke and I have been worried we might have been a bit hasty . . .

We've realized that maybe we really are better off as just friends . . .

We have a few things to work out regarding our future . . .

Personally, Audrey thought the first one was the best, and it was what she planned to announce on Instagram next week, when she went back to her regularly scheduled posts of lipstick recommendations and her latest skin-care regime.

She wasn't worried about it. If celebrities could get engaged and disengaged within the span of a month, then a pseudo-celebrity like herself could certainly do it in the span of a week.

But instead of getting the hell out of this mess, Clarke merely gave one of his trademark easy smiles.

"We'd love that. Thanks, Mom." He glanced down at Audrey. "Wouldn't we, Dree?"

What. The. Hell?

Wearing a pretend engagement ring for a week was one thing. Having an engagement party was an entirely different ball game.

But friends didn't let friends get trolled by smarmy Instagram jerks, *and* friends didn't leave friends to face manipulative mothers and scheming exes alone.

She looked up and found him studying her, his gaze thoughtful and a little pleading.

Audrey withheld a sigh. She would do just about anything for him. And he knew it.

She turned toward Clarke's mom with her warmest smile. "Absolutely. What date are you thinking?"

Chapter Four

Big decisions for the big night! Louboutins or killer Stuart Weitzman boots? Help! Comment below with your vote! ♥
—@TheAudreyTate

*T*he ankle-wrap Louboutin stilettos had won the vote, but Audrey still tilted her head back and forth in indecision.

The Loubs were darling and more bridal, definitely. But the thigh-high dove-gray Weitzmans, or Stuies, as she called them, were more practical given the forecast's call for a "wintry mix" tonight.

She made a mental note that when she got engaged for real someday, she'd time it so that her engagement party didn't fall in the middle of winter. Then, remembering just as quickly her resolution that marriage wasn't in the cards for her, she reached for the Louboutins.

If she only got to do this once, she was doing it right.

Her feet would be cold, but cute.

Pulling them on, she grabbed the white satin clutch she'd splurged on for the occasion. It perfectly matched the strapless white cocktail dress she'd also splurged on. After all, if one was "getting married" for show, why not put on one *hell* of a show?

Audrey retrieved her cell phone from the charger and was just about to slide it into the clutch when it buzzed with an incoming call. She did a double take at the name on the screen, then swiftly answered. "Anderson?"

"Little sister. You sound surprised."

"Only because you're the king of butt dials."

"One of my students showed me how to lock my phone when it's in my pocket."

"I'm so proud," she said with a fond smile as she went to her jewelry box. A necklace would ruin the neckline of the dress, but a simple bracelet would be perfect. "So what's new?"

"Well, let's see," he mused. "I got my hair cut. My favorite cereal brand changed the box, and I don't like it. Oh, and my youngest sister got engaged."

Audrey froze in the process of holding up a rose-gold bangle she'd gotten from Naomi. She didn't bother to hide the horror from her voice. "Oh, Anderson. It's not what you think."

"That you didn't bother to tell me the news?"

"No. I mean, yes." She dropped the bracelet and put a hand over her heart to ease the guilty squeeze in her chest. "Sort of. It's complicated?"

Damn. Her brother thought she was getting married and hadn't told him.

She and Anderson weren't close in age. At thirty-six, he was seven years her senior. The fact that he was a legitimate *genius* and had skipped a grade in school had widened the gap even further when they were growing up.

Add in that he lived in Seattle, and thus a different time zone, as well as that he was a biology professor at the University of Washington, and they didn't exactly have a lot in common. But that didn't mean she didn't love him to death, and he absolutely should have heard about her "engagement" from her. The worst part was, it hadn't even *occurred* to her to call him or that he'd even find out. Anderson had long ago left behind the New York social scene for West Coast academia.

An *actual* engagement he'd want to know about because he loved her. A fake engagement would go right over his brilliant head.

"How'd you find out?" she asked curiously.

"Instagram," he admitted.

She let out a startled laugh. "Seriously?"

"It's new," he grumbled. "Figured I would try to follow your world. Didn't realize just how enlightening it would be."

"Anderson, I am *so* sorry. But it's not what you think."

"You and Clarke aren't finally tying the knot?"

"No! Wait, what do you mean *finally*?"

He snorted. "I may be the family nerd, but I do have *some* social skills. Even I knew it was only a matter of time."

"Well, you're not so smart about *everything*," she said. "It's a fake engagement."

"A what now?" he asked, sounding completely at a loss, as expected.

"Short version, some social media troll somehow managed to accuse me of being a man-eater, a home wrecker, and a pathetic spinster all in the span of a handful of posts."

"And?"

"And, my skin wasn't as thick as it should have been," she admitted. "I got tired of the hundreds of comments rolling in about how I'd never posted about a boyfriend on social media, and I just . . . wanted to prove them wrong."

"Huh."

"It sounds stupid," she admitted.

"No," he said slowly. "I may be new to following you on Instagram, but even I can grasp that *the* Audrey Tate can't so much as fart without thousands of people knowing about it and having an opinion."

"Anderson. Girls never fart. I thought Adele and I taught you that early on."

He laughed. "You know what I mean. I can understand the need to self-protect. But . . . getting married?"

"*Pretending* to get married," she clarified quickly. "We're calling it off after the engagement party tonight."

"Audrey," he said with a laugh.

"I know," she said, laughing along with him. "Trust me, *I know*. It's insane. But because you love me, and because I'm vulnerable, can I ask for a week's delay on the lecture?"

He sighed. "I won't lecture. And, I guess . . . well, as always, I'm thankful for Clarke. He takes care of you in ways I can't."

"That's not true," she said loyally.

It was a *little* true. Anderson had been a good big brother, but the age difference meant that their childhoods hadn't overlapped much, much less their school lives. Even if they had, Anderson had been the lanky, nose-in-a-book teen who'd warranted social issues of his own. He'd hardly been the type of brother you could flaunt in front of your bullies and say, "My brother will beat you up."

Not that Audrey had had many social problems aside from the occasional playground bully and high school mean girl. But to her brother's point, maybe the reason her life had been relatively smooth sailing, save the Brayden incident, was because of Clarke. He'd always been her fiercest defender, her most loyal companion. Armed with good looks, ample confidence, and way too much charm, he'd been able to talk his way out of anything, both on his behalf and Audrey's.

"It is true," Anderson said gently, reading her thoughts. "But I appreciate that you'll still let me pretend to be your big brother."

"You *are* my big brother, and I am sorry I didn't tell you about my plan. And that you had to hear about it from Instagram, of all things. I should have told you when I told Mom and Dad."

"Oh God." He laughed. "I bet Mom is loving it."

"I think she was more excited about us all being in on a charade together than she would be if it were an *actual* wedding."

"Well, she does like to remind us about her acting aspirations. We can't go a single Christmas without hearing about her starring role in her high school's *Hello, Dolly!*"

"*Annie Get Your Gun.*"

"Whatever."

"Well, I guess I'll get to see tonight just how good of an actress she is."

"What's happening tonight?"

"Engagement party," she reminded him. "Mom and Dad flew in."

"They took a six-hour flight for a fake engagement party?"

"On the company jet, so not exactly a hardship," Audrey pointed out. "Plus, Clarke's mom more or less badgered them into it."

She could practically hear him shaking his head in disbelief. "You have a weird life, little sis."

"I do. I really do. But can I call you tomorrow to catch up on what's new with you? I have to go bride-to-be it up at the NoMad Hotel and somehow convince everyone that Clarke and I are madly in love."

"Don't worry. You will."

———

There were still two hours until the party started, but Audrey, Naomi, and Claire had agreed to meet up for a glass of champagne beforehand.

"You know, the weirdest part of this whole thing," Claire said, "isn't that you guys are fake engaged—though I will say Hallmark movie, much?—it's that everyone seems to believe it. I've had a half-dozen potential clients who seem more excited about the prospect of me doing *your* wedding invitations than their own."

"For the record," Audrey said, pointing her champagne flute at Claire, "if I were really getting married, you'd *totally* be doing my invitations."

In the past couple of months, Claire had dusted off her calligraphy skills and was already popular enough to have to turn down potential jobs.

"You know that digital invitations are in right now?" Claire asked. "Not like the 'pick a template and input your information' e-invitations that have been around for years, but like custom digital invitations by graphic designers and handwritten digital envelopes by yours truly."

"How does that work?" Naomi asked. "Do you have to scan everything?"

"Nope, I've been teaching myself how to letter with an iPad

and Apple Pencil," Claire explained. "There's a learning curve, but a fun one."

"Well, there you go, Aud," Naomi said. "If you and Clarkey decided to go through with this, Claire can make sure you do so in twenty-first-century style."

Audrey fished a cashew out of the complimentary nut bowl that had been served with their drinks. "I am not marrying Clarke."

"Says the woman dressed all in white just minutes before her fancy engagement party. You look great by the way."

"Thanks," Audrey said with a grin. "I'm glad you think so, because I'm totally going to have you take a photo before I leave."

"Okay, you know I say this without judgment," Claire said softly. "And I'm thrilled that Scandal Boy's backed off since you started this whole little charade. But do you feel at all weird letting your followers think you're engaged?"

"I did," Audrey admitted. "And I wouldn't say the lying feels *good*. But then I started getting so many comments from brides-to-be who've been loving my advice, who've asked a million questions about bridal hairstyles, makeup, venue ideas. The wedding market is huge and underserved, and there's a shortage of unbiased influences. Either you have the vendors, who are trying to sell you something, or you have the brides-to-be themselves, many of whom keep the details of their wedding planning secret, either because it's personal or because they don't want anyone copying their ideas."

"Ooh. You could influence them toward digital invitations!" Claire said.

Audrey laughed. "Precisely. It started out selfishly, but I've been shocked by the enthusiastic response, the way I can provide some insight into the process of planning a wedding in New York

City. I've reframed it. I'm not a *fake* bride. I'm an undercover bride."

"Very clever way to make sure you can sleep at night without any guilt," Naomi said, putting a hand over her chest. "I've never been so proud."

"I've learned from your business savvy," Audrey said, blowing a kiss to her wildly successful boss-babe of a friend.

"I love that we're all entrepreneurs," Naomi said happily.

"I don't know that I'm on the same tier," Claire said with a laugh. "Your company's valued at eight figures. Eight. And Audrey here's passed the million mark in followers. Literally, a *million* human beings follow her every move."

"But you love it, right?" Audrey asked. "The calligraphy business?"

Claire's hazel eyes were happy. "I do. Thinking of my life a year ago, it's hard to picture where I am now. A thriving little business doing something I love. A dog. A *husband*."

Audrey smiled as her friend shook her head in disbelief, content down to her very soul that Claire had found happiness in the aftermath of Brayden's betrayal with Audrey.

And Naomi, too, though of the three of them, Audrey suspected Naomi had been the least scathed by Brayden. Not unaffected—there was nothing easy about finding out your lover had (a) died and (b) been married the entire time.

Naomi had been seeing Brayden for a shorter amount of time and hadn't known that Claire even existed until he died. They'd never talked about it, but Audrey had always assumed that blissful ignorance meant that Naomi didn't carry around the guilt that continued to haunt Audrey to this day.

She should have done her homework, shouldn't have taken it at face value when he'd told her that he and Claire weren't even living in the same house. Shouldn't have believed him when he'd said that they were days away from signing divorce papers.

Audrey knew Claire now. Knew that none of it had been true. What had been brutally true was that Audrey was the other woman. The whole time she'd thought she'd finally found her happily ever after, she was destroying someone else's. A woman who, as Audrey had come to discover, deserved it more than anyone she knew.

"Okay, I have to ask," Naomi said. "How long are you going to keep up your undercover-bride thing?"

"Oh, not much longer. I imagine once we get through to-night—"

"Yeah, why *are* we doing this tonight?" Claire asked curiously. "Don't get me wrong, I'm thrilled to have the chance to get dressed up and go to a fancy party with my closest friends, but an engagement party seems . . ."

"Over-the-top?" Audrey said. "Tell me about it. Though it makes a little more sense if you've met Clarke's mom. Crazy as this is, I can kind of get why he wanted to call her bluff on this party. She was just so *smug* when we were there for dinner. I'd probably have agreed to just about anything to knock her down a peg."

"I'm dying to meet Clarke's parents," Naomi said.

"Same," Claire admitted. "I imagine they're a vital part of the puzzle that is Clarke."

Audrey blinked in surprise. "What do you mean?"

As far as she was concerned, Clarke was an open book.

"Just that when you first meet him, he seems so easygoing, without a care in the world," Claire explained. "But the more you get to know him, the more you realize something's going on beneath the surface. Based on the way he talks about his parents, I figured they had something to do with it."

"Yeah," Audrey said, looking down at her champagne. "They're very . . . I don't know. They're not bad people. I just think they're not suited to being parents. They've always treated Clarke like an extension of them rather than a person in his own right. His dad's blind to just about anything other than the company. And I know it bugs Clarke that Alton always just assumed Clarke would follow in his footsteps, and yet at the same time he makes it clear that it's not a foregone conclusion that Clarke will inherit the CEO title one day. It's like he wants Clarke to earn it but won't tell him how."

"What about his mom?"

"Control freak," Audrey said, taking a sip of champagne. "Her husband does everything she says, and it's always bugged her that even as a kid, Clarke would never comply with her demands the way his dad does. Clarke played baseball when she wanted him to study. He was prom king when she wanted him to be valedictorian."

"Classic rebellion," Naomi said knowingly.

"It didn't start that way," Audrey said. "I've known Clarke since we were kids, and I've seen him go through all the stages. Bewilderment that his parents were so against things that he loved. Sports, bugs, charming just about anyone who crossed his path. Then he went through an acquiescence phase, trying to learn to love science club and student council. That lasted about a month before the real Clarke burst out again, and then I think he just . . . gave up. Ironically, it's only in adulthood that he's gone full-on rebel. It's like he goes out of his way to do whatever they don't want him to."

"Including marrying you?"

Audrey grinned. "His mom hates me."

"I can't picture that," Claire said with a shake of her head.

"I've never seen friends as dedicated to each other as you two."

"Okay, she doesn't *hate* me," Audrey said. "But her feelings definitely top out at tolerance. She's always made it quite clear that her vision for Clarke's girlfriend is not a cheerleader turned sorority girl turned Instagram influencer."

"So, she didn't want him with someone hot," Naomi concluded.

"I think it's my flightiness that bothers her."

"You're not flighty."

"No, but I'm no Elizabeth Milsap," Audrey said, a little surprised by the edge in her own tone.

Her friends seemed surprised, too. They exchanged a look. "Who?"

She forced a casual shrug. "Clarke's ex and half the reason we're in this mess in the first place. She and Clarke broke up when she moved to DC a couple years ago. Now, she's back in town, and Clarke's mom's gotten it in her head that Elizabeth would be the perfect daughter-in-law."

"Would she be?"

Audrey hesitated. "I don't know. She's smart, ambitious, well-spoken."

"Yawn," Naomi said.

"But I don't dislike her," Audrey said. "I didn't know her well. Whenever we did hang out, she was interesting to talk to, and though mostly serious, she did have a sharp sense of humor that made rare appearances."

"But what does Clarke think about her?"

Good question. Audrey hated to admit it, but she wasn't entirely sure where Clarke stood when it came to his beautiful, if slightly mysterious, ex-girlfriend. On one hand, he was certainly going to great lengths to avoid his mother's scheming to push him and Elizabeth together. On the other hand, when his mother had tricked him into going to lunch with his ex, he hadn't walked away. When his mother had brought his ex to his engagement dinner, Clarke hadn't said a word against it.

Liz. She couldn't stop hearing him say it, couldn't stop seeing his face every time he'd uttered the nickname. How had she not noticed before that he was *different* when Liz's name came up? More importantly, why did she even care? It's not like they were really engaged. And they certainly weren't in love.

"I don't know," Audrey admitted. "I thought she was just another one of the billion women who have come and gone from his life, albeit with a bit more staying power. But maybe there's something I'm missing."

"Maybe she's his Meredith," Claire said.

"Or his Bridget," Naomi said in an ominous voice.

"Who?" Audrey asked, not recognizing either name.

"Scott and Oliver's ex-fiancées," Claire said.

"Oh, that's right," Audrey said, tapping her fingers on the glass. "I'd forgotten both those guys were engaged before they met you."

"I try to forget it," Naomi said, not bothering to keep the possessive note out of her voice. "Bridget bailed on Oliver after both his parents got sick within the same year. She's dead to me."

"And Meredith cheated on Scott, sooooo . . ." Claire trailed off, her statement pretty much saying it all.

"Jeez," Audrey muttered.

"Hence all those *delightful* trust issues that Claire and I get to work through with them," Naomi said with a grin. "Maybe it's the same with Clarke and this Elizabeth. Maybe *all* our guys have their individual female version of Brayden. You know. Their demon."

"Okay, crucial difference," Audrey pointed out. "Clarke's not *my guy*."

"Sorry, but who bought you that Tiffany ring?"

"And who's been your other half since, what, age seven?" Claire added.

"You know what I mean," Audrey said. "It's not the same. And if you're asking whether Elizabeth hurt Clarke the way those girls hurt your guys, I don't think so."

"He's never mentioned it?"

Audrey fiddled with her earring. "No."

"Well, he tells you everything, so maybe she really *was* just some girl who came and went, who he doesn't want to get saddled with now just because his weird mom has an agenda. Also, party starts in ten, and as guest of honor, a fashionably late entrance will be no good. We should go," Naomi said as she put her credit card down on the bill the server had just dropped off.

Claire was watching Audrey closely. "You're not sure how Clarke feels about this Elizabeth woman."

"I'm not," Audrey admitted, though it pained her. "I get the feeling maybe I underestimated the impact her leaving had on Clarke."

"You think she's the reason he agreed to let this fake engagement go so far as the fancy party we're about to go to?"

"I don't know," Audrey said as they stood. "But I'm about to find out, with your help."

"How's that?"

"Because," Audrey muttered, "you're about to meet her. Clarke's mother invited his ex-girlfriend to my engagement party."

Chapter Five

*W*here is your wayward groom?" Claire asked as the three of them stepped into the NoMad Hotel, just around the corner from their drinks location. "If you guys are going to sell this togetherness thing, shouldn't you walk in . . . together?"

"He'll be here," Audrey said, putting a palm against her stomach, surprised to feel the fluttering of nervous butterflies at the night ahead. Talking about wedding planning on Instagram was one thing. Walking into a room full of people who actually thought there would *be* a wedding was another. At least half of them were probably watching with an eagle eye to see if all the rumors about Audrey's bad luck with men were true.

She answered Claire distractedly. "He had a business trip to Miami. Or maybe Palm Beach?"

"Orlando, actually."

All three women turned to see Clarke just behind them.

Audrey's butterflies immediately vanished. Yes, she'd be walking into a room full of people as a fake bride-to-be, but she wouldn't be alone.

She looked down in puzzlement when she realized he was wheeling a suitcase behind him and had a garment bag over his shoulder. To say nothing of the fact that Clarke could pull off just about any look, she was definitely looking at *rumpled* Clarke right now. The hair was a little crazy, he needed a shave, and the jeans and wrinkled, untucked dress shirt were better suited for stumbling out of the club at 3 a.m. than they were for a formal cocktail party. Hosted by his mother.

"Is this just-woke-up look your newest way of pissing off Linda?" Audrey asked curiously.

He laughed and ran a hand over his face, which she belatedly realized showed all the classic signs of exhaustion. There were dark circles beneath his eyes, his smile less easy than usual.

"I just got into JFK an hour ago," he said by way of explanation. "And traffic was, you know, standard Manhattan fair."

"So, awful?" Naomi said sympathetically.

He gave her a fleeting smile, then apparently belatedly realizing he hadn't greeted his friends, pulled both Claire and Naomi in for a hug. "I haven't seen you beauties in forever."

"Rumor has it you've been busy and congratulations are in order?" Claire asked teasingly.

His smile was more genuine this time. "Hell of a game Dree and I have going on, huh?"

"Definitely," Naomi agreed. "Although, if I can be blunt—"

"Aren't you always?" he asked.

"Exactly. Which is why I'll tell you, you look like hell, and nobody is going to believe Audrey would marry a guy who shows up to his own engagement party looking like this."

"Try telling that to the family patriarch," he muttered.

Audrey frowned. "What did your dad do?"

"Sent me to a damn conference in Florida. Told me it ended yesterday. *Wrong*. The keynote speech was today."

"Couldn't you have politely bailed, saying you had a rather important *thing* you had to attend?" Claire asked, pointing at Audrey's clearly bridal-esque ensemble.

"I was *giving* the keynote," Clarke said. "Something my dad conveniently forgot to mention. I had zero chance of catching my original flight and barely got on standby for the flight I did."

Audrey laughed. "Oh dear. Your parents *really* don't want you to marry me, huh?"

"They just don't want me to do anything that wasn't their idea. My mother, however, did make a rather crucial mistake."

"Shoulder pads? Please tell me she's not one of those women who wears shoulder pads," Naomi pleaded.

"Not anymore," Audrey reassured her. "Now she just rocks a lot of pantsuits."

"Okay, but what was her mistake?" Claire asked Clarke.

"Well, no doubt they hoped I'd show up haggard without a chance to get ready. But if that were the case, she shouldn't have thrown this shindig at a hotel." He jiggled the garment bag that was slung over his shoulder.

"*Brilliant*," Claire said. "You can get a room and turn into your usual James Bond self."

"Actually, I don't think James Bond would even need a room. I'm pretty sure he could have managed to change and shave in the Uber . . ." Audrey said.

Clarke gave her a look. "Remind me again why I agreed to marry you?"

She blew him a playful kiss. "Okay, you go get ready. We'll hold down the fort."

"Uh-uh," Naomi said, already shaking her head. "Claire and I will hold down the fort. You will go off with Clarke. If you two want to sell this, you've got to show up at the party *together*."

"She's right." Claire nodded. "Audrey walking in with her two friends and Clarke showing up later is going to look strange."

"All right, Dree, you're with me," he said, already heading across the lobby toward the front desk to check in.

Audrey hesitated. "I thought you guys said I couldn't be fashionably late to my own engagement party."

"Generally, no. But being fashionably late because you and your fiancé just came from a hotel room together? Deliciously scandalous."

Audrey wrinkled her nose. "Eww. Everyone will think we were doing it."

"Audrey, you're supposed to be marrying the man. Everyone *should* think you're doing it."

"Right, right. Okay. You guys can make polite excuses for us?"

"Absolutely," Claire assured her. "Plus, Oliver and Scott are meeting us up there. Nobody does charming upper-crust chitchat like Oliver."

"You *do* realize that Oliver's there as my date. You're married to Scott," Naomi said, bemused.

"Yes, but do we *really* want Scott to be the one making small talk?" Claire asked, knowing full well that her husband, while sinfully rich and a pseudo-celebrity in the world of Manhattan real estate, had little tolerance for pretty manners.

"Right, okay. Go. Make sure you mess up your hair a little, like you were doing the nasty," Naomi said, gently shoving Audrey toward Clarke. "Oliver and Claire will make fancy talk. Scott and I will stomp around and glare at anyone that dares to grumble at your absence."

"You'd *better* not grumble," Audrey said. "There's a caviar and champagne bar up there."

"Ooh. Well, in that case, tell Clarke to hurry up," Claire said.

Audrey nodded in acknowledgment and headed toward a waiting Clarke.

"Hey, but, Audrey?" Naomi called.

She turned back toward her friend, who gave her a side grin. "Don't hurry too much. Clarke doesn't strike me as the type of man who would rush through *that*."

Audrey rolled her eyes and turned away. She had never spent much time thinking about her best friend's sex life, and she certainly wasn't about to start now.

———

"Do you really think your parents did it on purpose?" Audrey called from the bed, her feet dangling over the side. She'd kicked off the Louboutins. As expected, cute definitely did not equate to comfortable.

"Did what?" Clarke asked back through the open bathroom door.

"Arrange for you to be the keynote speaker on the same day as your engagement party."

There was a knock at the hotel room door before he could answer, and Audrey hopped off the bed. "I'll get it."

She opened the door to a smartly dressed hotel employee holding a tray with champagne in an ice bucket and two flutes. "Champagne for Mr. West and Ms. Tate, courtesy of Naomi and Claire," he said by way of explanation.

Audrey rolled her eyes, even as she stepped aside to let him bring the tray into the suite Clarke had reserved for the night.

"On the table okay?"

"Sure, that's great," she said, picking Clarke's wallet off the dresser and pulling out some cash for a tip.

"May I open the bottle for you?" the man asked.

"No, thank you, we've got it from here," Audrey said.

He nodded in acknowledgment, wished them a good night, and closed the door behind him with a quiet click.

Clarke stuck his head out of the bathroom, the lower half of his face covered in shaving cream. "Champagne?"

Audrey lifted the bottle out of the ice bucket to read the label. "Taittinger."

"Let's open it."

She glanced at the clock on the nightstand. "It's six oh five."

"Exactly. The party's been happening for all of five minutes. The majority of the guests haven't even left their penthouses yet."

He had a point. Fancy engagement parties in their world could go all night as people stopped by before dinner plans, after dinner plans, and so on.

"Besides," he called, disappearing back into the bathroom, "this party's really more about my mother than it is us."

"At least you're admitting it," she replied, pulling the foil off the top of the bottle.

"I never denied it."

"Well, I thought it might be at least a *little* bit about Elizabeth," she said, keeping her voice casual as she attempted to twist the cork off the champagne, but it remained stubbornly put. And Clarke remained stubbornly silent.

She gave the cork a few more twists before deciding it needed bigger hands and more muscle. Audrey took it into the bathroom, coming up short at the sight of a bare-chested Clarke. After taking a quick shower, he'd pulled on his suit pants but was apparently waiting until he finished shaving before putting on a shirt.

She swallowed, feeling strangely flustered.

Audrey had seen Clarke shirtless plenty of times over the years. Hot tubs, swimming pools, the beach, on a boat. But this felt decidedly different. His hair was wet, the bathroom was still steamy from his shower, and the gentle scraping sound of his razor against his jaw was surprisingly intimate.

He glanced over at her questioningly, then seeing the champagne bottle in her hand, jerked his chin in acknowledgment. With one last swipe of the razor, he set it aside and rinsed the shaving cream from his face.

Clarke grabbed a hand towel off the sink to dry his face and extended his other hand for the champagne bottle. "Hoping to get a look at the goods before you purchase?"

"Hmm?"

"It's very wifely. You creeping on me in the bathroom."

She rolled her eyes. "I'm here for the champagne, not your six-pack."

And it was definitely a six-pack.

She narrowed her eyes and gave his upper body a scrutinizing look. "Either you're suspiciously hairless or you wax your chest."

"The latter," he said, wrapping one hand around the champagne bottle, the other around the cork. "Women seem to prefer it." He twisted the top off with a confident pop.

"Plus, nothing to block your view of your chest muscles when you preen," she pointed out.

He grinned and handed her the bottle. "True. Why, you prefer your guys hairy?"

"Well, not when you put it that way," she said with a wince. "But I do usually prefer *man* over pretty boy."

He gave a sad shake of his head. "Damn. Our marriage is off to a rough start."

"Chest hair is our first irreconcilable difference," she agreed, retreating to the bedroom to pour two glasses of champagne. Well, actually, a half glass for herself. She was already one glass in, and she wanted to keep her head clear.

"So, what's our plan?" she asked, handing him his glass as he joined her in the bedroom.

"Hold on," he said. "Toast first."

"To what?"

He shook his head and, reaching out, unceremoniously clinked his glass to hers, which she had yet to raise before taking a sip. "I don't know. Friendship?"

"To friendship," she agreed, taking a tiny sip and setting the glass aside. "And to getting *back* to being just friends. How soon can we call this off after a fancy engagement party without it being weird?"

"The whole thing is weird."

"Well, that's true," she agreed. "I *still* don't understand why we didn't tell your parents that we'd changed our minds at dinner on Friday."

It had been bothering her all week, but with his work travel schedule, she hadn't seen him, and it hadn't seemed like a conversation to have by text or phone.

He settled on the foot of the bed, feet braced on the floor, staring down at the wine. The shower and shave had helped considerably in making him look more like himself, but they hadn't erased the dark shadows beneath his eyes.

"I don't know," he admitted, taking another sip of the wine. "For a minute there, standing in their living room, I felt like a seventeen-year-old kid again, desperate to piss them off the way they piss me off. I'm not proud of it."

"You know your mom only gets all up in your business because she loves you, right?"

He frowned and looked down, from side to side. "That's odd. I could have *sworn* I'm sitting on a bed, not lying on a couch."

Audrey rolled her eyes and went to sit beside him. "I'm just saying. Maybe if you tried talking to her, you could tell her you don't want to be with Elizabeth, rather than pretending to be engaged to me?"

He took a generous swallow of the champagne. "Quick refresher, Tate. This wasn't my idea."

"I know," she agreed quickly. "But it feels different now. Pretending to be engaged to get the Internet trolls off my back versus lying to family."

"All families are not created equal," he said, his voice a little testy. "Your family's an upper-class *Leave It to Beaver*. Mine's more like an East Coast *Dallas*."

"You watch *Dallas*?"

"I'm very evolved. You know this."

She smiled and looked down at her bare feet, wiggling her toes. "It's been sort of fun."

"What?"

"Being engaged this past week."

"Well, of course. I'm a fantastic fiancé."

"You're a *terrible* fiancé," she corrected. "I haven't seen you in days. But I'd forgotten how much I'd once dreamed of being a bride-to-be. There's a special sort of energy that comes along with an engagement, even the fake kind. Though, I imagine you're eager to be done with it."

He glanced down at her. "Why would you think that?"

"Well, you can't very well be wooing every woman in the bar the way you normally do while I've got this rock on my finger."

"If that's your way of asking if I've stepped out on my fiancée, absolutely not."

"Well, congratulations," she said dryly. "You've made it an entire week without sex."

"Thank you for noting my sacrifice." Clarke glanced down at his watch, then stood, refilling their champagne before taking his shirt off the hanger and pulling it on. "Guess we should go pretend to be in love, huh?"

"*You* pretend to be in love. I'm just here to show off my shoes," she said, reaching down to pull on the painful but beautiful pumps.

"And I need you to say it out loud, we're done after this, right?" she said, stepping toward Clarke and batting his hands aside to fix the tie knot he was mangling. "Your mom will get the message to back off with the Elizabeth stuff, and Scandal Boy and his minions have gotten the hint that I'm not a romantic pariah."

"How do you know they won't be back with a vengeance when we call it off?" he asked, studying her. "That they won't say, 'There she goes, losing another one'?"

"I thought about that," she admitted. "Which is why it's going to be crucial that I'm the one who dumps you." She gave his chest a friendly pat. "How's your fake cry?"

"How much time do I have to work on it?"

She shrugged. "This is your show now. We can either issue a peaceful statement in the next day or two, or we can put on a spectacular show tonight. We can have it be about something silly but real. Like, let's say, maybe I'm not so keen on the fact that you're texting another woman during our engagement party?"

Clarke grinned as he pulled on his suit jacket. "Spectacular. My playboy reputation could use a bit of a boost anyway. Shall we?" he asked, extending his arm to her.

She smiled and slid her hand into the crook of his elbow, though her smile slipped a little as they headed toward the elevator, wondering why Clarke seemed so eager to play the part of villain.

Chapter Six

Well, well, well, she's done it again. As if she didn't attempt to steal the late Brayden Hayes out from under his wife, it turns out our little home wrecker has been up to her old tricks . . .
—@ScandalBoyNYC

*C*larke was at the bar ordering himself a martini when his mother finally cornered him.

"Enjoying yourself?" Linda asked mildly. She held out her glass for the bartender to refill her chardonnay, not caring, or noticing, that she'd just cut in front of five people. Clarke knew that as the hostess of the party, it was her prerogative. Just as he *also* knew his mother would have cut in line regardless of whose party it was.

It never occurred to her that the Honorable Judge West would be treated with anything but deference to the point of worship. Though, in reality, most people fell in line. As a boy, his childhood friends had never spoken above a whisper in her presence. Even his teachers had spoken in almost hushed tones when they'd called his mother into the office for yet another *we have some concerns about Clarke's behavior in the classroom* talk. It hadn't gotten better as he'd gotten older. Girlfriends, colleagues, even his own father—*especially* his own father—acted as though Linda West's word was law, her agenda manifest destiny.

Everyone, except for Clarke himself.

Well, and Audrey. Even as a four-foot little girl with an ever-present bow in her hair, it had never seemed to occur to Audrey that his terrifying mother should be treated differently than her friends, her own mother, or her imaginary friends. It was one of the things he'd always liked best about Audrey. She simply saw people as people.

"Enjoying myself immensely," Clarke answered his mother as the two of them stepped to the side of the bar.

"Audrey seems to be in her element," Linda said, taking a sip of her wine.

Knowing that any mention of Audrey usually came with a side order of insult, Clarke scanned the room for his "fiancée."

Even if she hadn't been the only woman in the room wearing white, he'd have seen her right away. Not just because he always seemed to have a sixth sense for his best friend's presence, but because now, as always, everyone and everything seemed to revolve around her. Audrey had always been the very opposite of a wallflower, the center of attention, often in the literal center of every room. She didn't set out to have all eyes on her; all eyes just seemed to find her.

He smiled as the sound of her happy laugh reached him fifteen feet away, even with the conversation of fifty-something people buzzing around them.

"How nice that her parents could fly out for the celebration," Linda said.

Clarke didn't know where Audrey's father had disappeared to, but Audrey's mom was right by her side, an older version of her daughter, with the same bright smile and friendly presence.

Quick to laugh and easy to like, Kathleen Tate was the exact opposite of Clarke's own mother. Growing up, it had often been Kathleen that Clarke had turned to when he'd had a problem at school, with a girl, or with his parents. Something, Clarke was sure, Linda had taken notice of. In fact, he was willing to bet it was one of the many reasons why Linda seemed to dislike the Tates.

The other, of course, being that they were "party people who'd inherited their wealth and thus hadn't known a hard day's work in their life."

"Doesn't Audrey have a sister?" Linda mused.

"Adele," Clarke said, even though he knew full well that his mother knew everything there was to know about the Tates. "She just had twins a month ago and couldn't fly out."

"Kathleen and Richard must be thrilled to have grand-children. I understand that since neither of them work, they're able to care for the babies so that Audrey's sister could return to her law firm. I admire a woman who prioritizes a stable career and rearing children."

Clarke rolled his eyes. No way was he going to touch that conversational dynamite. It was almost impressive, the way his mother managed to load multiple land mines into a couple sentences. *Where are my grandchildren? Not that I'd be able to play nanny, since your father and I have real work, unlike the Tates. Oh, and wouldn't it be nice if Audrey had a real job instead of taking pictures all day?*

"Interesting," Clarke said, taking a drink of his cocktail.

"What?"

"You weren't entirely sure that Audrey had a sister, and yet you know said sister's career choice?"

"Lucky guess," she said, refusing to rise to the bait.

His mind now on the topic of attorneys, Clarke looked around for a different lawyer. The one who was half-responsible for his agreeing to this party in the first place. He hadn't seen Elizabeth all night and wondered if his ex had had the good sense not to play into his mom's manipulations by coming to his engagement party.

Without realizing it, his gaze specifically scanned for navy, which had been Elizabeth's go-to for everything from suits to casual wear to ball gowns.

Sure enough, there she was, dressed in a knee-length navy dress and matching heels. Basic short heels, he noted, not a hint of lace or frills or bows like Audrey tended to prefer. He was strangely disappointed in Elizabeth for attending the party, until he realized the hypocrisy of that thought.

He was the one who'd been so childishly annoyed by his mother's attempts to push him toward Elizabeth that he'd called Linda's bluff on this stupid party.

And Audrey had been right. Playing pretend-engaged as a joke to halt some Instagram moron's gossip chain was fun. Continuing the play to get back at one's mother at thirty-one was straight-up pathetic.

His mother must have read his thoughts, because she stepped slightly closer, lowering her voice to avoid eavesdroppers. "I was only trying to help."

Clarke didn't pretend to misunderstand. "By trying to force me back together with a woman I haven't seen or even talked to in years?"

"Are you sure you and Elizabeth weren't good together?" she asked, a thread of stubbornness in her voice.

Had they been? Truth be told, Elizabeth Milsap had always been a bit of a blind spot for Clarke. Despite being his longest relationship to date, he wasn't sure he'd ever really known the woman, and he *definitely* hadn't known himself when he was with her. She was different from every other woman he'd dated, or slept with. Driven, serious, a little bit quiet. She'd held herself, and everyone around her, to high standards.

And when she'd left, she'd made it quite clear that Clarke had never met those standards. And he'd told himself and everyone else that it hadn't mattered.

But the truth was, her dismissal had burned. Because though he hated to admit it, even to himself, Clarke had been *trying*. He'd been trying to be everything Elizabeth wanted, everything, even, that his parents had hoped him to be. For the first time in his life, he'd put in actual effort to please someone else. He'd learned how to cook. He'd brought home the damned *just because* flowers that women were always claiming were so important. He'd learned how to make the weird loose leaf French tea Elizabeth had loved so much, and he'd dutifully gone to every lawyerly dinner party and fund-raiser, no matter how boring, and they'd been excruciatingly dull.

The worst part was, Clarke had thought he'd been pulling it off. He'd thought they'd been on a steady, albeit slow, path to maybe ring shopping in the not-so-distant future. Elizabeth, on the other hand, had made it quite clear when she'd taken the job in DC without so much as a conversation, that he was the fun guy you dated before you married—not the guy you *actually* married.

In hindsight, he was relieved. He was fairly certain that they'd never have made each other truly happy. In the moment, though, it had hurt, both his pride *and* his feelings, and he had no interest in repeating any of it. Ever.

"Couldn't you have just asked me if I wanted to get back together with Elizabeth?" he asked his mom tiredly. "Didn't the engagement party feel a bit much?"

She smiled. "I was curious how far you and Audrey were going to take this thing. All the way, it seems."

"Well, not *all* the way," he said, smiling back in spite of himself.

"Good, because I'll happily host a fake engagement party, but I do draw the line at hosting a fake wedding."

"Noted. How'd you know?" he asked curiously.

"That your engagement wasn't real?"

He nodded.

"Well, that's the thing about being a mother. You get to know pretty quickly when your son is just trying to push your buttons."

"There's a little more to it than that," Clarke said, thinking of the petty Scandal Boy bullshit.

"I figured. Leave it to that girl to turn even marriage into a dog and pony show."

Defending Audrey to his mother had always been a waste of breath, but Clarke had never quit trying. And he wasn't going to stop now.

"You know," he said, taking another slow sip of his drink, "in all the years I've known Audrey, she's never *not* been there when I needed her."

"And?"

Clarke shrugged. "I'm just saying, there are two types of women. The ones who stay by your side. And the ones who move to Washington, DC, without asking you to go with them."

Leaving his mother to stew on his parting shot, and maybe,

just maybe, realize he could manage his own life better than she could, Clarke began making his way toward Audrey, stopping to shake hands and accept congratulations along the way. Strange, that although this party was all for show, the congratulations misplaced, none of this felt in the least bit odd. Shouldn't this advanced game of pretend feel wrong?

A hand caught his sleeve, and Clarke turned, smiling when he saw Naomi Powell and Claire Hayes. No, Claire *Turner*, he amended, remembering her spontaneous marriage to Scott Turner a few months earlier and her decision to take her new husband's name.

Clarke had thought Audrey's relationship with these two strange at first, considering how it had begun. Clarke had known enough women over the course of his life to think that a friendship between three women who'd all slept with the same man couldn't possibly be built to last.

He was wrong, though, and happy to be wrong. The three of them may have come together over their shared scorn for Brayden Hayes and their desire to protect one another from future heartache, but whatever had *kept* them together was much stronger than any man. Of all Audrey's friends, and she had dozens, these two ladies were perhaps his favorites.

Clarke cared for Audrey more than anyone, save perhaps her immediate family, but he knew Claire and Naomi came close in terms of being willing to do just about anything for her.

Which is why, seeing the troubled look on both of their faces, he dropped his smile immediately. "What's up?"

Naomi nodded her head to the side of the room, away from the crowd, and Clarke followed.

Wordlessly, Claire handed him her phone, Instagram already pulled up.

Clarke immediately went on high alert when he saw the account in question. @ScandalBoyNYC.

Alert turned to disbelief as he read, before finally settling on a deep and quiet anger.

He handed the phone back to Claire. "That bastard."

"Who, Randy or Scandal Boy?" Naomi asked.

"I want to pummel both, but Randy's first in line," Clarke said. "He was *married*?"

"Apparently," Claire said. "Even if Scandal Boy made it up, a rumor's every bit as damaging as the truth."

"Especially *this* rumor," Naomi said. "It's already all over that she was dating a married man. When people find out it happened twice . . ."

"They already have found out," Claire said glumly, thumbing through Instagram. "It's only been an hour, and already there are a thousand comments on Scandal Boy's post. Even worse, they've started commenting on her most recent post."

"What's the gist?" Clarke asked.

Claire's shoulders lifted. "About what you'd expect. Once a home wrecker, always a home wrecker. Find your own man."

"But she has found her own man," Naomi protested. "Or she has at least as far as they know." She pointed at Clarke.

Claire kept reading the comments and gave a sad shake of her head. "Apparently they're not buying it. Someone posted that at her 'engagement party'—that's in quotes—the so-called couple hasn't spent so much as five minutes together or touched even once. Now everyone's theorizing that you're her damage control 'beard,'" she told Clarke.

"Well, they're not entirely wrong," Naomi admitted, "but this also means that *someone* at this party is busy posting updates on Instagram."

"Who!" Claire demanded, looking up and glaring around the room, her anger palpable.

"Could be anyone. Probably a few of them," Clarke said, already thinking of a couple of catty attendees who'd always resented being the distant Plutos to Audrey's sun. He could think of a couple more whom he'd dated over the years who liked to imagine it was Audrey's fault that Clarke had dumped them.

"This is our fault," Claire said, the distress in her voice clear. "We agreed to protect one another. She's held her end up of the pact flawlessly for both of us, and we let this happen to her?"

"Simply suggesting Randy was a dud wasn't enough," Naomi said in glum agreement. "I *knew* there was something off about that guy. I should have handcuffed her to my side until that flea went to bother someone else."

"No," Clarke said. "You two have done plenty for her. I've got this one."

"You already fake proposed," Naomi pointed out. "I don't know what else you can do."

He handed his drink to Claire. "Hold this. It's time Audrey and I started selling this thing."

Audrey was a little surprised by how much she was enjoying herself. She'd always loved parties, but she'd expected this one to feel awkward given the circumstances. Instead, she was relieved to find it just felt like a group of people together in the same room celebrating love. And they were celebrating love. Friendship love, of the non-romantic variety.

"It's going great," her mother said, linking her arm with Audrey's and grinning happily. "Did you hear the story I told about you calling to tell me about the proposal?"

Audrey rolled her eyes. "I think multiple time zones probably heard that story based on the level of zeal in your voice."

"Was it too much?"

Audrey kissed her mom's cheek, more grateful than ever for her fun-loving, up-for-anything mother. "It was perfect. Though, I feel like one of us should inform Clarke that he rode a white stallion bareback through Central Park before someone else asks him to verify the story."

"You can fill him in right now," Kathleen said, patting Audrey's arm and nodding toward Clarke making his way over to her. She took Audrey's champagne flute out of her hand. "I'm going to go check on your father, and I'll get us some refills."

Audrey nodded in acknowledgment, then smiled at Clarke as he approached. "Hi! I haven't seen you all night."

"Yeah, that's sort of a problem," he said quietly.

Her smile fell as she registered the terse note in his voice and the tension around his eyes. "What's wrong?"

His gaze dropped to her clutch. "You haven't checked your phone?"

Audrey's stomach dropped. "No, I've been too busy making the rounds. Why? What's happened?"

Clarke looked up, noting, as she had, that people were done giving Audrey a reprieve and wanted a moment with the guest of honor. Guests, now that Clarke had joined her.

He stepped closer and gave her a fleeting smile, lowering his voice even further. "They're onto us, darling."

"What do you mean?" But she already knew what he meant. Knew that their engagement being a sham had somehow hit the rumor mill. And judging by Clarke's atypically serious expression, something beyond a little petty gossip was at play.

"Smile," he instructed, stepping even closer and sliding his hand around her waist. She smiled automatically, even as she registered that his hand had slid low on her back, his face needlessly close to hers.

"Clarke—"

"Brace yourself," he said out of the corner of his mouth.

"What—"

His lips closed over hers.

Audrey's eyes went wide in surprise before they fluttered closed, her hands waving helplessly for a moment as she tried to register the strangeness of Clarke's mouth against hers before they instinctively lifted to rest on his chest.

It was no big deal, she told her thundering heart. Just a perfunctory stamp of a kiss to get the doubters to back off. It'd be over before she knew it.

Clarke's lips moved against hers, his head tilting to the side, deepening the kiss slightly as his hand slid up her back, pulling her more firmly against him.

Audrey felt something strange and unfamiliar flutter in her stomach. Before she could identify it, Clarke lifted his head. His gaze stayed locked on her lips for a long moment, giving her a second to gather her thoughts.

Damn. He's *really* selling this, she realized. She knew it was all for show, but she still could have sworn she felt heat in his gaze, as though he were silently willing the rest of the room away so it was just the two of them.

His eyes lifted to hers, and she thought she saw a flicker of confusion before he straightened and grinned at his colleague and her husband, who were watching them with bemused smiles.

"Leslie!" he said in a cheerful voice. "So glad you could make it. Apologies for the, ah—moment," he said with a wink.

"I get it," she said with a laugh. "Chris and I were young once, too."

"You say that like I have a walker," her fifty-something husband grumbled.

"And yet, you don't kiss me like *that* anymore," she said teasingly.

Nobody kisses like that, Audrey thought.

She desperately wanted a moment to gather her thoughts, to find out what had prompted the kiss, but she couldn't let Clarke carry the show alone, so she linked her arm through his and chatted with the middle-aged couple. "I'm so glad you could make it. I haven't seen you since, what, Joel's wedding last summer?"

For the next several minutes, she made small talk and fielded wedding questions, all the while trying to ward off the sense of panic, the sense that things were spiraling out of control. Her panic escalated another notch when after her mother rejoined them, handing Audrey a glass of champagne, Clarke took her free hand, linked his fingers in hers, lifted her hand to his lips, and planted a kiss on the back of her hand as though it were the most natural thing in the world.

"You guys mind if I steal my fiancée for a moment?" Clarke asked the group surrounding them. Audrey noted the way his eyes sought out and found her mom's and the way her mom immediately took control of the situation, launching into an animated story about how Clarke had come home from college to accompany Audrey to prom after her high school boyfriend had come down with mono. She'd known then and there that he was *the one*.

Her mom hadn't known any such thing, but Audrey was grateful for the distraction as she let Clarke lead her through the crowd and out onto the rooftop patio. Since January was too cold to take advantage of the outdoor space, it was deserted. Clarke shrugged out of his jacket, dropping it over her shoulders. She didn't protest.

"What's going on?"

He shoved his hand into his pocket and pulled out his cell phone, scrolling until he found what he was looking for. She wasn't surprised when she saw the issue stemmed from Instagram, but she was surprised by what she saw there.

Audrey's eyes watered automatically. "He was *married*? Randy was married?"

"Apparently."

She looked up at Clarke, blinking quickly to keep the tears from falling and smearing her makeup. "Why?"

He sighed. "Damn, Dree, I don't know. Men are shits."

She wiped her nose with the back of her hand. "How did Scandal Boy know?"

"I'm guessing his network outnumbers the rats of this city and is just as gross."

"And now everyone thinks you and I are just doing this as damage control." She let out a quick laugh. "Though, I guess they're right, aren't they? And now they're just waiting for us to call it off so they can prove they're right."

"So, let's not," Clarke said.

"Let's not what?"

He smiled. "Call it off."

"Clarke."

"Don't worry, I'm not suggesting we get *married*. I'd make a terrible husband, and I certainly wouldn't wish that upon my best friend. I'm just saying, what's the rush in ending the charade? You said yourself that it was fun. Just a few more days. Until this blows over for real."

"Yeah, but . . . it's fun for me because I'm obsessed with bridal magazines, and yeah, okay, I've sort of always dreamed of taking my Instagram game into the wedding world. But don't pretend it doesn't put a major crimp in your love life."

"It does," he admitted. *"But."* He leaned forward so they were face-to-face. "Turns out I care about you more than I do sex."

Her eyes narrowed in suspicion. "You do?"

"Eh." He grinned. "Mostly."

He held out his hand for her. "Come on, bride. Let's go tell people about how I proposed."

"Oh, about that," she said, setting her hand in his and letting him lead her back inside. "Do you know how to ride a horse . . . ?"

Chapter Seven

*N*ow, you're sure you don't want me to stay here in New York a few more days?" her mom asked for the fifth time since they'd sat down at the dining room table. "I always imagined that when you got married, I'd be dress shopping with you!'

"And if I get married, you will," Audrey reassured Kathleen. *If I ever do.* "But for the hundredth time, Clarke and I are not *actually* getting married."

Her father made a grumbling noise from behind the *Wall Street Journal*.

"Something to say, dear?" Kathleen asked, smearing raspberry jam onto her croissant and taking a dainty bite as she glanced at her husband.

He took his time folding the paper and setting it aside. "Well, it just seems that in my day—"

"Oh no," Audrey said, reaching for a cranberry scone on the pastry plate her mother had had delivered from one of their long-time favorite bakeries. "That's never a good opener."

"In my day," her dad said, undeterred, "matrimony was taken very seriously between two people who were committed to each other."

"Can it, Richard," Audrey's mom said, wiping her mouth. "You and I got married because I was pregnant with Anderson."

"I *knew* it," Audrey said in a dramatic, scandalized voice.

Actually, everyone knew it. Her older brother's birth certificate pretty much said it all. But shotgun wedding or not, her parents had made it work. No, that wasn't quite right. What her mom and dad have went far beyond mere contentment or making the best of their situation. They were the sort of couple that somehow managed to maintain their individuality while simultaneously hating to be away from the other person.

It was love, pure and simple. The sort of love Audrey had once imagined she'd had with Brayden, and the sort of love that Audrey now approached with extreme caution.

"You already know why they're doing this," Kathleen said in defense of her youngest daughter. "Some jealous twats have gotten Audrey in their crosshairs and are trying to take her down. You know all too well what this world can be like. Though, I do miss this house. And Orwashers," she said, looking lovingly at her pastry.

Audrey's parents still owned the penthouse on Madison Avenue, and even now that Audrey had moved out, they kept a live-in housekeeper to ensure it was always ready for when they came into town, or when friends needed a place to stay while visiting the city. Audrey had come over for brunch to spend some time with them before they flew back this afternoon.

"I *do* know how this neighborhood can be," Audrey's dad said in agreement. "It's why I moved to California." He looked at Audrey. "*You* should move to California."

"Yes, because LA is so wonderfully free of superficial gossip," Audrey pointed out.

He wagged his head from side to side in acknowledgment of her point, then picked up the paper again, then put it aside once more, as though he couldn't decide whether he wanted to continue the conversation or not.

He apparently decided yes, because he gave her a pointedly fatherly look. "I don't understand why we don't just confront these people head-on. Tell them to stop telling lies about you."

"They're not lies," Audrey said. "I *was* dating Brayden while he was still married. And I was dating this Randy guy, too."

Audrey's parents had always made open communication with their children the highest priority. They'd been one of her first phone calls after learning of Brayden's betrayal, and she'd told them first thing this morning about what was going on with Randy and the Instagram aftermath.

"But you didn't know they were married."

"I did," Audrey said, nibbling on her scone. "Not that Randy was. I didn't have a clue. But I knew about Claire, remember? I just thought they had separated."

Kathleen sighed. "Oldest snake line in the book."

"That I fell for," Audrey said, refusing to absolve herself of all blame for her role in destroying Claire's illusion of a happy marriage.

"I still don't get what this has to do with Clarke and you two pretending to get married."

"He's protecting my reputation, Daddy," Audrey said in her best Cher Horowitz voice, "so people don't think I'm damaged goods."

"They are calling her Tarnished Tate," Kathleen chimed in.

"I spent two hours this morning seeing what was going on. It was vicious."

Audrey covered her face with her hand. Sadly, the Tarnished Tate moniker was all too true.

To her surprise, her joking and her mother's needling seemed to mollify her father. "I guess it could go a long way to defuse the gossipmonger's energies."

"Not exactly the way I'd phrase it, but yeah, that's the idea," Audrey said.

"Yes, but only if you step it up," her mom said, pushing her plate away and looking at Audrey with a pointed look.

"Uh-oh," Audrey said, sipping her coffee. "What's that look for?"

"In order for them to believe you're getting married, they have to believe you're in love. You can't just say you're in love. You have to *show* it."

Audrey fiddled nervously with the handle of the mug. "Was I not?"

"The only thing close to heat I saw last night was that kiss. He sold it. But you looked like it was the first time you'd ever kissed the man."

"Because it was!"

"Really?" Kathleen titled her head curiously. "I just assumed you two had fooled around back in the day. Teenage curiosity and what not."

Audrey groaned. "Mom. Don't be gross."

"Yes, don't," Richard said, retreating once more behind his newspaper.

"No heavy petting? Nothing? Okay, well, whatever. You and Clarke need to, you know . . . get a little handsy. Stare at him like you can't wait to drag him home."

"Please stop," Richard said.

Kathleen ignored her husband, keeping all of her attention on Audrey as she leaned forward. "And, honey, a little advice from someone who once got into a catfight with a hussy ex of your father's—"

"Ooh!" Audrey sat up straighter. "I haven't heard that story."

"And you won't," Richard said, giving his wife a meaningful look over the top of his paper before resuming his reading.

"Later?" Audrey mouthed.

"Later," her mom mouthed back, nodding in agreement.

"But I'm serious, Audrey," her mom resumed in her normal voice. "Never underestimate the power of an ex-girlfriend with an agenda, especially when that ex-girlfriend has a shark like Linda West on her side."

"What do mean?" Audrey asked in trepidation.

"I mean, that Clarke's brainy-looking ex in the blue dress didn't take her eyes off of him the entire night. The only time she did was to glare at you. I know when another woman means trouble. And that one had it written all over her."

Chapter Eight

*C*larke had to give his mother credit. The woman did not back down. And when she raised the stakes, she raised them all the way. Hence, why he and Audrey were sitting across the table from an honest-to-God wedding planner.

His mother had called him at work to give him "the good news" and then droned on and on about how she'd booked the crème de la crème of wedding planners as a gift for Clarke and Audrey.

Clarke could have easily named nine hundred things he'd rather do with his Thursday evening.

Lobotomy.

Colonoscopy.

The opera.

But, his mother apparently hadn't been exaggerating about the wedding planner's merits because when Clarke had told Audrey, expecting her to be as disgruntled as him, she'd gasped in surprised delight, knowing the name of the wedding planner even before Clarke said it aloud:

Alexis Morgan.

Just like that, Clarke's plans of backing out of his mother's prearranged appointment had evaporated. Audrey had been so excited just to meet the damned woman that Clarke had somehow found himself traveling to the West Side in the middle of rush hour to meet a wedding planner for a wedding that would never be happening.

Based on the female reverence and his experience with the general stuffiness of Manhattan weddings, Clarke had been braced for a theatrical diva who'd come at them with suggestions of live butterflies, crustless sandwiches, and hot air balloons.

Instead, upon arriving at the Upper West Side townhome where the Wedding Belles was based, he was pleasantly surprised to find that the wedding planner was reassuringly *normal*. A slim brunette with a no-nonsense face and a quiet competence, Alexis Morgan seemed the consummate professional, more concerned with getting to know them than pushing her own agenda.

Not that he'd gotten a word in anyway. Audrey and Alexis had hit it off immediately, talking not just about their "wedding" but about the latest fashions, a new wine bar on Central Park South, and Alexis's husband, who used to be Audrey's accountant.

For an island with a couple million people, Manhattan was a tiny-ass world.

Alexis seemed to notice his silence and turned slightly toward him with a smile. "Clarke, I was so pleased to hear from your mother."

His eyebrows lifted, and he smiled. "Truly?"

She laughed, not pretending to misunderstand his skepticism. "She's a frequent speaker at a women-in-business group I belong to."

He felt Audrey stiffen slightly beside him. He knew that as hard as Audrey worked—and she put in more hours on the job than anyone he knew—she would never earn the respect she deserved. Never mind that she near outearned him, never mind that she was named on just about every most-influential list around. People didn't know what to do with jobs that didn't have set hours and a regular office space. She'd never be invited to Alexis's and Linda's women-in-business groups or anything even close.

Without really thinking, he reached out and took her hand, giving it a squeeze. Audrey gave him a surprised look but then squeezed back, playing her part of the in-love couple. Something tightened in his chest that he couldn't identify—and that he didn't want to examine.

"All right, now in these early stages, I'd just like to get a very high-level vision," Alexis was saying, "so we won't be talking dates or details. I want to know the type of wedding you envision. Who's there, how do you feel, that sort of thing. And. I like to start with the groom."

Clarke looked at her in surprise. "What?"

"I know, it's the cliché for the bride to have all the visions, and it's a cliché that often holds true," Alexis said with a quick smile at Audrey. "But I find that the guys often have some thoughts of their own. They just need to be asked."

"Ah—"

Clarke casually slid his hand away from Audrey's, clasping his together and leaning forward slightly. "I hate to break it to you, but I don't know that I've done much thinking about it."

"Never?" Audrey asked in surprise.

"Not unless you count the times you made me play wedding when I was ten."

"You were childhood sweethearts?" Alexis asked. "Your mother didn't mention that."

No, I bet she didn't, he thought before remembering that they weren't *actually* childhood sweethearts.

"Clarke would sit for hours while I tried to learn how to tie my dad's bow tie on him," Audrey reminisced with a grin. "My dad was less than pleased to find Cheez-It fingerprints all over the imported silk."

"And you never did learn to tie the bow tie," he pointed out.

"That's true. Regular ties are much easier. Clarke doesn't have to wear a tux, does he?" Audrey asked the wedding planner.

"That's up to Clarke," Alexis said, smiling. "It's okay if you haven't thought about it before, but if you let yourself think about it now, your ideal wedding day, what are you wearing?"

He resisted the urge to quip "sweatpants," guessing he wouldn't be the first groom-to-be to think he was hilariously original to joke about bucking the trend of formal wear.

Clarke shifted awkwardly in his seat, both women watching him expectantly. Realizing the sooner he played along, the sooner he could get out of this, he reluctantly answered the question.

"A tux. I guess."

Alexis nodded. "So, more formal. Do you see yourself getting married here in the city? Or a destination wedding?"

"Here," he said without hesitation. He was a New Yorker through and through and rarely found reason to leave the city. He didn't even like vacationing much. Everything he wanted from his life was right here, starting with Audrey.

"Church?"

"Yes," he said, again without hesitation. Then he frowned. "I mean, I guess. It doesn't have to be."

"Gut reactions are valuable," Alexis said. "Even if you haven't consciously envisioned your wedding, chances are your subconscious has sort of chewed on it over the years in the back of your mind."

She was right, he realized. He had never sat and daydreamed about his future wedding. In fact, any time he *had* thought about his future wedding, it was in terms of the one he wouldn't have.

It wasn't so much that he couldn't envision a wedding day; it was that he had never been able to envision a marriage. He'd flirted with the idea just once. Once, when he thought maybe he and Elizabeth could make a go of it.

But then she'd left, and he'd come back to his senses. Clarke loved women. He respected them. And because of this, he couldn't imagine shackling any woman to him.

He glanced over at Audrey, the best woman he knew.

Not a real wedding, he reminded himself. And so he played along.

"I want big," he told the women with an unabashed grin. "None of this small and intimate stuff. I want the spectacle. I want everyone I know to see that the most amazing woman in the world chose me. And then I want a hell of a party to celebrate it."

Alexis nodded. "Audrey? How's that sit with you?"

Audrey looked his way and smiled. "Pretty much my thoughts exactly. I've always been the big-white-wedding girl. The princess dress, the wedding march, all eyes on me, the Plaza, doves—"

"Doves?" Clarke interjected.

"Metaphorical," Audrey said, waving a dismissive hand. "Or real. I don't know. It's like you said. The spectacle."

"We can do spectacle," Alexis said confidently. "And we can

do doves, too. Real ones. Though I should warn you, the *level* of spectacle depends on the timeline. Have you two talked dates yet?"

Clarke watched Audrey's wide smile dim as reality set in. There wouldn't be a timeline, there wouldn't be a spectacle, because there wouldn't be a wedding.

"We're still sort of mulling things over," Clarke said quietly, realizing they needed to nip this meeting in the bud before things got out of hand.

"Of course," Alexis said immediately. "There's absolutely no need to rush into anything, and this was only an initial consultation. There's no pressure to commit to me or the Belles or a date today."

The wedding planner stood to indicate the meeting was over. "The only thing I want from you two right now is for you to go out to dinner and just enjoy being engaged. There's plenty of time for the other stuff. I'll give you my card, and if you decide to go with the Belles, I'd love to hear from you when you're ready."

Relieved, Clarke and Audrey stood, and Audrey took the card Alexis pulled out of a white cardholder on the desk, slipping it into her bag.

"Just one more thing," Audrey said, "and you can totally say no. Would you mind if I took a picture on the steps in front of the Wedding Belles plaque on the porch and posted it on Instagram? I'd tag you guys, if you have an Instagram account. Or not. Do you have a policy on that?"

Alexis's eyebrows arched. "I'm a businesswoman. My policy is that having *the* Audrey Tate post a picture of the Wedding Belles is better than any marketing budget."

"I just want everyone to know how fabulous you are," Audrey said as Alexis walked them to the front door. "And I can't believe how hungry for Manhattan wedding details my followers are. My engagement rate has gone through the roof since I started talking about wedding stuff."

"There's a lot of mystery in it for such a big industry," Alexis agreed, opening the front door. "Brides are so used to being sold to. I imagine there's absolutely room in the marketplace for someone to show the process of planning a wedding without any agenda beyond peeling back the curtain a bit."

Audrey handed Clarke her phone as they stepped onto the porch. "You know what to do."

He took her phone without hesitation, having played the role of photographer so many times that he knew exactly where the camera app was on her phone. A photographer he was not, but even as Audrey's follower numbers grew into seven digits, she had refused to upgrade to a fancy camera, wanting instead to show that anyone could make a career out of Instagramming with only an iPhone and a decent photo editing app.

He hopped down the steps to take the photo as Audrey dug her lipstick out of her purse. "How's my hair?" he heard her ask Alexis.

"Perfect," Alexis said, giving Audrey a once over. "I'll head back inside so I'm not photobombing, unless . . . do you want me to take the photo? Of both of you?"

"No," Clarke said, just as Audrey lit up.

"Oh, that would be fantastic."

He groaned. "Dree."

"I know, I know I promised never to show you in my photos. But that was before we got engaged," she said pointedly, giving him a look.

He looked up the steps at her, seeing the stubborn glint in her eyes and knowing exactly what she was thinking. The more togetherness they presented, the less ammunition Scandal Boy had to call their bluff.

He jogged back up the steps, handing the phone to Alexis as they traded places.

Clarke slipped his arm around Audrey's waist as she did the same, and he smiled dutifully as Alexis held up the phone.

"Can you see the Wedding Belles sign?" Audrey asked.

"Scoot a little to the left. There, perfect," Alexis said. Then she lowered the phone, giving them a careful look. "Just a suggestion . . ."

"Tell me," Audrey said.

"What if you turned and faced each other," Alexis said. "This pose looks a little buddy-buddy right now."

"Imagine that," Clarke said out of the corner of his mouth.

"Oh, be quiet," she said, pulling away and turning toward him. "Here, face me."

He sighed and did as instructed.

"Already better," Alexis encouraged. "Audrey put your arms around his neck, looped kind of casual—yes, perfect," she said as Audrey locked her wrists around the back of Clarke's head.

"I hate your job," he told Audrey, preempting Alexis's next command and setting his hands on his friend's waist.

"Hush. Look in love," Audrey commanded.

"Easy to do when you're so bossy," he said sarcastically, though he let his mouth curve into a genuine smile because holding Audrey in his arms wasn't *so* bad.

Audrey smiled back, lifting her eyes to his.

"Perfect, stay just like that while I find the best angle," Alexis muttered, almost to herself.

Out of the corner of his eye, he saw the wedding planner

scoot back and forth on the sidewalk, trying to perfect the photo.

And then, something odd happened. He quit seeing Alexis. He stopped thinking about how annoyed he was at his mother for making this appointment without his and Audrey's consent. He quit resenting Audrey's job.

All of that disappeared until there was only Audrey. Clarke became acutely aware of the way her fingers brushed against the hair at the back of his head, the shape of her waist beneath his palm, even beneath the bulk of her winter coat. He heard a distant ringing in his ears and felt the same disorientation he experienced after their engagement party kiss, when the ground had felt slightly unsteady under his feet.

Audrey's lips parted just slightly as though she was suddenly short of breath, and he wondered if she felt it too, wondered if she knew better than he what to do about it—

"*There*," Alexis said confidently. "I think I got it. You want to take a look?"

The wedding planner began walking up the steps, and Clarke immediately dropped his arms, putting distance between himself and Audrey, grateful for the interruption.

Audrey stayed still a moment longer, then gave a quick shake of her head before turning to Alexis and taking her cell phone back. She scanned the photos. "Oh, perfect!" she said.

Clarke's eyes narrowed slightly, because Audrey's voice was higher than usual, the way it got when her mind was somewhere else and she was operating on autopilot.

"Thank you so much. These are great," she said, locking her phone and dropping it into her purse. "I'll absolutely be sure to tag the Belles."

"Thank you. I appreciate it," Alexis said, giving her arms a quick rub against the cold since she hadn't grabbed her coat on the way out. "Now, I meant what I said. Clarke, take this woman to dinner."

"Will do. I'll even let her pick the place."

"You say that as though I don't always pick," Audrey said, linking her arm in his as they walked down the steps.

"True, though if you pick one of those obnoxious small plate places, I *will* exercise veto power," he said, relieved when he felt the world right itself again as they became Audrey and Clarke once more, friends and *only* friends.

The last thing Clarke wanted was for the most stable relationship in his life to turn upside down.

Chapter Nine

Could @TheAudreyTate's "fiancé" be ANY more bored
to be at dinner with her? Looks like she's about to lose
another one (but did she ever have him . . . ?)
—@ScandalBoyNYC

*H*appy now?" Audrey asked as she set her menu aside and
took a sip of her red wine. "They have steak on the menu."

"Very," he said. "Want to start with the oysters?"

"Sure," she said distractedly, picking up her cell phone and
holding it up. "You mind if I'm rude for a second? I'm dying to
edit the Wedding Belles photo and post it."

He waved his hand, used to Audrey spending time on her
phone and not minding in the least. Her phone was her job, and
her job wasn't nine-to-five. He knew that if he needed her full attention, he'd have it without a second thought. That if he needed

her in any way, she'd have tossed her phone into a fire and given him every ounce of her energy.

But he didn't need her now, was content to have a moment to catch up on his own work. Clarke was second in command behind his father at York, Inc., a media conglomerate that had done well to keep its head above water even as competitors bit the dust. As vice president of strategy, Clarke knew full well that much of that success was due to him. When other media companies had clung desperately to their print publications, their bread and butter in the twentieth century, Clarke had been one step ahead of everyone else. He'd been the persistent twenty-something who'd annoyed his more senior colleagues in every meeting, not just by virtue of being the CEO's son, but because Clarke had been relentless in his insistence that the company make a name for themselves in the digital space back when the digital space was still forming.

Eventually the old farts had simply turned the entire digital department over to him, probably hoping he'd fail. He hadn't. As competitors were just starting to notice the decline in print sales, York was ahead of the game, already primed to serve content to an ever more device-reliant public via apps and an optimized website.

Clarke's colleagues and superiors hadn't hesitated to give credit where it was due, and Clarke had risen through the ranks quickly, he liked to think, because of his contribution rather than his last name.

Especially since the one person who stubbornly resisted giving Clarke even a modicum of praise was his own father. Alton made it clear every chance he got that Clarke didn't hold the second-in-command spot alone. He shared it with the vice president of operations, Maria Folse, who had her eye on the CEO position.

Clarke respected Maria. Hell, he *liked* her. He enjoyed wine-filled dinner parties with her and her wife every bit as much as he enjoyed butting heads with her in the conference room.

But he had zero intention of conceding the company to her, no matter how often his father tried to undermine him. Not that Alton ever undermined Clarke in front of Maria or anyone else in the company. His father, for all his flaws, was a professional.

In private, however, he never let Clarke forget the boy he'd been. The teen who'd sworn up and down he wanted no part in the family business. The frat boy who'd ignored his mother's wishes that he go into law and his father's wishes that he get his degree in business.

Clarke had instead gone into computer science, partially, yes, to dodge his parents' expectations, but also because he'd found the classes to be enjoyable. And Clarke had always figured, even from a young age, that life was supposed to be enjoyed, even if his parents had never seemed to get the message.

The biggest irony was, it was probably the computer science degree his father had been so damn set against that had saved his precious company in the first place. Without that degree, Clarke wouldn't have had nearly enough know-how to push York in the right direction. And because fate was a tricky beast, what had started as Clarke wanting to prove his father wrong—or maybe just prove himself—had turned into a genuine love for the company. Growing up, he'd never understood how his father could be so consumed with a company. And while he still vowed never to let a job matter more than people, a part of him understood. When you poured your energy into something, it became a part of you. Like it or not—and most of the time he didn't like it—this company had become a part of Clarke. Something worth fighting for.

Clarke winced as he checked his email, noting that the

number of unread messages was nearing triple digits, just in the couple hours since he'd left the office.

A handful of them were from Maria, who hadn't wasted any time in taking advantage of Clarke's distraction with his upcoming "wedding" over the past couple weeks. He had no doubt she was making sure Alton knew she was still in the office while Clarke was off sipping wine with his fiancée.

Clarke had no idea how much his father knew about the fake nature of his and Audrey's arrangement. He certainly hadn't given the old man the details, and as far as he could tell, Linda rarely told her husband anything about her master plan for the family. Clarke did know, though, that even if Alton thought the engagement was real and that Audrey was about to become his daughter-in-law, it wouldn't have mattered. Clarke would have been penalized for choosing anything over the company. Including his own wedding.

Most of Clarke's incoming emails were merely FYIs, and he made quick work of archiving them. A few necessitated easy responses, which he fired off, and a handful more required more mental energy than he had at the moment. He flagged those to deal with first thing in the morning.

He glanced up at Audrey and saw that her tongue was tucked into the right side of her cheek, the way it always was when she was focusing, so he turned his attention back to his phone, pulling up Instagram to see just how ridiculous he looked in the photo.

She hadn't posted yet, still doing whatever she did that made her photos look far more impressive than he'd thought a camera phone capable of. Killing time, he mindlessly scrolled through photos of friends' happy hours and workouts and a couple of taillights with the usual griping about the city's rush hour traffic.

The photos more or less blurred together, until one in particular caught his attention.

Clarke had been idly leaning back in his chair, but he slowly sat up straight, feeling his blood pressure rise at the photo of *himself*.

In the picture, Clarke was glaring down at his iPhone, wearing the exact suit he was wearing now, in the exact restaurant he was currently sitting in, drinking the exact martini he'd just taken a sip of. It had to have been taken within the past few minutes.

Clarke didn't even have to see the handle to know which account it was. He'd started following @ScandalBoyNYC under a fake account the moment the twerp had started giving Audrey trouble. The guy hadn't posted anything in the past couple of days relating to Audrey, but the text below the photo of him scowling made him see red.

How dare a complete stranger assess what he was thinking, what he was feeling, or dare to imply that Audrey could ever lose him.

He took a deep breath to fight for control, resisting the urge to look around the room to find out who the hell had crossed the line into such a blatant invasion of privacy.

Instead, he focused his energy on Audrey. Judging from her thoughtful look with her tongue still in her cheek, she was editing her photo or writing her caption and hadn't yet seen the story.

Casually, as though he hadn't a care in the world, Clarke set his phone aside, keeping his expression deliberately bored and reaching out to take a sip of his cocktail as though not in the least bit perturbed by what he'd just been viewing on his phone.

Relaxing his posture, he leaned forward slightly.

"Audrey."

"Mmm," she said distractedly, not looking up from her phone.

He resisted the urge to say her name more sharply, to let her know they were being watched. Having her full attention on her phone was not exactly selling them being madly in love.

He reached slowly across the table and touched her hand. She jerked in surprise, but he wrapped his fingers around hers, hoping no one noticed how startled she'd been to have her *fiancé* casually hold her hand.

She looked up at him in bewilderment, and he forced an easy smile, even as he lowered his voice to let her know what was going on.

"Seriously?" she said after he'd dropped the bombshell. "Someone's here? Watching us?"

"Apparently. No, don't look!" he admonished. "Honestly, you're not very good at this whole clandestine romance thing."

"Believe it or not, pretending to be in love with my best friend doesn't come all that easily," she snapped, clearly rattled.

Clarke's thumb stopped idly stroking her knuckles, a little surprised by the stab of . . . hurt?

Not that he expected her to be in love with him. He wasn't in love with her. But it didn't exactly feel good to know that the one person he cared about more than anything thought him such an unworthy romantic partner.

Could he blame her, though? Audrey knew him well. Knew exactly just how cavalierly he treated relationships. Suspected, even, Clarke's deepest shame.

He hadn't even known his darkest secret until she'd told him about the pact she'd made with Naomi and Audrey to protect one another from heartbreakers. But the moment she'd told him, he'd *known*. He'd known that he was one of those men.

Not one of the good ones. He was a *Brayden*. He was one of the men the women had sworn to protect one another against.

All this time, he'd wondered if Audrey realized. Now he was fairly certain.

She knew.

Still, knowing who Clarke *really* was didn't mean she couldn't pretend to be enamored with who he was pretending to be. Saving her reputation was the least he could do for her, but he needed her to sell it a lot better than she was currently. Her spine was straight, her eyes wide, her face white.

"Put your phone away," he commanded gently. "Slowly, indifferently, like whatever's happening on your phone doesn't matter one way or another to you."

She did as he instructed, leaning down and dropping the phone into her bag.

"Good," he murmured. "Now give me your other hand."

His right hand still holding hers, he set his left palm up on the table. She hesitated only briefly before setting her right hand lightly atop his.

"Smile," he said, holding both her hands now. "No, not a big grin, just a little private smile, like we're having a nice conversation."

"But we are *not* having a nice conversation. You're being bossy," she pointed out.

"You look nice today," he said, stroking his thumbs over her knuckles. "Is that a new lipstick?"

Her eyes narrowed. "What are you doing?"

"Showing interest in my fiancée and hoping the Peeping Tom in the restaurant with us notices. Your turn."

She sighed slightly. "Fine. How was your day?"

"Do better," he said in exasperation.

"How'd your presentation to the board go?"

"Solid wifely question," he praised with a wink. "And good.

Maria couldn't find much to nitpick about, so that's always positive."

She watched him closely. "And your dad? What did he think?"

Clarke shrugged. "Hard to read. He didn't seem displeased by my team's suggestions, so that's a start."

"He'll come around, you know. He's just making you earn your stripes before he hands over the company reins."

"Maybe."

"You're good at your job," she said, squeezing his hands. "And more important to me, it's obvious that you love it. Something, by the way, I never thought possible back when you wanted to be a safari tour guide as a kid."

"I maintain that that was a solid career track."

"Yes, but it's mostly honeymooners," she teased. "Whomever would you sleep with?"

His grin slipped slightly. "Is that all you think I care about?"

She looked surprised at his tone. "No. Of course not. I mean, I don't know. You said yourself today you'd never thought about your wedding. I guess I realized I've never been able to picture you getting married either."

Clarke started to withdraw his hands, but Audrey tightened her grip.

"Hold on," she protested. "I didn't mean to say that you wouldn't make a great husband. I mean that you've never shown interest in a long-term relationship. Outside of Elizabeth."

He heard the question in her voice, but he didn't answer it.

"Did you mean what you told the wedding planner?" he asked. "Is the *spectacle* your dream wedding?"

She hesitated, clearly tempted to press him to talk about his ex, but instead she smiled and shrugged. "Yeah. I don't know how you're surprised. I mean, you saw my wedding scrapbooks when I was twelve."

"Saw? You once made me spend an entire afternoon gluing pictures of wedding cakes into a spiral notebook."

"An even exchange for me passing that note to Steffi Miller at ballet class."

"That took you five seconds. Those damn cake pictures took hours."

"I seem to remember that the result of that note passing was you and Steffi making out in Bryant Park. I got exactly *nothing* out of those wedding notebooks."

"Not true. You just started your wedding planning really, *really* early. Now you have a head start."

"Yeah, for a wedding that won't be happening."

"Well, I mean, no, not yours and mine. But your *real* wedding."

Even as he said it, the thought felt strange. Objectively, he'd always known Audrey would likely get married someday just as sure as he'd known that he likely would not. But now he realized just what Audrey's inevitable marriage would mean. No more dinners like this one, just the two of them. No more being each other's last-minute dates to events and fund-raisers. No more casual Friday nights binging on *The Fast and the Furious*.

"Wait, my real wedding?" she said, looking surprised. "I thought out of everyone you would understand."

"Understand what?"

"I don't want to get married."

Clarke blinked. He'd known this woman his whole life, and she very rarely surprised him. But she shocked the hell out of him now.

"Why the hell did I have to glue those wedding cake pictures, then? Since when have you not wanted to get married?"

Her smile was a little sad. "Since Brayden."

His fingers clenched hers, and he noted out of the corner of his eye that their server was doing yet another walk-by, but wisely read the situation and kept moving so as not to interrupt.

"Dree, you know better than anyone that he was *actual* human waste. I'm not glad he died, but I'm glad you're not with him anymore. You can't let him ruin your life."

"I'm not!" she insisted. "I'm perfectly happy single."

"What happens when you meet someone?"

She hesitated. "Well, that hasn't happened, has it? The closest has been Randy, and look how that turned out."

He shook his head. "You were never going to marry Randy, even if he hadn't turned out to be a married weirdo. But, and I mean this as a compliment, you're marriage material."

"Says the man who doesn't want to get married."

"Says the man who knows you. And I know you've always wanted a husband and a family and a dog."

She pressed her lips together, seeming to gather her thoughts. "You said I couldn't let Brayden ruin my happiness."

He nodded. *Damn straight.*

"Well, the thing is, Clarke, I . . . I've never been able to forget about the fact that I ruined Claire's happiness."

"What the hell are you talking about? What's Claire have to do with whether or not you get married?"

"Because I was so busy believing in happily ever after and buying into the prince sweeping me off my feet. I was so selfishly absorbed with being in love with Brayden that I never stopped to realize that I was stomping on someone else's happily ever after. That I was stealing someone else's prince."

Her voice was so genuine, her expression so open that Clarke felt a surge of frustration with himself for not realizing sooner how deeply she'd let the Brayden thing affect her. He'd known, of course, that it had. How could it not? The man she'd thought she'd marry had been married to someone else the entire time.

But he'd also thought that through her friendship with Claire and Naomi, she'd made peace with the fact that no part of it had been her fault. He told her that now, but she immediately shook her head.

"I should have checked," she persisted. "I shouldn't have taken his word that his divorce was nearly final. How dumb could I have been?"

"Don't let yourself feel guilty because you believe the best in people. A jaded person might have second-guessed his claims, sure. But you're not jaded."

"Well, I wasn't then," she said with a cheeky grin. "Now I've got my guard up."

He smiled back, but he felt a stab of regret and a fresh wave of anger that Brayden had taken someone as trusting and optimistic as Audrey and dulled her ability to always look for the best in people. She wasn't a cynic now, by any means, but it bothered the hell out of him that the girl who still had dreams of a white wedding dress and doves assumed she wasn't worthy of any of it.

"Hey!" she said happily. "At least our conversation made me forget all about the whole Scandal Boy thing. Do you think they got a picture of us holding hands?"

Clarke looked down, a little surprised to see that they were indeed still holding hands. And more than a little surprised that for the past few moments of their conversation, he hadn't been holding them for a photo op.

But he was most surprised of all that he didn't want to let go.

Chapter Ten

O-M-G you guys!!! You will never guess where I am today! Be sure to check my stories for all of the white, poofy details. 😏
—@TheAudreyTate

*N*o," Claire and Naomi said at the exact same time as Audrey came out of the dressing room.

She feigned confusion. "What do you mean?"

"Honey, is there no mirror in there?" Naomi asked, aghast, as she stared at Audrey.

"What, do you not like it?" Audrey asked in dismay.

She shuffled toward the big mirrors in the main dressing area, then tried and failed to hold in her laugh at the absurd wedding dress. "Who made this?"

"Oh, thank God," Naomi breathed. "I thought you were serious."

"Yes, definitely serious," Audrey said, plucking one of the dozen buttons that made up the front of the bodice. Not *functional* buttons. But decorative, mismatched, randomly scattered buttons. "Country quilt is so very me."

"It *does* sort of look like a quilt," Claire said, champagne glass in hand as she circled Audrey. "It's like they took all the scraps and buttons from every other wedding dress in existence and put them all together on this dress."

"I couldn't resist trying it on. I thought it had to look better on me than on the hanger, but . . . no. It's worse. So much worse."

"At least it makes your boobs look good!" Naomi said cheerfully.

"Sorry about the delay," the saleswoman said as she came back into the dressing area. "I had to— Oh. Oh my."

"I don't think this dress style is quite *me*," Audrey said diplomatically, not wanting to insult the woman's inventory.

"I think that particular dress is probably for very few people," the woman said with a smile. "It was custom-made for a bride whose wedding fell through. She paid full price, and even though we don't offer refunds on custom gowns, she insisted we keep it in case some other bride fell in love with it."

"Well, it won't be *this* bride," Audrey said, scooping up the fabric of the skirt and heading back toward the dressing room.

"Wait," Naomi commanded. "Picture!"

Audrey struck several dramatic poses as Naomi took photos. It was, after all, the reason they were here.

One of the city's top bridal shops had called Audrey and offered her the shop to herself and champagne for her and her friends if she did a casual fashion show to share with her followers.

After being assured there would be no pressure whatsoever to buy or commit to a gown, Audrey had agreed. The bridal shop was extremely elite, with reservations usually made months in advance. Most of Audrey's followers would never be able to see it in person, and she was thrilled to be able to give them a glimpse inside, as well as to hopefully offer brides-to-be inspiration on designer gown wear.

She wasn't exactly sure who would find inspiration from the button and lace explosion she was currently wearing, but she supposed it took all kinds.

"Okay, so the fan favorite so far is definitely the strapless A-line with the pink sash around the waist," Claire called from the other side of the dressing room, apparently having taken over monitoring Audrey's phone. "Did we like that one?"

"The cut, yes," Naomi said. "I don't know how I feel about the pink. Audrey, did you like the pink?"

"I didn't hate it," Audrey called over the dressing room door as she wiggled into a slim-fitting halter. "It was fun, but maybe a little too trendy. I've always sort of envisioned the traditional all-white dress."

She got the zipper as far as she could, then gave up. Some she'd been able to yoga her way into zipping up; others she needed help.

"Agreed on the all-white thing," Naomi said as Audrey came out of the room and turned so someone could zip her up. "Though I *hate* the fact that it's supposed to represent purity."

"Yeah, because what percentage of brides do you think are actually virgins?" Claire asked as she pulled up Audrey's zipper and fiddled with the halter neck.

"It's been so long for me, I may as well be a virgin," Audrey grumbled as she stepped in front of the mirror to see the dress. It was pretty, but a little simple for her tastes. She turned and struck a couple of poses for Claire to take a picture.

"How long is so long?" Naomi asked, bringing Audrey's champagne glass to her. "Exactly how long is your sex hiatus?"

Audrey took a sip. "Um."

"Oh no," Naomi said, her eyes wide in horror. "I'd known you'd been on a *sort of* dry spell since Brayden, but are you telling me . . . *all the way* dry spell?"

"Well, I tried to break it with Randy," Audrey defended herself. "Look how that turned out."

"Yes, but, sweetie," Claire said, looking concerned. "Brayden passed a year and a half ago."

Audrey resisted the urge to snap that she was *well* aware of just how long it had been. Audrey had never considered herself an overtly sexual creature. She liked sex, definitely, but she'd found herself missing the companionship, the romance, and the butterflies of being with Brayden much more than she'd missed the sexual aspect.

But in recent months, she'd officially rounded the bend. Her body's cravings had caught up with her heart and mind, and she'd decided to do something about it. Hence, Randy. Yes, the guy had turned out to be a creep—a married creep. But one with laugh lines, a great smile, and excellent shoulders. More importantly, the guy had known his way around a romantic phrase or two, and for Audrey, good sex *was* all about the romance.

"I just haven't quite figured out how to have sex without romance," Audrey said, spelling it out for her friends.

"Oh, it's easy," Naomi said. "Before Oliver, I—" She broke off. "Actually, Claire. You take this one."

"I get it," Claire told Audrey, taking over. "I had the same realization last year. Remember when I was going through my whole no-strings-attached aspirations?"

Audrey smiled. "I remember. You were dead set on having a fling."

"I was dead set on not getting my heart broken," Claire corrected. "I didn't realize it at the time. Needless to say, I was not counting on Scott being so . . ."

"Dreamy?" Audrey fluttered her eyelashes.

"Something like that," Claire said with a private smile.

"Well, I'm already there on that realization," Audrey pointed out. "I already know that I'm not cut out for sex without romance. The romance is my favorite part!"

"So why aren't you *seeking* romance?" Naomi asked. "You're gorgeous. Successful. Sweet. Smart. Funny."

"Blushing here," Audrey said, pretending to fan her cheeks.

"I'm serious. We're onto you, Tate. We know exactly the looks you get in bars, and I could name at least ten men who would kill for a shot with you."

"Same," Claire said.

"I haven't been interested," Audrey said, sipping the champagne.

"You haven't *let* yourself be interested," Naomi persisted stubbornly. "Why?"

Audrey gave them both an exasperated look. "Was I this pushy when you were fumbling your way through things with Oliver and Scott?"

"Yes," they answered in unison.

She laughed. "Fair enough. But I'm doing fine, I promise."

"Sweetie, you're trying on wedding dresses for a wedding that you have no intention of going through with," Claire said gently. "Not that this isn't fun," she was quick to add.

"It does sound sort of depressing when you put it that way," Audrey said, checking to make sure the saleswoman wasn't nearby before sinking onto a puffy blue cushion, doing her best not to wrinkle the dress.

"Having second thoughts?" Naomi sat beside her.

"Weirdly, not really," Audrey admitted, looking down at the bubbles rising in her champagne glass. "I'm having so much fun with this. My followers are loving it, and it *does* feel weirdly good to keep calling Linda's bluff."

"But?" Claire asked.

Audrey looked up, surprised to realize her friend knew her well enough to sense there was something lurking beneath the surface, then realized she shouldn't be. She sometimes thought she knew these two women better than they knew themselves—she'd certainly known they were falling in love before they had. She supposed it made sense that they'd know her pretty well, too.

She bit her lip. "It's probably nothing. Maybe my imagination. But I keep having these fleeting moments where things with Clarke feel a little . . . weird."

"Weird how?"

"It's hard to describe. Like, when we kissed—"

"Oh, thank God," Naomi said, flopping back in relief. "I thought I would die if you didn't talk about that, but Claire said I couldn't bring it up unless you did."

"Why would you bring it up?" Audrey asked in confusion.

"Because it was *hot*," Naomi said. "He all but bent you over backward in front of everyone. And the way he looked at you after . . ."

Audrey's eyes rolled. "He just puts on a good show."

"Mmm-hmm," Naomi said, not bothering to hide her skepticism. "If it was just a show, then what was weird about it?"

Audrey huffed out an irritable breath. "I don't know. It was just . . . I guess we've kissed before. Pecks. Playful smacking kisses. But we've never *kissed*. Not like that."

"It was pretty great, huh?" Claire asked.

"It was a good kiss," Audrey admitted. "Though, the guy's had lots of practice, so I sort of keep trying to chalk my butterflies up to his sheer *skill*. But then . . ."

"Oh, there's more. Did he touch your boob?" Naomi asked gleefully.

"*Boob?* How old are you? And no. He just . . . we held hands."

Out of the corner of her eye, Audrey saw Naomi's nose scrunch in disappointment, but Claire seemed to have the opposite reaction, her gaze sharpening slightly. "When?"

Audrey filled them in on dinner and Clarke doing damage control after Scandal Boy posted a picture of him looking horrifically bored to be in her presence.

"The moment in the restaurant was just like the kiss," she said, frowning. "It started out almost jokingly, very pretend, and then something shifted. And I don't really know what."

"Do you think he noticed the shift, too?"

"Maybe? I don't know, and that's what bothers me more than anything. I keep getting the sense that there are things he's not telling me. He's holding back, and he's *never* held back around me before."

"He might be right to keep his distance," Claire said gently, coming to sit on Audrey's other side. "You guys are playing with fire here. Blurring the lines of your friendship with romance is dangerous territory. Maybe he knows, even on an instinctive level, that it's smart to keep some distance."

Audrey swallowed, the thought of Clarke keeping his distance feeling totally depressing.

"Okay, I'm going to ask something that's not my business," Naomi said.

"Now, *there's* a surprise," Claire said.

Naomi gave Claire a toothy smile and turned back to Audrey. "Have you ever thought about trying this whole romance thing for *real* with Clarke?"

Audrey groaned. "Not this again. I've told you two a thousand times that we're really, *truly*, just friends."

"Yes, but that was before."

"Before what?"

"Before you knew he was a good kisser. Before you held hands. Before you had *feels*," Naomi said, lowering her voice to a whisper.

"I do not have *feels*," Audrey said shortly, standing to indicate the conversation was over.

She handed over her champagne to Claire and headed back into the dressing room.

I do not have feels, she repeated to herself. *I do not have feels.*

Swallowing, she put a hand to her stomach, realizing with dismay that saying it aloud and thinking it repeatedly didn't seem to make it true.

Chapter Eleven

*Y*eah," Clarke called, not looking up from his computer at the knock on the door. Clarke didn't close his door very often, preferring to keep the exact opposite work environment his father offered.

If Alton West could have built a moat around his top-floor office, he would have. Instead he settled for regulating the elevator. Nobody could even *get* to the CEO's office unless personally escorted by Clarke's father's longtime assistant.

Clarke's own office was on the floor just below the CEO's, and he made a point of keeping it as open and accessible as possible. Not because he particularly relished interruptions, but because he found that people worked harder and worked better when they felt heard.

Still, the open-door philosophy, while ideal in theory, wasn't always ideal for Clarke's productivity. The past month in particular, Clarke had been scrambling to keep up with the constant influx of questions and demands crossing his desk.

As a result, he'd been closing his door more and more lately in an attempt to block out the noise. He didn't like it, but he needed to keep his performance from slipping.

Clarke knew why Maria was flooding his inbox and calendar— she knew her opponent was distracted with a wedding, and she saw her chance to prove her dedication to the job. What he didn't fully understand was why his *father* seemed to be in on the misery.

Not that he was complaining, really. Clarke had been waiting years to feel like his father trusted him enough to lean on him. And it was finally happening. He just didn't understand why it had to be *now*, when Clarke was trying to balance cake-tasting appointments with budget meetings.

"Yeah," Clarke said again, louder this time, when whoever knocked didn't enter. He was careful to keep the impatience out of his voice. His team knew better than to knock on the closed door unless it was urgent.

He glanced up as the door opened, his fingers freezing over his keyboard when he saw the familiar face. "Liz."

His ex smiled tentatively. "Can I come in?"

"Sure," he said automatically. Not because he wanted to see her, but because he was damned curious. Elizabeth had rarely come to see him at work when they'd been dating. She'd been too immersed in her own career. That she'd take time out of her busy workday now was . . . interesting.

"My mother sent you?"

Liz had the decency to flinch as she shut the door. "I deserve that."

"Ah," he said, smiling slightly and leaning back in his chair. "So you admit you've been working with her."

She lifted her chin slightly in defense. "She knows I've been wanting to see you since I've been back in town. To catch up."

"We caught up over the lunch you two tricked me into." Clarke kept his voice light, but there was a note of steel to his tone, too. "I know you've moved back because you're up for a nomination at the AG offices. I know you've just bought a place on West 70th and that you've had a year to mourn Lucy and think you're about ready to get a new cat. I know you still pick cucumbers off your salad, even though I maintain they have no taste and are thus harmless."

She gave a fleeting smile and approached his desk. "And I know *you* still live in that place off Madison you bought after I moved. I know that if there's a cheeseburger on the menu, you order it. I know that Priscilla is still your assistant and that you got a promotion. Congratulations." She lifted her hands and gestured around the large office, the Midtown view.

"And yet"—her hands lowered so all ten fingertips braced lightly on the opposite side of his desk—"you didn't mention one very crucial detail at that lunch."

Clarke stayed silent and still, not giving an inch.

She leaned forward just slightly. "You failed to mention you were getting married."

"Must have slipped my mind," he said with a noncommittal smile.

"Must have."

Their eyes locked, and as he had at the aforementioned lunch, Clarke waited for the punch of rightness. Hell, he'd take a *flicker*. Anything to remind himself that he'd once cared about this woman. Not that he didn't care about her *now*. Elizabeth had once been important to him, and he wished only good things for her. But whereas before he'd found her beautiful, now she was merely attractive to him, in a detached, observational kind of way. Not because she'd changed, but because the way he felt about her had changed. She was merely a mostly fond memory now, and her being back in New York didn't change that.

Still, Elizabeth gave him a knowing smile. "How long are you two going to keep it up?"

He tilted his head, feigning confusion.

"Cut the crap, Clarke," she said, sitting down without being invited. "I know why Audrey's playing bride. It's *literally* her career to pose. But what I can't figure out is why you're going along with it. To get back at me, to irritate your mother, or because Audrey still has you wrapped around her finger?"

"Careful, Liz."

"Oh, I don't mean any offense against Audrey," Elizabeth said. "She's always been nice to me. I even started to like her once I quit being jealous of her. But I was jealous in those early days, and I can remember quite clearly that you spent the first several months of our relationship trying to ease my jealousy by reminding me that she was like a sister to you."

It was on the tip of Clarke's tongue to issue his usual knee-jerk reaction. To insist that Audrey *was* like a sister to him. Today, however, the words wouldn't come. He tried to tell himself it was because he wanted to get under Elizabeth's skin, but he was becoming increasingly aware that things between him and Audrey had nothing to do with Elizabeth.

"Does it surprise you that I'm marrying Audrey?" he asked. "Or that I'm marrying at all? Because I seem to remember you made it quite clear I wasn't marriage material."

"You weren't marriage material *then*," she clarified softly. "You had some, um, growing up to do. Manhattan was your playground, and you treated it as such. You and I both knew you wouldn't be happy settling down with me in DC."

You never even asked.

But the thought lacked its usual punch of bitterness. For years he'd been bothered that Liz had underestimated him the way his parents had. Assuming that because he was quick to smile, because he prioritized fun and liked to do things on his own timeline in his own way, that he wasn't serious about anything, or anyone.

"Maybe I wouldn't have been happy there," he agreed. "Maybe New York has always been my place. And maybe Audrey's always been the one."

He said it to push Liz's buttons, but the moment the words were out of his mouth, Clarke felt thunderstruck. Not because the statement felt absurd, but because it *didn't*.

Maybe Audrey's always been the one.

Stunned, Clarke sat back all the way in his chair, finally registering what had been nagging at him for weeks. That in spite of Elizabeth and his mother's manipulations, and even with the sheer savage annoyance of Scandal Boy, Clarke had never felt more centered than he had this past month.

As though his life was finally on track.

Clarke gave a quick shake of his head. *Clearly* this whole game he and Audrey were playing had started messing with his mind.

Elizabeth studied him closely, then frowned as though frustrated he wasn't an open book.

"Clarke." She started to reach across the desk, then, sensing her mistake in trying to touch him, pulled her hand back and simply looked at him steadily. "I miss you."

Clarke couldn't figure out if he was surprised by the announcement or not. On one hand, he wasn't. Liz hadn't been exactly subtle in her attempts to reconnect with him recently. But on the other hand, the Liz he'd known, or at least thought he'd known, had rarely expressed emotions, much less vulnerability, and he couldn't quite figure out how he felt about this whole thing.

"Why?" he asked.

She laughed. "*Why*? Because you're, well . . . we were good together."

"Were we?"

"Clarke." She was exasperated. "You know we were. We dated for a year. You don't stay together that long if there's not something there."

"True. You also don't leave town if there's something there."

"You know I had to leave. The opportunity—"

"You couldn't turn it down, I understand that. I respected it. But you made it clear I didn't have a part in that chapter of your life. Long distance wasn't on the table, and you didn't ask me to come along for the ride."

"Would you have?"

He looked down at the desk, considering. "I don't know," he answered finally. "But the fact that you didn't ask spoke volumes."

She inhaled and held her breath for a moment, before releasing it slowly. "Well, I'm asking now. Not for you to move to DC with me, but to give us another chance, here in New York. To finish what we started."

And with that, Clarke knew how he felt about this woman: gently indifferent.

"You're too late, Liz," he said softly, standing to indicate the end of the conversation. "I'm marrying Audrey."

"Oh, please," she snapped. "You're only pretending to marry her to get back at your mother for bossing you around, and maybe to punish me, but—"

"You're wrong," Clarke interrupted sharply. "My relationship with Audrey doesn't have anything to do with you. Now, if you'll excuse me. I have to meet my fiancée for a cake-tasting appointment. I'm sure you remember your way out."

———————

The bakery was elite, even by Manhattan standards. Clarke had to get past a security guard in the lobby, an intercom outside a locked door, and now a receptionist who seemed to be on the verge of asking for identification after he'd said his name.

"Ms. Tate didn't indicate that anyone would be joining her," the blonde said coolly, giving him a once-over.

"I told her I couldn't, but I managed to rearrange my schedule."

"Hmm." The receptionist looked less than impressed.

"Is she here yet?" Clarke asked patiently. "Actually, you know what? I'll just call her and let her explain to you that I'm her fiancé, and then *you* can explain why I'm late to join her because I'm still out here in the lobby."

He pulled out his phone, and the receptionist relented with a sigh. "This way, please."

Clarke followed her down a short hallway, unsurprised to see that the space, while small, was swanky. Glossy photographs of elaborate cakes lined the walls, and the lighting was soft and strategic instead of the usual harsh fluorescent light in a Midtown high-rise. It looked nothing like any bakery he'd ever been in and didn't smell like one, either.

"It doesn't smell like cake," he pointed out.

The icy blonde didn't turn around. "This is our showroom and tasting space. The baking takes place elsewhere."

She didn't add the word *obviously*, but Clarke heard the silent addition just the same.

The receptionist stopped and motioned him through a doorway.

Audrey sat at a round table, preoccupied with her phone, and her eyes widened in surprise when she saw him. "Hey! What are you doing here?"

The blonde pounced. "You weren't expecting him?"

"Oh, for the love of . . ." Irritated at being treated like a person of interest at a *wedding cake shop*, Clarke marched toward Audrey and, planting both hands on the arm of her chair, bent down and stamped his mouth over hers.

He meant the kiss to be cursory and brief, and solely for the benefit of the Stormtrooper blonde in the doorway, but the second his lips touched hers, they were in no hurry to leave.

Clarke realized then what he'd actually been hoping for with this kiss was confirmation that the kiss the night of the engagement party had been a fluke and that the addictive sweetness of Audrey's lips had been his imagination.

This kiss shot that hope to hell. Her lips parted slightly in surprise, and Clarke had to fight the urge to deepen the kiss all the way, to kiss her for real. Strange, that as well as he knew Audrey, as much as he thought he knew everything about her, he hadn't known *this*. That her lips would be so soft or feel so . . . right.

He forced himself to pull back, his point more than proven. Sensing Audrey's confusion and avoiding her gaze, he turned around and gave the receptionist his cockiest grin. *See? I belong to her.*

Finally satisfied that Clarke was actually supposed to be here, the blonde gave them both a polite nod. "A team member will be with you as soon as possible to begin the tasting. We're running just slightly behind schedule. Can I get you anything to drink? Coffee? Tea? Wine?"

The wine was extremely tempting, given how his day was going so far, but he and Audrey both shook their heads. Audrey waited until the receptionist's clicking heels faded away, then gave him a searching look. "What was that about?"

"What is this, the Fort Knox of bakeries?" he grumbled, hooking the leg of the chair with his shoe and pulling it out so he could sit beside her. "I seriously thought she was going to hit the panic button because my name wasn't on her approved list."

"Well, you told me you had a meeting and couldn't make it, so I told her I was alone."

"I did have a meeting," he said, rubbing his temples.

"It got canceled?"

Something like that.

In reality, he'd been so thrown off balance by Liz's visit and the strange storm of realizations it had wrought, that he'd stomped out of the York office building and was halfway to the cake shop before he remembered the reason he'd declined the tasting appointment in the first place.

He'd thought about turning back around to take the scheduled vendor meeting, but instead had called one of the guys on his team who'd been requesting more responsibility in an unsubtle bid for a promotion and asked him to take the meeting on his behalf.

"You okay?" she asked.

Clarke lifted his head, intending to tell her about the office drop-in from Elizabeth, but then . . . didn't. Audrey and Clarke didn't *not* have secrets, per se, but they also stopped short of telling each other *all* the details of their romantic lives. They tried as best they could to make their friendship and respective relationships work alongside each other, either with the rare double date when they'd both been seriously seeing someone at the same time, or the slightly more uncomfortable third-wheel scenario, when he'd been with Elizabeth and she'd been with Brayden.

However, they'd never shared intimate details of the physical or emotional variety. They limited it to the highlight reel—creepy Randy and his room of mirrors or the time Clarke had gone home with a woman who'd had *twelve* birds and their cages in her bedroom. But that was the shallow stuff—the entertaining bits.

The emotional stuff? Not so much. Clarke had known, of course, that Brayden's death and betrayal had ravaged Audrey, but her friendship with Claire and Naomi had been her rock during that turmoil. As for him, his only serious relationship had been Elizabeth, and he'd told Audrey next to nothing about her leaving. Not about the conversation leading up to it and not about the fact that it had *hurt*.

She reached out and gently pressed the tip of her index finger between his eyebrows. "What is this? You're frowning. You never frown."

He instinctively lifted his hand to capture her fingers in his. He didn't let go. "Sorry. Rough day."

"Well, you've chosen the right way to make it better. This cake company is super exclusive, and the cake itself is insanely delicious. They made this bourbon pecan cake for Diana Collier's wedding, and it was—"

"Dree," he interrupted, his grip tightening on her fingers. "How long are we doing this?"

"The cake tasting? It shouldn't last more than an hour or so—"

"Not the cake. This." He gestured between them. "How long are we keeping up the charade?"

Audrey exhaled slowly. "I don't know. It's all starting to feel a little real, isn't it?"

He gave her a half smile. "Let's just say in the early days of our little game, people would tell me congratulations, and it would take me a full ten seconds to remember what they were referring to. Now, they tell me congratulations, and I actually half listen when they start offering marriage advice. Now, it takes me a full ten seconds to remember that I'm not *actually* getting married."

She laughed. "I know what you mean. I spent an hour on the phone with the wedding planner this morning. I felt guilty until I went back and looked at her contract and confirmed that she'll get paid no matter what. And paid quite well, I might add."

"Contract? You signed a contract with the Wedding Belles?"

Audrey groaned and tugged her hand away from his to cover her face with both palms. "I know. I know! I've officially lost all touch with reality and control of the situation."

So have I. He sat back in his chair, tapping his fingers against the table. It didn't even particularly bother him that they'd spent so much time, energy, and money on their charade. What bothered him was that the further along they got in this game of pretend, the less it was about the wedding, and he was starting to see all too clearly what it could be like *after* the wedding.

It was increasingly easy to imagine what that life with Audrey would be like.

"Hey," Clarke said, waiting until she'd lowered her hands so he could see her face. "Did you mean it the other night at dinner? When you said you weren't planning to get married?"

"Yes," she said automatically. "If the past year and a half have taught me anything, it's that while the idea of Prince Charming and happily ever after is pretty great, it's hardly without risk. And when those things go wrong, they can go *really* wrong. The thrill of falling in love isn't worth the risk of ending up on the wrong side of the divorce statistic, or worse, getting your heart shattered."

Clarke's brain was humming with protests. *What if the marriage's foundation was on something far more stable than any romantic love? What if it was founded on a lifelong friendship?*

Clarke felt an idea forming, one of the better ideas he'd ever had.

He opened his mouth. "Audrey—"

"There's the happy couple!"

Audrey and Clarke both turned toward the doorway, where a tall, wiry man wearing a mint-green bow tie sashayed over to them, hand outstretched.

"I am *so* sorry to make you wait," he said, giving them both a handshake before sitting down at the table beside them. "We had a bit of a frosting emergency. Doesn't happen often, but when it does, it's all hands on deck. Now," he said, opening an enormous binder, "I have your profile right here, and it says you haven't yet narrowed down your cake flavors, which is good news for me, as it means we'll get to sample *all* of them this afternoon . . ."

Audrey immediately leaned forward in excitement as Clarke slumped back slightly, tuning out as the exuberant employee droned on about ganache and raspberry coulis.

For the life of him, Clarke couldn't figure out if he was relieved or disappointed that the man had interrupted what he'd been about to propose to his best friend.

Chapter Twelve

*C*larke returned to the office an hour later, his temper vastly improved by large quantities of sugar and the usual mood boost he got by spending time with Audrey. Even with plenty unsaid between them, even as he felt himself rethinking everything, one thing never changed: simply being around her, Clarke always felt all the shit of the world fade away.

The reprieve from the real world, however, was temporary. No sooner had Clarke's ass settled back into his desk chair than his assistant buzzed his phone.

He picked up. "Yup."

"Mr. West would like to see you in his office."

Not *your father*. Always *Mr. West would like to see you.*

Priscilla had always made a habit of referring to Clarke's father as *Mr. West*. Though, now that he thought about it, Clarke wouldn't be surprised if the instructions came straight from Alton himself, in an attempt to maintain distance. It's not as though

Alton had ever been eager to call attention to the fact that he and Clarke shared a bloodline.

"Let me guess," Clarke said, tiredly rubbing his eyes, "he expects me up there ASAP."

He heard the smile in his assistant's voice. "Ten minutes ago, actually. I called your cell. And texted."

"Sorry about that," he said, pulling his phone out of his suit pocket and taking it off the Do Not Disturb setting.

The stairwells in Manhattan high-rises didn't get much use, save for the occasional torturous fire drill, but since his VP title meant he was a mere one floor beneath his father's top-of-the-top office space, he'd taken to using the staircase. Partially because taking the elevator one floor seemed lazy and indulgent, partially because the cold stairwell was sometimes the only solitude he got during the workday.

But *mostly* because it drove his father crazy.

The staircase ensured Clarke entered the executive floor *behind* the desk of Alton's assistant. He had nothing against Roberta, but one-upping his father was a rare bonus Clarke enjoyed taking advantage of.

Today, however, Clarke was denied the pleasure of catching his dad off guard. Alton's office door was open, and instead of looking surprised to see Clarke, he seemed to be waiting for him.

Clarke lifted his eyebrows. He'd never known his father to wait on anyone. He'd never been able to figure out if his father was a study in indifference or actually *was* indifferent. Indifferent to his wife, indifferent to his son . . . indifferent to his whole damn life outside of work.

Alton nodded in relief when he saw Clarke. "Come in. Shut the door."

Clarke did as instructed, then bowed. "You rang?"

"Cut the crap, son."

Clarke did his best to hide is surprise. Alton had called him *son* plenty over the years, but almost never in the office. He gave his father a closer look, noting that he seemed almost distracted.

"Everything okay?" Clarke asked.

"Sure. Sure. Sit."

Clarke did, a little unnerved and surprised he hadn't been summoned to receive marching orders or to answer a barrage of questions about his quarterly report or to get lectured about how if he really wanted the company, he had to stay hungry.

"You were out to lunch?" Alton asked awkwardly.

"Sure." Cake counted as lunch, right? Clarke refused to explain how he chose to spend his time. He wasn't some fresh-out-of-college analyst. He didn't need his schedule managed by his boss *or* his dad.

Again, his father surprised him, nodding agreeably instead of pointing out that Maria always ate at her desk, or not at all, and if Clarke wanted the company as much as she did, he'd survive on PowerBars and Tums, too.

"How was Audrey?"

Clarke sat back in his chair, tapping his fingers together as he studied his dad. "How do you know I was with Audrey?"

"Seemed logical. What with her being your future wife and all."

His father's gaze locked on Clarke's as he said it, a slight mocking emphasis on *future wife*. Well, that answered his question. His dad may be aloof, but he wasn't entirely oblivious. He knew all about the battle of wills happening between his son and his wife.

"You wanted something?" Clarke asked, not feeling up to playing whatever game Alton was trying to play. He already had his hands full managing his mother.

Alton leaned forward. "I've always liked Audrey."

Clarke blinked. "Really?"

Alton smiled. "You sound surprised."

"Well. Can't say I've ever felt the waves of approving warmth rolling off you when she's around."

"Have I *ever* given off approving warmth?"

Clarke bit out a sharp laugh. "True."

"Just because I'm not some teddy bear father figure doesn't mean I don't see that she's good for you. That she's always been good for you."

"Dad," Clarke said, shifting uncomfortably. "You know that this thing with me and Audrey, it's all—"

"A sham?" Alton said, his smile widening slightly.

"Well . . . yeah," Clarke said. He and his father might not have a warm relationship, but he drew the line at outright lying to the man. "It started as a joke mostly, because Internet trolls were giving Audrey a hard time, and then we kept going because—"

"Because your mother tried to coerce you into a relationship with her vision of the perfect partner for you."

"Pretty much," Clarke admitted.

Alton nodded slowly, turning his head and gazing out the window for a while. "She's wrong, you know."

"About trying to control her grown son's love life? Yes, I'm aware."

"That, but also about Elizabeth being the better partner for you."

His dad was still looking out the window. Clarke studied his father's profile, trying to figure out what had brought on the odd mood. He had never discussed any relationship with his father before, much less a romantic one. That his father even noticed

Clarke's ex-girlfriend or best friend was unexpected. That he *commented* on it was unsettling.

"You don't like Elizabeth?" Clarke asked cautiously.

Alton waved a hand. "I like her fine."

"But not for me."

His father turned back to Clarke, his expression serious. "Elizabeth reminds me of your mother in many ways."

Clarke smiled. "Probably why Mom likes her so much."

"Yes. Probably." Alton didn't smile back. "And *your* mother in many ways reminds me of *my* mother."

Clarke winced. "Jesus, Dad. You've got to warn a guy before you go all Oedipus complex."

Alton leaned forward again, his expression intent, ignoring Clarke's discomfort. "Your grandmother was not a soft woman. She had strong opinions, and she was very good at getting her way."

"Okay?" This was hardly a surprise. Clarke's grandmother had passed a few years ago, but he remembered her well as a fearsome, unyielding woman.

Alton looked down at his hands for a moment. "Your grandmother introduced me to your mother. Did you know that?"

"I did not."

Alton nodded once. "She introduced us. Urged me to court her, even though I was dating someone else at the time. A pretty, sweet girl who made me laugh."

Clarke looked up in surprise.

Alton gave a fleeting smile. "Yes, son. I know how to laugh. Or at least I used to."

"What happened?"

Alton merely held his gaze.

"Mom happened," Clarke said flatly.

"Your mother is a good woman. She loves you very much. She

wants what's best for you, just as my mother wanted what's best for me."

"But you think she's wrong."

Alton hesitated. "I think they were both wrong. I'm sorry if that's hard for you to hear."

"You forget we all lived under the same roof," Clarke said quietly. "You don't have to shield me from the fact that your and Mom's relationship isn't exactly . . . affectionate."

It was an understatement, but Alton surely didn't need his son to relay just how chilly his own marriage was. Clarke couldn't remember his parents touching unless it was to pose for a photo, couldn't remember them going out to dinner unless it was with another couple for networking purposes. Couldn't remember them even *talking* unless it was to discuss Clarke's grades or their social calendar or a monotone summary of their respective workdays.

"Why did you get married, then?" Clarke asked.

Alton was silent for a long moment, looking out the window once more. "I'm ashamed to admit that I can barely remember. I suppose it felt like the path of least resistance, and I had both my mother and yours reminding me that it would be an advantageous match. We were from the right families, and on paper, Linda and I are well suited. Serious, committed to our careers . . ."

"Dad. If you're trying to warn me not to follow in your footsteps, you don't have to worry. I have no intention of marrying Elizabeth."

"I know."

"Really?" Clarke said doubtfully. "Then what the hell has this entire talk been about, if not to warn me not to follow in your footsteps?"

"I don't want you to make my mistakes—"

"Right, I got that. Don't marry someone Mom picks out for me. Check."

"Not *just* that," his father said, impatient. "I want you to marry the girl who makes you laugh. Don't let her get away . . ."

"What do you— Wait, Audrey? I already told you, we're just friends. We were just messing around with the engagement thing—"

"Marry that girl, Clarke. You won't regret it."

Clarke gave a good-natured eye roll. "Fantastic. Now both my parents are trying to rush me to the altar with different women."

"It's not the same thing," his dad said quietly.

"How's that?"

Alton studied him with a cryptic, knowing look. "You'd figure it out in time, but because I'm not a particularly patient man, maybe I can help speed you along."

Clarke gave his dad a wary look.

"Marry Audrey," his father said, looking him straight in the eyes. "Marry Audrey, and the company is yours."

Clarke had been idly tapping his fingers against one another, but he went completely still at that. "*What?* Jesus, Dad, and I thought Mom was the master manipulator, but this . . . this is a whole other level of . . . I don't think there are words."

His father said nothing. Or maybe he did. Clarke was too busy trying to gather his reeling thoughts.

When he finally got ahold of them, he stood and looked down at his dad. "I deserve this company because I've earned it. Because I've done a damn good job. I don't want it handed to me because of some game you and Mom are playing with my future."

"Your mother and I may be the ones playing the game, but you'd be the one with the prize."

"Only you would describe your own company as a prize," Clarke replied, turning away, disgusted.

"No," Alton said, his voice so sharp that Clarke froze. "Audrey, son. *Audrey* is the prize."

Chapter Thirteen

*A*s far as man caves go, it's a damn good one," Clarke said approvingly, looking around the upstairs loft area of Oliver and Naomi's apartment.

"I guess that's a pretty good compliment from a guy whose entire house is a man cave," Oliver said.

"Is it?" Scott asked curiously, taking a sip of beer and eyeing Clarke. "You know, I've never seen your place."

"Me neither," Oliver said. "I've only heard from Naomi who's heard from Audrey that it's basically man-heaven."

"If you're hoping I'll be appalled at my oversight and invite you two over for tea, you're going to be disappointed," Clarke said cheerfully, settling onto the black leather sofa. "I know better than to invite an architect and contractor into my home."

"What exactly is it that you think we're going to say?" Oliver asked.

Clarke shrugged. "That the foundation's shaky. The drywall's shit. My floor's crooked. That my ceiling doesn't have the right support beams. I don't know, something that will necessitate me moving out while it gets fixed."

"You'd think you'd *want* to know all of that about your own house," Scott pointed out.

"Nope." Clarke sipped his beer. "Ignorance is bliss."

"What if we promise not to utter anything other than 'it's nice'?" Oliver proposed, leaning back against the pool table and crossing his feet at the ankles.

Scott was already shaking his head. "I do not agree to that. If your ceiling's about to cave, I'll tell you. Which, by the way, is a compliment. It means I count you as a friend."

"What if I weren't a friend?" Clarke asked curiously. "You'd just let me be crushed by shoddy house construction?"

Scott grunted. "Let's just say if I'd walked into Brayden Hayes's house when he was still alive and saw a wall about to fall on him, I wouldn't have said a single word. Assuming, of course, Claire wasn't in the house when it came crashing down around the bastard."

Oliver reached out and clinked the neck of his beer bottle against Scott's. "I've had some fantasies in a similar vein."

Same, Clarke thought. Hatred for a dead man was a strange thing to form a friendship on, but it had formed one all the same. Though, technically, Oliver and Scott had been friends since architecture school, long before Clarke had met either of them. But in the past year, their friendship had been cemented even further as Oliver had moved in with Brayden's ex-mistress and Scott had married the man's widow.

Clarke had joined the crew at first on the periphery, as Audrey's occasional tagalong, but over time, he'd become friends with Oliver and Scott in his own right. He and Oliver had run loosely in the same circle for years. In fact, on paper, he and Oliver had plenty in common. Born and raised on the Upper East Side, fathers established business leaders. Had they not been sent to different prep schools, Clarke expected they'd have been friends long before now. As it was, though, it had taken Oliver falling in love with Naomi, and Naomi and Audrey becoming fast friends, to bring them together.

Scott was a bit more of a mystery to Clarke. He was from Vermont or New Hampshire or some place with a population of twelve, but he had made a name for himself, not just in the New York real estate world, but internationally, as a contractor in charge of some of the most prestigious skyscrapers and landmarks of their lifetime.

The result was a man who looked as comfortable in a tuxedo with champagne in his hand as he did with a leather jacket and beer. Actually, that wasn't entirely true. The leather jacket, jeans, and boots Scott wore now seemed a far more natural fit. But Scott fit into their world when it suited him. Which wasn't often.

"You know, maybe the bachelor party would be a good time for us to see the house?" Oliver said with a smirk as he looked at Clarke.

"Yeah, tell me you at least get a stripper out of this whole fake wedding thing," Scott said. "I thought Claire was joking when she told me about it."

"Not a joke. You were at the engagement party," Clarke pointed out.

"I was," Scott drawled. "Didn't see much about it that looked fake."

Clarke sat forward and ran this thumb over the label of the bottle.

"He's referring to the kiss," Oliver said.

"I know what he's talking about," Clarke said irritably. "Is this why I got invited to your dinner party? So you could interrogate me about it?"

"No, Naomi invited you to the dinner party so *she* could interrogate you. I'm merely giving you a reprieve," Oliver said. "Though I suspect our man cave moments are limited before we're summoned to the salad course, or some shit, so if you want to spill, do it now."

"I don't want to spill," Clarke said. He realized the moment the words were out that it was a lie. He *did* want to talk about it, and these two guys were as good a bet as any. He stood and paced the room, looking around without really seeing Oliver's big-screen TV, the pool table, the built-in fridge, and the wet bar filled with an assortment of whiskies.

"You guys think I'm nuts."

"To be willingly going through the wedding planning process without even getting sex out of it?" Scott said. "Yeah. A little bit. Wait, you're not getting sex out of it, are you?"

"No," Clarke said.

"You don't sound entirely pleased about that," Oliver observed.

Clarke ignored this. He did *not* want to talk about sex. Or the fact that he wasn't having any. Or the fact that he'd been thinking about it more than a teenage boy lately. To say nothing of the fact that the subject of his rather vivid fantasies was entirely off-limits.

"Did you at least get to taste cake?" Scott asked. "That was my favorite part."

"I thought you and Claire eloped."

"We did. I meant cake tasting at my first wedding. Well, *almost* wedding."

"That's right," Clarke mused. "I forgot you guys were both engaged."

Clarke didn't know all the details, but if he was remembering correctly, Scott's fiancée had cheated on him, and Oliver's had bailed when she'd learned that being married to Oliver meant she'd also have to deal with his sick parents.

"Well, good news, you'll soon be joining our club," Oliver pointed out.

"What club?"

"The broken engagement club."

"Ah," Clarke said lightly.

Scott's eyes narrowed slightly. "What was that?"

"What's what?"

"You know what," Oliver said, straightening. "That 'ah' was loaded."

"It wasn't."

"You and Audrey are engaged for pretend, right?" Scott asked, frowning. "I didn't miss some crucial development?"

"No, you've got it right," Clarke said distractedly.

"Okay, I've heard the women's version of why," Oliver said, "but what's your story. Something about your mom being sort of . . ."

"A bitch," Scott said unabashedly. "No offense."

"None taken. She can be."

"And your ex, too, right? She and your mom are in cahoots trying to, what, rush you down the aisle?"

Liz's plea whispered through Clarke's mind. *I miss you.* But that little bombshell was nothing compared to the wallop his father had delivered hours later.

He and his father hadn't spoken since the bizarre meeting in his office a few days earlier. Clarke had been half hoping it had all been a dream, that his father hadn't actually dangled the company in front of him like a carrot to entice him down the aisle.

But though his father hadn't pushed him on the issue, he also hadn't retracted it.

Clarke was terrified—and quite certain—his father had meant every word. That York would be his if he and Audrey went through with the wedding.

The idea was preposterous and . . . not nearly as unappealing as it should have been.

"Can I have another?" Clarke asked Oliver, pointing at the beer bottle.

"Help yourself."

"So who is this ex of yours?" Scott asked. "Anyone I know?"

"Elizabeth Milsap."

Both men shook their heads.

"We dated for a year or so. A few years back. We broke up when she went to DC."

"You didn't want to go with?"

"I wasn't invited."

It was Oliver's turn to utter a telling *ah*.

"You want her back?" Scott asked with his usual bluntness.

Clarke popped the top off another beer, though he didn't take a drink. "I don't. In fact, this whole fake-engagement thing started as sort of a childish need to tell her she was wrong about me."

Oliver shook his head. "Not following."

Clarke sighed and leaned against the wet bar, facing his friends. "When Liz left, it wasn't acrimonious, necessarily, but it didn't exactly feel good, either. She's always been very career fo- cused, goal-oriented. The type of woman who's got her life plan outlined in an Excel spreadsheet. She made it clear that I hadn't made the necessary growth to warrant a spot in that plan."

"What sort of growth?"

Clarke shrugged. "You know. Not marriage material."

"And you thought you were?"

"I thought I deserved a chance to try. Back then, at least. Now, I know I'm not. *Now*, I know she had it right the first time."

"Bullshit. You're a good guy."

"I know," Clarke said with a smile, appreciating the compliment. "But I'm also sort of a man whore."

"We're all man whores until we're not," Scott said. "I had a different woman in every city and never promised a single one that I'd call again."

"What changed?"

Scott looked at him like he was an imbecile. "Claire."

"Right. Of course. But how did you . . . why did you—"

"I didn't even really think about it," Scott said, preempting Clarke's question. "I just woke up one day and felt that ending that wild-oats part of my life wouldn't be a sacrifice in the least. Given the choice between sleeping with a dozen different women or sleeping with *the* woman for the rest of my life? No-brainer."

"Why, are you thinking you might be the marrying type after all?" Oliver asked Clarke curiously.

"Maybe," Clarke admitted, somewhat surprised to hear himself say it out loud and even more surprised to realize that it didn't fill him with immediate terror. Maybe it was just getting older, but the thought of coming home to someone—the same someone—sounded a lot more appealing than it ever had before.

"So this Elizabeth woman. You think she's changed her mind about you as husband potential?"

"What? Oh," he said, shifting his thoughts back to Liz. "I don't know. I guess. She came to my office on Wednesday and made some definite noise about wanting to get back together."

Scott whistled. "That's ballsy. As far she knows, you're engaged."

"Yeah, well, I think she's got a pretty good sense of just how engaged Dree and I really are."

"Which is to say, not at all."

"Exactly. But—"

"Hiya, boys," Audrey said, bounding into Oliver's man cave. Dressed in dark jeans, a plain white T-shirt, and her usual ponytail, she was the epitome of the girl next door.

His girl next door.

No. Not his. Not for real.

Not in the way that mattered.

"Whew, testosterone in here." Audrey waved her hand in front of her face. "I'm surprised there's not a dartboard and a humidor."

"They're getting delivered on Monday," Oliver said with a grin.

"Figures. Anyway, Naomi sent me up. Appetizers are done."

"*Real* appetizers or fussy canapés?" Scott asked skeptically.

Audrey tilted her head. "I think a man with scruff on his chin, wearing a faded bomber jacket, who also says words like *canapés*, might be just about the sexiest thing I've ever seen."

Scott laughed and hooked an arm around Audrey's neck as they headed toward the door. "You like that? I've got more fancy words. Hors d'oeuvres. Foie gras. *Indubitably*."

"If I swoon, you'll have to carry me down the stairs," Audrey said, laughing as they left the room, Oliver at their heels.

Clarke took a moment longer, staring after them with a frown as he tried to place the unfamiliar emotion settling in his stomach. When he finally identified it, his scowl deepened. It was a first for him, and he understood now why it had a reputation for being so unpleasant.

Jealousy.

Chapter Fourteen

*A*udrey managed to keep her smile in place throughout the entire dinner party. She'd laughed at the right times, complimented the fresh flowers on Naomi's table, gushed over the food, and delighted along with Claire and Naomi in watching the men do the dishes. There was something downright amusing about watching big hands attempt to hand-wash dainty white wineglasses.

But under the surface, she'd been reeling. Ironically, the only person to notice was the same person who was at fault.

You okay? Clarke had murmured during dinner. She'd nodded.

You sure? he'd said out of the corner of his mouth as he'd cleared the table.

She'd nodded again, even as her brain screamed no.

She was *not* okay. She was not okay at all about what she'd overheard Clarke telling the guys, and worst of all, she couldn't even identify exactly *why*. So what if Elizabeth wanted him back? It's not as though Clarke wanted Elizabeth back, and even if he did, Audrey should be happy for them.

But try as she might to be happy for Clarke, or at least butt out of his business, she couldn't stop her chest from aching at the knowledge that he hadn't confided in her. He'd told the guys about Elizabeth's proclamation, but not her.

And it had happened on *Wednesday*, the same day as their cake tasting, when there'd been *plenty* of time to share—if not at the tasting itself, then certainly when they'd gone out to dinner that same night. Or yesterday when they'd gone to lunch. Or earlier tonight, when they'd shared a cab on the way to Naomi and Oliver's house.

She was baffled. Angry. *Hurt.* Three emotions that were all foreign as they related to Clarke. She didn't have a clue how to sort out the unfamiliar feelings, and she certainly didn't know how to do so in public, so throughout dinner, she'd played the same role she always did: laughing, cheerful, optimistic Audrey.

But the facade dropped the moment she and Clarke stepped onto the sidewalk outside Oliver and Naomi's place. She'd have preferred to leave alone, but since Claire and Scott were headed to Scott's apartment on the West Side, she and Clarke were the only ones heading to the Upper East Side, and she couldn't think of a good reason why they wouldn't go together. They were Audrey and Clarke. Clarke and Audrey. They'd been a unit long before they'd gotten "engaged," and now they were . . . she didn't know what they were.

"Okay," Clarke said with a smile, gently snagging her arm as they stepped into the evening air. "*Now* tell me what's wrong."

Audrey jerked her arm away, and his expression flickered in confusion.

She crossed her arms and stared down at her boots as she had an alarming realization. She'd been wrong, earlier, in thinking she was okay with his ex's office visit. She wasn't *just* upset that Clarke didn't tell her about Elizabeth. If she were brutally honest with herself, the idea of Clarke and Elizabeth spending time together made her stomach twist.

"Why?" Audrey finally asked aloud, once she's tamped down the unexpectedly nauseous feeling.

"Why what?"

"Why didn't you tell me that Elizabeth came to see you on Wednesday?"

He frowned. "How did you know that?"

"Well, not from you!" she snapped.

His eyes narrowed slightly. "Spy much, Dree?"

"Secrets much, Superman?" she shot back, deliberately wielding his least favorite nickname.

He threw up his hands in exasperation. "Sorry. Okay? It's not like I meant it to be some big secret."

"And yet you told the guys and not your fiancée?"

She winced as soon as she said it, well aware of just how *jealous* she sounded. His eyes narrowed again in speculation.

Audrey held up her hand. "Don't. No need to correct me. I know I'm not actually your fiancée. But I am your friend. I thought your *best* friend."

"You are my best friend. Seriously, what's the big deal?"

She huffed. *Such a guy.* "Whatever. Forget it." She started to whirl toward the curb to hail a cab.

He reached out and grabbed her hand. "Hold on. We're not done yet."

"Fine." She turned back around and waited. "I'm listening."

She could practically hear his teeth grind in frustration. "It's just . . . having your ex-girlfriend stopping by isn't something you tell your fiancée. It felt strange to bring it up."

"Especially since she didn't *just* stop by. She said she wanted you back," Audrey challenged.

"Wow, you were *really* thorough with that eavesdropping."

"Well, she does, doesn't she?" Audrey pressed, not letting him off the hook. "Want you back?"

He looked down at his feet, then back at her, shrugging. "So she says."

Audrey looked at him carefully. "Whatever happened with you two anyway? Back then? You never talked about it. I thought maybe there wasn't much to tell, but now that I know you and I have secrets—"

"Will you stop with that? We don't have *secrets*. How old are you right now, eight?"

She didn't rise to the bait. "What happened with you and Elizabeth?" she asked again.

"Oh my God, *this* is why I don't have girlfriends," he said, plowing his fingers through his hair. "They're demanding and pushy."

Audrey's lips parted in hurt. "I wasn't asking as a girlfriend. I was asking as—"

"A friend, I know," he said tiredly. "I shouldn't have said that. I just . . . I don't want to talk about this, Audrey. It was a long time ago. She moved on, I moved on—"

"Except she didn't," Audrey persisted, not sure why she was pushing so hard. She only knew that she felt something strange burning in her stomach, and she wanted it to stop. "Elizabeth didn't move on. She thinks you're engaged, and she still came and made a move."

"Because Liz knows *this*," Clarke said, gesturing between the two of them, "is fake."

The words weren't meant to hurt her. They *shouldn't* hurt her.

But they did.

"Got it. Well, if this is so *fake*, I guess this is as good a time as any to call it," she said, suddenly exhausted down to her very bones.

"Call what?"

"The 'engagement,'" she said, lifting her hands into air quotes. "Scandal Boy's backed off, your mother got a lesson in not sticking her nose where it doesn't belong, and your ex-girlfriend got the wake-up call that she let a good one get away."

"That's not why I've been doing this," he snapped.

"No?" she asked.

"No!"

Her frustration burst out. "Well, how am I supposed to know when you don't tell me!"

"Because I don't tell you everything, Audrey!" he shouted. "I'm sorry, but I don't. We can be friends without me having to fucking spill my guts every minute of the damned day."

The hurt was stronger this time. Not the sting of a paper cut, but the throb of something much deeper.

"Got it," she said, turning away.

"Dree, wait—"

"No, Clarke." She turned back, keeping her face expression-less, her tone calm. "I think separate cabs would be a good idea. Let's just take a night to cool down."

"And then what?" He shoved his hands into his pockets, looking as lost as she felt. They *never* fought.

She shrugged. "Then we figure out how to get ourselves out of the mess we got ourselves into."

Clarke said nothing for a long moment. "Sure. Okay. Let's get you a cab."

Wordlessly they walked to the curb. It was late on a Saturday, so it took a few minutes to find an available cab. She was relieved when he opened the door for her but didn't follow her into the taxi.

"You sure this is what you want?" he asked quietly before closing the door. "To end the engagement?"

She looked into his familiar gold-brown eyes and nodded. "I'm tired of pretending."

He held her gaze, then jerked his head in understanding. "Sure. I get it."

Audrey pulled the door shut, not looking his direction as the cab drove away. She squeezed her eyes shut. Clarke wasn't the only one who was keeping secrets.

Audrey was tired of pretending, but what terrified her down to her very soul was that she wasn't tired of pretending to be engaged.

She was tired of pretending she wanted it to end.

Chapter Fifteen

A week later, the ice between Audrey and Clarke hadn't yet thawed. It was fitting, Audrey figured, that the next time they saw each other would involve copious amounts of snow.

"You're *sure* you won't come with?" asked Erin Ratliff, a society darling whom Audrey was friendly with. Erin positioned her designer ski goggles atop her head and gave Audrey a worried look. "I feel so bad leaving you behind. I thought you skied!"

"Oh, I do ski," Audrey said with a reassuring smile. "I like skiing. I just love a good book, a hot toddy, and a roaring fire even more."

Audrey gestured behind her at the resort's après ski lounge area, which truly was her version of heaven, a hideaway with plenty of cozy corners and comfortable furniture tucked around an enormous fireplace.

Erin gave her another skeptical look before stepping closer and lowering her voice. "I am *super* sorry. This must be so awkward. When I invited you and Clarke a while back, I didn't real-

ize you were together, and then one of the other girls invited
Clarke's ex—"

"It's fine," Audrey cut in quickly. "Clarke and I are adults, and
Elizabeth and I are fine."

Not quite as fine *as Clarke and Elizabeth*, a traitorous little
part of her brain whispered, as her gaze skimmed over the small
group pulling on gloves and dabbing sunscreen on their noses as
they prepared for a day on the slopes. Audrey's eyes found Clarke
almost immediately, and she was unsurprised to see that Elizabeth was glued to his side.

Audrey looked away, wising she'd have found a way to get out
of the ski-trip invitation she'd accepted weeks ago. The worst part
was that even as of last night, Audrey had been looking forward to
the weekend. She'd figured it'd be the opening she and Clarke
needed to resolve things after their fight.

When Erin had picked Audrey up at the crack of dawn,
Audrey had all but skipped to the car, her stomach aflutter at the
thought of seeing Clarke again. She'd *missed* him and had run to
open the door of the SUV, only to find the back seat full, all three
seats taken.

By Erin's cousin. By Clarke. And by Elizabeth Milsap.

The worst part hadn't been seeing Elizabeth's thigh pressed
familiarly against Clarke's. It had been the fact that Clarke had
barely *looked* at Audrey. And they hadn't spoken even once.

She looked back toward Clarke and Elizabeth again, watching as a laughing *Liz* reached out and swiped a glob of sunscreen
onto Clarke's nose. Audrey felt like throwing up as Clarke smiled
in response, tugging off his glove to rub in the sunblock.

"You'd think she could be a little more subtle," Erin said loyally, under her breath.

Audrey forced a smile. "Oh, it's fine. We're all friends."

Though at the moment, she wasn't quite sure what she and Clarke were. They'd gone a week without talking or texting before, when they were busy with work or on vacation, but this felt *different*. There was a gap between them that they'd never experienced before, and Audrey didn't have a clue how to bridge it. Somewhere in the past couple of weeks, things had started to skid out of control, and she was terrified that even if and when they did manage to get things back on track, everything would feel different.

"Everyone ready to head out?" Erin's cousin Mike asked the group.

He was met by an enthusiastic chorus of yeses as they began filing out the door.

Erin gave Audrey's arm one last squeeze. "I'll come check on you in a couple hours?"

Audrey rolled her eyes. "I'm fine. I promise. I brought reading supplies." She held up her e-reader.

"Okay, okay, I'll stop mama-bearing you. And for what it's worth, I'm totes jealous that you get to rock the snow bunny look without the bulk." She patted the thick padding of her down jacket and gave Audrey's black yoga pants, fur boots, and cozy oversize sweater a covetous look.

"*Go*," Audrey commanded with a laugh, pointing her friend out into the bright, frigid sunshine with the rest of the group. "They'll leave without you."

Erin turned away, and Audrey allowed herself one last look at Clarke. Other than Erin, he was the last one out of the lodge. He glanced her way and hesitated. For a second, Audrey thought—*hoped*—that he was going to walk over and finally address the weirdness between them.

But just as he stepped forward, Elizabeth poked her head back into the lodge. "Clarke. You coming?"

Clarke stopped in his tracks, glancing over his shoulder at Elizabeth, then back at Audrey. As she silently begged him to choose her, Audrey saw the indecision in his gaze and knew him well enough to know which path he was going to choose: the easy one. She was disappointed in him, but more so, crushed to realize which side of the coin she fell on. Not so long ago, Audrey had been his easy path, his safe space.

Now *she* was the one he didn't want to deal with.

"Yeah, coming," Clarke said to Elizabeth with a grin. He turned his back on Audrey and walked outside without a backward glance.

Audrey swallowed, a little alarmed to feel a lump in her throat. Apparently, they were really, truly done pretending to be engaged, even though neither had explicitly said it to the group. She could handle that. But at the moment, it felt like they were done being friends. And *that* felt like it would kill her.

Taking a deep breath, she turned on her heel and scanned the mostly empty lodge. There were a handful of people who apparently had the same idea as her and had staked their claim on various chairs and couches with a laptop or book in hand. But for the most part, she had her pick of places to sit and opted for a cozy chair near the window facing opposite of the way her friends had gone. The last thing she wanted to do was watch the group get on the chairlift. Each chair seated two, and it didn't take a genius to know who Clarke would be paired off with.

Audrey ordered a hot chocolate with extra whipped cream, and though it took her a few false starts, she finally managed to lose herself in her book, a psychological thriller that everyone had been talking about but that she was just finally getting around to reading.

She eventually became so engrossed that she jumped when she realized someone was standing in front of her, trying to get her attention. Audrey looked up and saw a man dressed in ski pants and a black sweater smiling down at her, a bit sheepishly. "Sorry. I didn't mean to startle you."

Audrey blinked. The man was attractive. *Extremely* attractive. Tall and lean, with a dash of silver at his temples and smile lines indicating he had a few years on her. But the years looked good on him. He seemed vaguely familiar, though she couldn't quite place him.

He pointed toward her feet. "You mind if I sit? I hate to invade your space, but as far as I can tell, you've got access to one of the only power outlets in the place."

"Oh, of course," she said, noting the laptop under his arm and waving at the chair opposite her.

He smiled and sat, pulling a charger out of his jacket pocket and shrugging out of his coat. "Good book?" he asked, nodding at her Kindle.

"Apparently," she said, looking at her watch, surprised to see how many hours had passed.

"Not a skier?" the man asked curiously, bending down to plug in his charger.

"I am. I just never learned to love it enough to choose being out in the cold over being cozy by the fire. You?"

"I *did* learn to love it. But I've got two loves, and this is the other one." He tapped a long finger against his closed laptop.

"Your computer?" Audrey asked dubiously.

"Work," he said, his eyes doing that attractive crinkling-in-the-corner thing again.

Audrey couldn't help her gaze dropping to his left hand, a little surprised to see there was no ring. She wondered if he was newly divorced or a rare late-thirties/early-forties bachelor who was, well, *hot*.

"Your husband ski?" he asked casually, opening his laptop.

"Hmm? Oh," she said, realizing that he had apparently checked out her left hand as well and found it adorned with Clarke's ring. "Fiancé. And yeah, he does."

The man gave a noncommittal smile and turned his attention to his screen.

Audrey turned her Kindle back on but looked up when she sensed eyes on her. She was a little surprised that the man didn't look away or make any effort to pretend he hadn't been curiously studying her.

He leaned forward, right hand extended. "Jarod Lanham."

"*Ohhh*," Audrey couldn't help but say, as the name confirmed why he looked so familiar.

He flashed her a smile, white teeth gleaming, as she noted his face looked to have gotten a bit of color out on the slopes that morning. "I see the name rings a bell."

"The world's most eligible billionaire? I've heard of you," she teased lightly, then promptly felt a wave of dismay when she heard the flirtatious note in her voice.

She and Clarke may not be actually engaged, or even on speaking terms, but she was still wearing his ring.

But, to give herself credit, it was hard not to be at least a little bit dazzled to be talking to *the* Jarod Lanham. Growing up on the Upper East Side, Audrey was no stranger to extreme wealth, her own family included, but this man was on another level entirely. Self-made and richer than Audrey's and Clarke's families combined, Jarod was a bit of a legend in Manhattan social circles, especially since he had homes all over the world and spent a limited amount of time in the city.

Despite being frequently photographed with gorgeous models and actresses, generally on a yacht or in glamorous mansions in Monaco, the man was famously elusive when it came to relationships. It was also hard to miss that he was better looking in person than he was on the magazine covers. In pictures, he was attractive enough, but in a generic stock-photo-of-a-businessman kind of way. In person, he had a sort of raw masculinity beneath all the polish. And then, of course, there was that smile . . .

Realizing she was staring, Audrey felt herself blush and glanced down at her book, just as a waiter came over to ask if Jarod wanted anything to drink.

"I'll have an Irish coffee, extra hot, light on the whipped cream."

The server nodded, then turned to Audrey, who looked down at her empty hot chocolate mug and figured what the hell. "Same. Though don't you dare go light on the whip."

Jarod surprised her by closing his laptop once the waiter left, even though he couldn't have possibly done any work in the two minutes it had been open. "You left me hanging."

"What?"

Another smile. "When someone introduces himself, it's customary for the other to do the same."

"Ah," she said with a laugh. "Forgive me, I was dazzled by your celebrity status."

"It happens." He winked.

Audrey smiled and extended her hand. "Audrey Tate."

They shook hands for a second time, and Audrey was a little surprised to realize that despite his attractiveness and appealing charm, she didn't feel *it*. There was no electric current when their palms touched, no butterflies beyond the slight excitement of meeting someone who'd graced the cover of *People*.

"So, who is Audrey Tate, other than a ski-indifferent whipped cream enthusiast? I'm guessing . . . a New Yorker."

"That obvious, huh?"

"You've got the look." The admiring glint in his gaze told her it was a look he approved of, though she appreciated that his flirting felt harmless rather than propositioning. After Brayden, she was extra appreciative of a man who respected a ring on the left hand.

"Manhattan, born and raised. And actually, it's my job to have the look."

"Model?"

"Flattering, but not exactly. Instagram influencer."

He shook his head, and she explained. "It's a newfangled fancy way of saying that I make money as a lifestyle blogger. Basically, I have a lot of Instagram followers, and companies pay me to utilize my reach, to attend their parties, and so on."

"Clever. Are you working now?"

"Nope, this is purely a vacation," she said. "Though once my friends get back, I'll probably coax one of them into taking a picture of me. I try not to go more than a day without posting a photo to keep people engaged."

"I could do it. Take the picture, I mean."

Audrey lifted her eyebrows, "You *want* to take a photo of me?"

"Sure, why not." He set his laptop aside and held out his hand. "Give me your phone."

"Um, all right." She shrugged and picked up her phone from the side table near her elbow.

"So how does this work. I just . . . point and shoot?"

"Well, ideally I'd have had time to go back to my room for lipstick," she said with a laugh.

He took a picture.

"Hey!" She laughed again as he took yet another picture.

"That is *not* how this works," she said, grinning as she leaned forward to grab the phone. "I have to pose. Maybe by the fire . . ."

He took another photo, just as Audrey grabbed the phone, giving him a chiding look, then laughing even harder as she looked at the handful of photos.

"These are terrible! My mouth is open in all of them!"

"People like candid photos," he said with an unrepentant grin.

"Not when they can see my molars!"

Still, she locked her phone instead of deleting them straightaway. He *was* Jarod Lanham after all.

"So, Mr. Lanham—"

"Jarod," he corrected. "I've seen your molars, remember. I think we're on a first-name basis."

"All right then, Jarod. Tell me—"

"Dree."

Audrey jolted and looked up, surprised to see that in the time since Jarod had sat down, the lodge had grown crowded and noisy with skiers coming in for a midday lunch break, including her group of friends.

And her *fiancé*.

Clarke was hovering over her, looking both irritable and a little unsure of himself. She met his gaze and narrowed her eyes slightly in a silent challenge. *Where's Elizabeth?*

He narrowed his eyes back, then turned toward the man sitting across from her. "Hey. I'm Clarke. Audrey's fiancé."

Audrey looked up in surprise at Clarke's hard profile, startled by the possessive note in his voice, the emphasis on the word *fiancé*. Her surprise shifted quickly into irritation. Um, no. He did *not* get to come in here acting like a jealous jerk after the way he'd been behaving.

Jarod seemed unperturbed by Clarke's sharpness. He gave an easy grin and shook his hand. "Jarod Lanham."

Audrey saw from Clarke's quick blink that he recognized the name. He looked back at her, his expression conflicted, but the question in his gaze was clear. *Good-looking bachelor. Should I back off?*

It was a silent exchange they'd had a million times before, each taking care to know when they should make themselves scarce, *or* when they were needed to make the unwanted suitor scarce.

This time, there was an extra something in his gaze. A vulnerability along with the question. And Audrey was surprised to realize that she didn't have an answer for Clarke. Or for herself. The obvious answer, of course, was that now would be a really good time to announce the end of their fake engagement. She was clicking with a very eligible man, and Clarke was clearly enjoying Elizabeth's company.

And yet, no part of her was eager to take Clarke's ring off her finger.

For all their recent antagonism, Clarke still knew her better than anyone and read the indecision on her face. "Will you excuse us for a moment?" Clarke asked, glancing down at Jarod.

"Of course," the billionaire said with a polite smile, already reaching for his laptop.

Clarke extended a hand to Audrey, and she hesitated only a moment before taking it and letting him pull her to her feet.

"I'll be right back," she told the server with a smile as he approached with two Irish coffees.

Clarke looked down at the matching drink order, his jaw

tightening along with his fingers as he led her around the throng of boisterous skiers.

"Where are we going?" she asked as they stepped into a quieter hallway outside the great room.

He released her hand and turned to face her, arms crossing defensively across his chest. He must have left his jacket with their group because he was wearing only a dark green Henley with his gray ski pants. His hair was wind tossed, his cheeks were slightly red from the cold, and his eyes were unreadable as he looked down at her.

Audrey gave him a pretty, fake smile. "It's good to see your nose didn't sunburn. Good old SPF."

His gaze suddenly became very readable: *wary*.

Good. He should be.

"Where *is* Elizabeth?" Audrey asked, leaning forward and pretending to look around. "I'm surprised she let you out of her sight for more than thirty seconds. Wouldn't want you running off to speak to your fiancée."

"Looks like my fiancée found someone else to chat up."

She gave an incredulous laugh. "Seriously? You're going to give me crap for having a conversation when you ditched me to flirt with Elizabeth?"

"I didn't ditch you," he snapped. "We were invited up here to ski, and that's what I did. Not my fault you prefer to sit around the lodge in your tight pants and bat your eyelashes."

Stung, she could only stare at him before shaking her head. "I can't figure out what you're worse at these days, playing fiancé or actually *being* a friend."

He flinched, and she knew her jab had hit home. But she was glad about it. Something needed to wake him up from whatever was going on with him.

"Look," she said, gentling her voice, "if you want to publicly announce that we've ended it so you can get back together with Elizabeth, just say so. You're my friend. I'll be happy for you, no matter what."

"You're the one who said you wanted to call it off. Just in time, too," Clarke said, nodding in the direction of the main lodge area where they'd left Jarod Lanham.

Audrey threw up her hands in exasperation. "All right, Clarke. I give up. I don't know what the hell is going on with you, but you're going to have to work through it without me. I don't know who or what this version of Clarke is, but he's not my best friend. Let me know when you want to have an actual conversation and go back to being Clarke and Audrey, because *this*"—she gestured between them—"isn't working for me."

Audrey started to brush past him, but he reached out and grabbed her hand, the way he had outside Naomi and Oliver's. She looked down in surprise at their joined hands, then glanced up at him. He was still scowling, but his expression had shifted into frustration.

"What?" she asked when he said nothing to break the silence and didn't release her hand. She tried to tug it away, but he tightened his grip.

"Clarke, what—" His expression shifted again, into a look she'd never seen before. She didn't have a chance to identify it before he pulled her slowly and purposefully toward him, his head dipping down, his lips brushing over hers.

Audrey exhaled at the unexpected kiss, then gasped as his free hand came around to cup the nape of her neck, pulling her all the way against him as his mouth slanted over hers. She kept thinking she'd get used to the jolt at these faux kisses, but this was the third one and she felt a little more confused every time.

Confused as to why he tasted so good, why his lips against hers felt like a piece of her life she hadn't realized she was missing.

Audrey's hands lifted to his chest, her fingers instinctively gripping his shirt, pulling him closer. He went slightly still, as though surprised she was responding to the kiss, but when he moved again, it was to wrap an arm low across her back until they were pressed together hips to hips, belly to belly. Mouth to mouth.

Her lips parted, and Clarke took full advantage, gliding his tongue forward to brush against hers as she felt the touch all the way down to her toes and everywhere in between. Clarke nudged her backward, pushing her against the wall, never breaking the kiss as he tilted her head back farther, demanding more. Demanding *everything*.

Her hands slid further up his chest, her fingers tangling in his thick hair as she whispered his name. The second she did, Clarke's head snapped back up, and his eyes locked on hers for a moment, smoldering before he abruptly stepped back.

They were both breathing hard, but only Audrey seemed to be disoriented. Clarke seemed otherwise unaffected, as though it had been just another one of their playful, just-for-show kisses, as though everything hadn't just changed.

Slowly, he turned his head, glancing down the hallway. Audrey followed his gaze, her heart dropping into her stomach when she saw what he was looking at. *Who* he was looking at.

Elizabeth stood in the middle of the hallway, staring at them with a stricken expression before turning on the heel of her ski boot and marching back into the lodge.

Audrey closed her eyes, feeling slightly queasy as she realized that the kiss *had* been for show after all. He'd known Elizabeth was watching. He'd been kissing her as part of their game, while she'd been kissing him . . .

She closed her eyes unable to even finish the thought.

When she opened them, she forced a bright smile and gave a brief slow clap. "Well, congratulations, Clarke. Hell of a show you put on. I'm sure Elizabeth definitely got the message this time."

She started to walk away, then turned back around, angry now. "Actually, just so I'm clear, what *is* the message you're trying to convey? What role am I playing here?"

He pushed his thumbs against his eyes. "I don't know, Dree. I don't fucking know."

"Right, well," she said in a light tone. "Let me know when you figure it out."

Chapter Sixteen

*I*f a man had to eat an enormous slice of humble pie, Valentine's Day was a good time to do it. Not that Clarke couldn't find whatever he wanted in a place like New York on *any* day of the year, but the stores had made it especially easy for him to arrive at Audrey's armed with groveling supplies.

And Clarke most definitely had some groveling ahead of him.

He paused on the sidewalk outside Audrey's brownstone, tapping the bouquet of pink flowers against his hip, stalling for time as he tried to think through his game plan. Clarke knew he was good with words, skilled with charm, but groveling was one area he'd never mastered. Never really *had* to master, actually. He'd pissed off plenty of women over the years, to be sure, but usually the source of their ire was lack of attention, and the reason for the lack of attention was that he'd already had one foot out the door anyway. No point in groveling when you didn't plan to see the woman again.

If he were brutally honest, he'd never cared about a woman

enough to grovel. Except for Audrey. And Audrey had never been mad at him.

Until now. And justifiably so.

He exhaled and rallied his courage. It wasn't that he didn't want to have this conversation; it's that he didn't know where to start. The list of things they needed to discuss was long and hefty. For starters, he needed to tell her about his father's ultimatum: that if they went through with the wedding, he'd get the company. That was a doozy.

They also needed to talk about the fact that he hadn't told his father to shove his ultimatum outright. *That* was a whopper. They needed to have a conversation about Elizabeth. About what had gone down with them years ago, and he had to apologize for his behavior on the ski trip, where he'd been an unpardonable ass for reasons he hadn't even fully sorted out yet.

Nor had he sorted out that damned kiss. Audrey had been wrong about his reasons for it. He hadn't kissed her because Elizabeth was watching. In that moment, he hadn't even remembered that Elizabeth existed. The only thing he'd been aware of was Audrey and the way he'd felt when he'd seen another man making her laugh.

Clarke had never really understood the concept of jealousy, but he'd felt it twice now in the past couple weeks, and it was brutal. Audrey's easy flirting with Scott had been mildly annoying. He'd been able to remind himself that Scott was happily married to Claire and that Audrey was merely being her usual charming self.

But on Saturday, he'd known *real* jealousy. There was nothing gentle or subtle about the ache that came from his bones, from his very soul. The need to stake his claim, to remind the other guy *and* Audrey that she was his. Except she wasn't. Not in the way he'd wanted her to be in that minute. The way he'd wanted her to be a lot, lately. He couldn't remember the last day—the last hour—that he hadn't grappled with the uncomfortable realization that the way he felt about Audrey was shifting with every kiss, with every smile, hell, with every *glance*.

But that was for him to deal with, on his own. In the meantime, he had something more important to do than get over the fact that he couldn't stop wondering what her skin would feel like if he slipped a hand beneath her shirt, wondering what sounds she'd make if he kissed her neck.

None of that mattered as much as their friendship. That came first. Always.

"Shit," Clarke muttered, and tapped the bouquet against his thigh again, this time hard enough to lose a few petals. He forced himself to jog up the steps to her front door, and with his other hand, which was holding a fussy pink gift bag that cost him six dollars—not counting the sparkly tissue paper the saleswoman had insisted he needed—he knocked.

Clarke sucked in his cheeks and waited. He was fairly certain she was home, since she'd posted an Instagram Story showing off her latest purchase in her closet less than an hour ago, but he was decidedly *less* certain she'd open the door once she realized it was him.

He let out a breath of relief when the front door opened, only to have that same breath catch in his chest again at the sight of his best friend. She was clearly gearing up for an evening in, dressed in cropped sweatpants, a red T-shirt, and her long dark hair in a messy knot atop her head. She looked . . .

She looked so damn good.

Clarke was braced for the anger he knew he deserved, but instead he saw only curiosity on her face. No, not just curiosity.

Audrey also looked a little wary at the sight of him, and that made his chest ache.

Audrey was wary of *him*. Clarke had spent his entire life doing his best to never hurt Audrey, and he knew in this past week, he'd failed horribly. In some ill-gotten attempt to protect her, he'd done the exact opposite.

"Hi?" she said when he didn't move or speak.

"Can I come in?" he said roughly.

"Of course," she said, sounding slightly affronted that he'd thought he had to ask. He felt his hopes lift as she stepped aside without hesitation.

Clarke couldn't ever remember feeling nervous around Audrey, so he was more than a little appalled to realize he had sweaty palms and something akin to . . . butterflies?

"Here." He shoved the flowers at her, and she glanced down at the bouquet he'd thrust against her chest, a little smile playing around her lips that went a long way to ease the butterflies.

Her brown eyes lifted to his. "You brought me Valentine's Day flowers?"

Clarke shrugged. "Valentine's Day. Apology. *Clarke's an ass* flowers. Take your pick."

"The first one," she said, rubbing a finger over one of the rose petals. "I'm going to pretend they're the first one. Nobody's ever brought me Valentine's Day flowers before."

A strange feeling tugged in his chest. "Nobody?"

"Well, my dad always used to buy my mom two dozen red roses, and he'd bring a single long-stem rose home for me and my sister. But flowers from my *dad* don't really count."

"What about these? Do these count?" he asked, remembering all the times she'd described him as a brother.

"Well, depends," she said, looking up at him once more. "Did you buy them for me as a sister?"

She was smiling, but Clarke couldn't quite manage a smile back, at least not the carefree, teasing kind to match hers.

"No." Clarke's voice was a little gruff. "I did not."

They were not brother-sister flowers. And for all his intentions of this being about salvaging their friendship, they weren't friend flowers, either. Friends bought friends cheerful, casual flowers. He knew, because he'd bought her flowers countless times, though apparently not on Valentine's Day, which he was currently regretting.

Even as a guy, Clarke recognized that these flowers were different. Indulgent, lavish, expensive, and . . . sensual?

Pull it together, man. They're just flowers.

Clarke followed Audrey into the kitchen, watching as she set the flowers on the counter and walked over to flick open the high cupboard door above the fridge. She teetered on her toes for a moment, waving her hand futilely.

She rocked back to her heels and pointed a commanding finger at the shelf. "Hey, six-one. Make yourself useful."

Clarke easily grabbed the vase, setting it on the counter beside the sink as Audrey began clipping the ends off the flowers.

"These are beautiful," she said with a little sigh, lifting one of the blooms to her nose.

"Brayden didn't get you anything for Valentine's Day?" he asked, then flinched, realizing it probably wasn't a happy memory.

She merely shrugged and dropped the rose into the vase. "We were only dating for one Valentine's Day, and he said he was traveling for work, that we'd celebrate later. We never did, and I guess I didn't think much of it." She spun a tulip around, studying it. "Though, I suppose, thinking about it now in hindsight, he was spending it with Claire. Tuesday-night trysts are for mistresses, but Valentine's Days are for the wives."

"And the fiancées."

She let out a mirthless laugh. "Of course. Is that why you're here?"

Clarke had been leaning backward against the counter, watching her trim the flowers, and he reached out and gently took her left hand, realizing how often he'd been doing that lately. Realizing how much he liked the feel of her small hand in his.

He ran his thumb over her bare fourth finger. "Apparently, I no longer have a fiancée."

She tugged her hand away and didn't meet his eyes. "Come on. I thought we agreed that night after Naomi and Oliver's dinner party to call it."

"We talked about it. But you were still wearing the ring the day of the ski trip." He knew, because it was the first thing he'd looked for when she'd entered the car that morning.

"Yeah, well, that was before."

"Before Jarod Lanham?" he asked, hating that he had to ask, hating how much he dreaded the answer.

"What?" She gave him a baffled look. "Oh. No."

"Really? You two seemed to be hitting it off."

"Well, as far as he knew, I was engaged, and he didn't make a move on someone else's woman."

"But *you* knew you weren't engaged."

"True. But I also knew there wasn't any spark. And even if there was, I'm not looking for a fling with a billionaire."

"What are you looking for?"

She looked puzzled by the question. "Nothing. You know that better than anyone."

"You used to want it all. The spark. The prince on the white horse. Happily ever after."

She shrugged, and instead of pushing her, he reached for the gift bag he'd set on the counter and handed it to her as she finished arranging the flowers.

Audrey looked surprised. "For me?"

He rolled his eyes. "Who else would it be for?"

She didn't reply, but he'd gotten damn good at reading Audrey Tate over the years and knew who she'd been thinking it was for: *Elizabeth.*

She'd thought the gift was for Elizabeth. As though he were the type of man to bring flowers to one woman and a gift to another, all in the same night.

But wasn't he? Hadn't he always been *exactly* that type of guy? The one that went out of his way to make sure women knew he wasn't playing for keeps?

Why, then, did it feel so important to prove to her that he could be a one-girl kind of guy, that he might have a solution that would make both of them happy, even if it was entirely crazy?

Don't be an idiot, he chided himself, as he did every time the insane idea popped into his head.

"It's for you," he said simply, handing the gift to her.

Clarke had given Audrey plenty of presents over the years, but this was the first time he'd felt nervous about it. He'd gone with his gut, but as he watched her shove away the tissue paper, he had doubts. He should have gone with jewelry or something fun and frivolous. Something she'd never have bought herself. Wasn't that the general rule on buying gifts for women? Something indulgent and pampering?

Audrey's gift had three parts, and she laid them down on the counter one by one, as a faint line formed between her eyebrows.

Clarke resisted the urge to grab the items, stuff them back in the bag, drag her to Tiffany's or Chanel, and tell her to pick out a new pair of earrings.

"What is it?" she asked, looking up at him.

Clarke cleared his throat. "It's ah . . . it's for your iPhone. The middle one is a lens that allows you to take better quality photos on your phone since you don't carry around a separate camera. The other is the case that you clip the lens onto, and the third is a filter to give you more options. You mentioned a few months ago that you wish you had more photography options, without always having to switch to using a camera, and I researched—"

Audrey threw her arms around his neck.

"Thank you," she murmured, burying her face into the nook beneath his jaw.

Clarke's eyes closed as he wrapped his arms around her, returning the hug. "I am really sorry. You know that, right?"

He felt her smile. "I know. It's okay."

He gave a quick shake of his head. "You shouldn't make it that easy for a man, Dree. You deserve the groveling."

"I don't need the groveling. I got flowers, a heartfelt apology, and the most thoughtful gift anyone's ever given me."

He smiled in indulgent disbelief. "It's a camera lens. Not even the expensive kind, but a clip-on."

"That fits into a clutch *and* that won't require me to change my workflow," she said, pulling back and looking up at him with a smile. "It's perfect."

He smiled back, but it was fleeting. He knew he was getting off too easily. "About Elizabeth . . ."

Her grin slipped. "We don't have to talk about it. You're right, you don't have to tell me everything about your life, and I'm sorry I badgered you, making you feel like you had to."

"It wasn't that. That's not why I held back from telling you."

She frowned. "Then why?"

"It was just . . ." He frowned, realizing he didn't know how to explain, or even what he was trying to explain.

He wanted to tell her that he hadn't mentioned Elizabeth stopping by because when he was in the same room with her, Elizabeth was the last person he was thinking about. He wanted to tell her that the day of the ski trip, he'd let Elizabeth stay glued to his side because, like an idiot, he needed a buffer. *From her.*

But he couldn't tell her that in a strange, twilight zone twist of fate, his ex-girlfriend felt bland and safe, whereas the mere thought of Audrey was conjuring up dangerous, intense emotions.

Looking down at her face now, trusting and understanding, he realized how wrong he'd been. There was nothing dangerous here. Intense, yes. But even amid their recent complications, one thing was simple: This woman was the best part of his life. The rock he could always count on.

Without thinking, he tucked a loose strand of hair behind her ear. "Can I take you to dinner?"

She smiled. "On Valentine's Day? Our options will be limited without a reservation."

"I've made three. You've got your choice between Italian, French, or a pretentious little place in the West Village deemed the 'most Instagram-able place in the city.' I figure we're due for a preemptive strike against Scandal Boy and his minions."

"Yes, he *has* been suspiciously quiet. I thought for sure someone would have caught a picture of you and Elizabeth swooping down the slopes together," Audrey said.

"Swooping?" he asked, eyebrows arching even as his guilt gnawed at him. "For the record, I have never swooped in my life, and it wasn't like it was just the two of us holding hands down the mountain while singing our love. We were with the group the whole time."

"Well, it was going to be either that or a shot of me and the hot billionaire. But maybe that's the benefit of getting out of the city. I guess Scandal Boy's army of sycophants don't hang out in the Poconos."

"Bet they'd love to get a shot of us on Valentine's Day, though." Clarke kept his voice casual. *Don't beg, man.*

She hesitated. "I'm sure. But what's the point if we're no longer engaged?" She held up her bare left hand. "Might as well let people know sooner rather than later.'

"I realize I'm not the most romantic of guys, but maybe Valentine's Day isn't the ideal day to announce to your followers that love is dead?"

She laughed. "Good point. I guess I could suffer through wearing the gorgeous diamond on my finger for one more night. Or . . ."

"I'm listening," he prompted.

"We could stay in?" she asked hopefully. "Order sushi or pizza, no false eyelashes for me, you could ditch the tie," she said, flicking a playful finger over the knot of his suit tie.

"A photo op *in*. Solid strategy," he said. "Behind-the-scenes always gets big likes, right?"

"Actually, I could use a break from being @TheAudreyTate," she said. "What if it was just us? Like it was before Instagram, before Elizabeth, before the fake engagement and Scandal Boy, back before things got . . ."

"Got what?" he asked, pulling her closer and registering that neither of them had stepped out of their embrace for the entire conversation.

"Complicated," she said slowly, choosing the word carefully.

"Things got complicated, and I want to go back to simple. I want to go back to *us*."

"I want that, too," Clarke said without hesitation.

It was true. He did want that. He was just afraid he was starting to want other things, too.

Later, as they sprawled on her couch, sipping red wine and picking at leftover lo mein, her calves draped casually over his thighs and his hand resting easily on her shin, Clarke had the fleeting thought that he couldn't remember the last time he'd been this content.

And then he glanced over at Audrey and realized he *could* remember.

It was every time he was with her.

Chapter Seventeen

*A*udrey figured if there was any place to have to confess to the city's most exclusive wedding planner that there wasn't going to *be* a wedding, it might as well be at the Plaza.

Alexis Morgan had called her that morning, her usually cool voice more animated than usual as she'd asked if Audrey could meet her at the Plaza at three today, assuring her that it would be well worth her while.

Truthfully, Audrey was a little surprised at the wedding planner's insistence. It wasn't as if Audrey had never been inside the Plaza or wasn't aware of its reputation as *the* elite wedding venue in Manhattan.

It was just that Audrey didn't really understand the point. Anyone who had seen *Bride Wars* knew that the place was booked up years in advance. Even if Audrey and Clarke were getting married for real, they wouldn't be doing it at the Plaza unless they wanted to get married two years from now or on a Tuesday.

Ultimately, though, Audrey had agreed to meet Alexis, mainly because her confession was past due and she needed to free up the wedding planner's time for someone who would actually be getting married, and she wanted to do it in person.

And, selfishly, she'd never seen the Plaza through the lens of a potential bride. She might as well have her final performance as the future Mrs. Clarke West at the reception site of her childhood bridal fantasies.

Dressed in an emerald-green dress and L.K. Bennett wedges, with her hair extra bouncy thanks to the pricey Bergdorf blowout and with her makeup professionally applied by the skilled hands at the Charlotte Tilbury counter, she sauntered up the familiar steps and smiled in thanks as the doorman opened the door for her.

She'd taken extra care with her appearance today, wanting to look her best when she posted on Instagram that she and her fiancé had opted to go their separate ways. If she was going to open herself up to Scandal Boy's claws again, at least her hair would be on point when he took a swipe at her.

Stepping into the Plaza lobby, Audrey was so busy looking for the petite Alexis that she didn't register that someone else was coming her way until he was right in front of her.

"Hey! What are you doing here?"

Clarke shrugged. "Alexis called me. Said I had to be here."

"Oh. Did she tell you why?"

"I think we're about to find out," Clarke said, nodding toward the approaching wedding planner.

Alexis smiled at them. "Good. I'm so glad you were both able to make it."

She gestured at someone behind Audrey and Clarke, and a hotel employee approached with a tray holding two champagne flutes. "Our congratulations on your upcoming nuptials," the woman said with a polite smile.

Audrey smiled back, even as her stomach sank at the reminder of why they were really here. To end it, once and for all. Still, the crowded lobby wasn't the place to do it, so she and Clarke both took a flute. This was one of the things she'd miss most when they called it off—the champagne.

She glanced at Clarke, and her stomach flipped just at the sight of him. Maybe champagne wouldn't be the thing she'd miss *most*, and that was utterly terrifying. And to be dealt with later. Alone.

Alexis motioned for Clarke and Audrey to follow her, and they headed toward the private event spaces.

"So, I know you've probably attended events here over the years," Alexis was saying. "But I wanted you to come today specifically, for two reasons. The first . . ."

She motioned to an open door, and Audrey let out a delighted gasp. Alexis smiled knowingly. "So you could see it set up for a Friday reception that I think is *very* much in line with the vision you two have described to me."

"Oh, it's perfect," Audrey breathed, stepping into the space and spinning slowly in a full circle. It was more than perfect. It was everything she'd ever envisioned for her wedding. The ceiling had been festooned with soft waves of tulle and twinkle lights that gave the room a fairy-tale look. The centerpieces on the table were nearly three feet high, the assorted white flowers arranged to look like they were fountains overflowing with blooms instead of water. The sashes on the backs of the chairs were a delicate pink, and the name cards were handwritten in what looked like gold ink.

She smiled at Alexis. "You're so right. It's a princess wedding." *It's my wedding.*

Alexis smiled back. "I thought you'd love it."

"What's the second reason you wanted to see us today?" Clarke asked, with a touch of male impatience. "To see Audrey's perfect wedding and . . ."

"Well," Alexis said, tapping her nails against her iPad, looking thoughtfully between the two of them. "I'm sure you both know that the Plaza books out very far in advance, unless you want to get married on a Wednesday morning off-season."

Audrey nodded knowingly. "Is it really true it gets booked by women who aren't even dating anyone yet, or is that Manhattan urban legend?"

"It's been known to happen," Alexis said. "But the Belles are on very good terms with the event coordinator here, always on the first-to-call list when there's been a cancellation."

Audrey couldn't help it. Caught up in the moment, she gasped. *A cancellation.*

Alexis smiled in confirmation. "One of their scheduled Saturday events fell through, and I'm sure I don't have to tell you that a last-minute Saturday opening at the Plaza is rare."

"I was *just* thinking about *Bride Wars*," Audrey said.

"I'm not following," Clarke said.

"It's a movie where—never mind, it's not important," Audrey said as reality crashed down on her. Excited as she'd been, she remembered just as quickly that it wouldn't matter that there'd been a cancellation at the Plaza now or ever.

Audrey took a deep breath. Now was as good a time as any. "So, Alexis, Clarke and I really appreciate that you thought of us, but—"

"How last-minute?" Clarke interrupted, looking at the wedding planner.

Alexis pursed her lips. "Well, that's the catch. Things would have to happen soon."

"How soon?"

"The last Saturday in March. The twenty-eighth."

"*March?*" Audrey squeaked. She couldn't fathom a fake wedding at the Plaza happening in under two months, much less a real one. Not that that was her problem.

"Is that even doable?" Clarke asked Alexis, still not looking at Audrey.

"Anything is doable," Alexis said. "Like I told you at our consultation, there are always sacrifices that have to be made with shorter timelines, and that's not even mentioning the increased costs. But Audrey's reputation is more valuable to a lot of vendors than the money. Though it would be expensive," she clarified with a smile.

"Sure," Clarke said distractedly.

"I know this is a lot to think about," Alexis said, looking back at Audrey. "I can put a twenty-four-hour hold on it, but after that—"

"Put the hold on it," Clarke said.

Audrey's eyes went wide. *"What?"*

How had they gone from agreeing to call this whole thing off to pretending they were going to book the Plaza?

"Actually, we don't need twenty-four hours to decide," he told Alexis. "We just need one hour."

"Clarke." If he were closer, she'd kick him.

He met her eyes, and Audrey was alarmed that she couldn't read him—didn't have a clue what he was thinking or what the hell he was doing.

Clarke took a deep breath. "Dree. Can we talk?"

———

The wide-eyed, appalled look Audrey was sporting as she sat across from him in the Plaza's champagne bar wasn't the strong start he'd been hoping for. Neither were the first words out of her mouth.

"Clarke, if you want to keep the charade going for a bit longer, I'm game, but I draw the line at taking this spot at the Plaza. Even if the deposit is refundable, which I doubt it is, I am *not* taking that spot away from someone who will actually use it. Saturdays in the wedding world are precious currency."

"I know." He picked up the cocktail menu and scanned the expansive sparkling wine options. "Moët or Veuve?"

"I don't care," she said distractedly. "If you keep acting crazy, the only sparkling beverage I'm letting you drink is water."

He merely smiled as he flagged down a server and ordered them two glasses of the most expensive champagne on the menu. It seemed to fit the occasion. What he was about to suggest was nuts, and yet it also felt exactly right.

Clarke waited until the server moved away, then met Audrey's gaze. "I'm sorry."

"For being a weirdo?"

"For Elizabeth. For not telling you about her."

She waved her hand. "We already went through that. Water under the bridge. It's fine. I told you, you don't have to share every detail—"

"No, I mean, I'm sorry I didn't tell you what happened with me and Elizabeth before. Years ago."

"Oh." She blinked. "*Oh.* Why?"

"I've been thinking a lot about that lately." He waited until the server had placed the champagne in front of them and moved away. He took a sip, barely tasted it.

"And?" Audrey nudged.

He lifted his gaze. "I didn't want you to know."

"Know what?"

"What Liz thought of me."

"She wants you back," Audrey said softy. "I'd say she thinks pretty highly of you."

"Not what she thinks *now*. What she thought of me back then." He continued to watch his friend. "I'm not marriage minded. You know that. *I* know that. But the truth is, I didn't really know that until she told me I wasn't."

"Elizabeth told *you* you didn't want to get married?" Audrey asked skeptically.

"Not exactly. She told me I wasn't marriage material."

Her eyes bugged a little in outraged surprised, and she scowled. "That horrible—"

"No," he said, holding up a hand. "She was right. But the real kicker is, I was actually *trying*. When she and I were dating, for the first time in my life, I was trying to be different. Better. You know how I was as a teen. And in college. I was a classic playboy who thought the world couldn't hurt me, and I didn't care who I hurt."

"You never hurt me."

Which is sort of my point.

"I was a nightmare of a kid, but right around the time I met Liz, I got the job at York and decided if I was going to be a grown-up in my professional life, I should be one in my personal life as well. So I dated exactly the sort of woman my mother wanted me to find. I bought the flowers. I didn't so much as look at another woman. I learned to cook."

"You did?" She looked fascinated, as though she didn't even know him.

"I didn't say I learned to cook *well*. But I did every damned husbandly thing I could think of."

"And she threw it back in your face," Audrey said quietly.

"Worse," Clarke said with a wry smile. "She didn't even *notice* any of my efforts. She got that job offer in DC, and selfishly, I wasn't thrilled. I didn't want to leave New York. But I was thinking, 'Okay, this is what committed people do. We'll figure it out.' Only she didn't want to figure it out. Not with me. That burned the most. I don't even think she *considered* it. It seemed to be a non-option in her mind."

He took a gulp of the champagne, annoyed that though the memory had dulled over time, it still hurt his ego. At least now he could admit that it *was* ego, and not something far more damaging.

He hadn't wanted to marry Elizabeth. Then or now. But it had been a valuable lesson in how women saw him—the same way his parents saw him. He was the fun guy, the unpredictable party boy. The one you brought home to your parents as arm candy because of his name and bank account, not because your dad would be impressed by his moral fiber. Even the women who'd made noise about coaxing him down the altar had been far more interested in the challenge, the inheritance, and the last name West.

"Liz told me I wasn't marriage material, and she was right."

"She was wrong," Audrey protested. "Just because she couldn't see your value doesn't mean someone else won't." She reached a hand across the table.

Clarke took a breath and placed his hand over hers, feeling the diamond of her engagement ring dig lightly into his palm. The fact that she'd decided to put it back on for one last day gave him the courage he needed.

Here goes nothing. "Someone already has."

Audrey blinked and tried to wriggle her hand away, but he pressed more firmly. "You've met someone?" she asked, sounding both thrilled and surprised.

"I've known her awhile, actually."

This time she was successful in jerking her hand away, dropping both hands into her lap, out of reach. "Well, that's great. Oh my gosh, you should have told me. I put your ring back on for God's sake. I just wanted one last hurrah, and—never mind, none of that's important. *Clarke.*" She leaned forward, eyes wide. "Are you thinking of marrying this woman? Is that why you told Alexis to reserve the Plaza? Oh my God, can I be your best woman? You have to say yes!"

Huh. This was not how he envisioned this going.

Clarke tried again, starting over. "I said that Liz was right when she said I wasn't marriage material, but only partially right. I'll never fit into her mold of marriage. Or society's mold of marriage. I don't know how to *dote*—I've never met anyone I want to *dote* on. Even if I did, to your point about divorce rates, I don't have faith that I, or any of us, really, can count on love to last."

"Or that the guy you're in love with isn't *also* in love with his wife," she said glumly.

Clarke was pretty damn sure Brayden Hayes had only ever been in love with himself, though he didn't point this out to her. Deep down, she probably already knew.

Audrey was frowning at him. "Okay, so you don't believe in love, and you don't think you're marriage material. So help me understand . . . *Why* are you letting Alexis think you're going to book the last Saturday in March at the Plaza?"

"I said I wasn't marriage material for *that* kind of marriage."

"The *regular* kind?" she asked.

His head dropped forward with a laugh. "You are really not making this easy."

"You're not being particularly clear," she countered.

Fine. She wanted clear? He'd give it to her:

"I think we should get married."

He braced himself, half expecting the sky to fall or the ground to split open or Audrey to bust up laughing. But strangely, the moment the words were out there, he knew it was the greatest idea he'd ever had, the best thing he'd ever said.

Audrey said nothing, so he pushed forward.

"You've said yourself that Brayden ruined the idea of marriage for you, and I've never particularly wanted it myself. But that doesn't mean we can't get married *our* way."

"Which is . . . ?"

His heart pounded harder. *She wasn't saying no.*

He forged ahead, desperate to convince her. "We enjoy each other's company. We don't get on each other's nerves. We understand each other. We look out for each other. We care about each other. Not to mention, neither of us would have to deal with friends pushing us into blind dates or parents setting us up with family friends, and Scandal Boy would be completely thrown off his game."

Audrey laughed. "I'm not going to get *married* because some Internet troll has it out for me."

"Why not? You got engaged for that reason."

"That's different. *Temporary.*"

She was right. It was very different. But he wasn't ready to back down. If she said no, fine. It's not like he'd walk away with a broken heart, which was kind of the point. With Audrey, there'd never be a risk of that.

Except . . . there was.

With the old Audrey/Clarke dynamic, their hearts had never been on the line, but now? Now he'd never wanted anything as badly as he wanted this.

"We're social people, Dree. We may have sworn off fairy-tale romance, but we're not meant to be alone, either. Tell me it wouldn't be fun to have someone to eat with every night. To have a built-in date to all these damned events we get invited to. To have a partner in life."

"We can be all of that without being married. We're already halfway there."

Clarke's heart sank slightly at the skepticism in her tone, but he smiled. "You know you can just say no, right? You don't have to spare my feelings."

Please don't say no.

"I'm thinking," she said, sipping her champagne. "I'm trying to figure out why it's somehow the craziest idea I've ever heard in my life, and yet it doesn't feel that crazy."

His heart lifted once again. "And . . . wedding at the Plaza?"

"What happens if one of us meets someone?" she asked. "I mean, I know we both think we're not cut out for that sort of thing, but we can't predict the future."

"Then we'll deal with it when that happens. We'd also probably win some award for being the most amicably divorced couple on the planet if it does."

"What about . . ." She hesitated. "The physical part? Would it be an open relationship? Because I know you, and you may talk a good game about someone to have dinner with, but you also want someone to . . . *you know* with."

An image of Audrey naked beneath him, her dark hair spread out on his pillow caused an immediate tightening of his entire body, and he nearly groaned as he faced the fact he'd been avoiding for weeks.

He wanted her. He wanted his best friend in ways that had nothing to do with friendship.

To deflect and distract, he teased her. "You can't say the word *sex*? You're twenty-nine."

"I can say it," she said with a stubborn pout.

He grinned. "Say it."

"I'll say it when you tell me where you'll be getting it in this little scenario of yours."

"Touché," he said. "Fine, I guess I hadn't really thought about that, but yes, we'd just . . . discreetly take care of business."

"Now who can't say the word *sex*?" she said smugly.

"We'd figure it out," Clarke said, realizing that he hadn't quite figured out the whole physical part of their arrangement, either, but not wanting it to deter the plan. "We always figure everything out together. You can't tell me that's not a solid foundation for a marriage. On top of an already rock-solid friendship."

"But you're not in love with me," she pointed out.

He hesitated. "And you're not in love with me."

They held each other's gazes for a long time, and she finally looked away with a breath of disbelief. "You're seriously suggesting this? Getting married?"

"Why not?"

She gave a startled laugh. "Because it's crazy. It's *beyond* crazy."

"Which has always been our favorite way to do things. I could get down on one knee if it would help?"

He started to move out of his chair, but Audrey held up a hand. "Don't you dare."

Clarke froze, then hopped off his chair as Audrey came around the table and flung her arms around his neck. "Let's do it. Let's get freaking married."

He laughed along with her, more certain than ever that the craziest idea of his life was also his best one.

Chapter Eighteen

I'm sorry, but are we in *The Matrix*?" Naomi asked. "*What* is going on here?"

Claire looked as stunned as Naomi, though true to form, she was quieter about it, merely staring across the table at Audrey after she'd dropped her bombshell.

Claire finally found her voice. "You're getting married. At the Plaza. In a month?"

"To Clarke?" Naomi added, for good measure.

"Yup," Audrey said, taking a sip of her iced tea.

"Isn't that taking things a bit . . . far?"

"If we were just doing it for the reasons we got engaged—to thwart his mother, to get back at Elizabeth, to tell Scandal Boy and all of social media to suck it—then yes. That would be going a bit far," she said with a smile.

"So if not that, then why?"

"Oh my God," Naomi said, reaching across the table and giving Audrey's arm an excited squeeze. "You finally figured it out."

Audrey frowned. "Figured what out?"

Naomi opened her mouth, then jolted and glared at Claire. Audrey looked between Naomi and Claire, then narrowed her eyes at the latter. "Did you just kick Naomi under the table?"

"Certainly not," Claire said smoothly, reaching for a roll from the bread basket. "But, seriously, do tell us what's going on."

As if I know.

One moment Audrey had been trying to figure out how to tell Alexis Morgan that they wouldn't be needing her services after all, and the next she'd been watching Clarke hand over his credit card to reserve March 28 for his wedding date.

Their wedding date.

She was marrying Clarke.

It had been nearly a week since she'd agreed to his spontaneous suggestion, and she'd deliberately not told anyone, thinking—assuming—that she'd come to her senses, that she'd wake up one morning and realize how ridiculous it was, that she'd call him and they'd laugh at the insanity of it.

Instead, every day, things felt a little clearer.

She could *see* it. And not just the wedding, though that would be spectacular.

But she could see the *marriage*. She could see them having coffee together every morning. Planning the day ahead, giving each other pep talks when necessary, sharing a cocktail at the end of the day, arguing over what kind of takeout to order.

Claire and Naomi were waiting impatiently for an explanation, but all she could do was smile and say, "I don't know. I don't know how to explain it."

"Is it a marriage of convenience," Claire asked around a bite of bread, "or a marriage of . . ."

"Lust?" Naomi supplied hopefully.

"Definitely not the latter," Audrey said.

"Well, then what's the point!" Naomi said, throwing up her hands. "Why would someone get married if not for constant access to sexy times. Claire, tell her."

"It's a definite perk," Claire said slowly. "But you don't have to be married to have regular sex."

"Well, that's true," Naomi admitted. "I suppose I know that firsthand. But are you and Clarke doing the nasty?"

"No," Audrey said emphatically.

"So, you're, what, saving yourself for the wedding night?" Naomi asked skeptically.

"It's not that kind of marriage," Audrey explained quickly.

"What sort of marriage is it?"

"Well. I guess Claire's description of a 'marriage of convenience' is as apt as any," Audrey said, "though it's not so cold as that. But you always hear that the best marriages are the ones based on friendship, right? Everyone imagines that when they get married, it'll be to their best friend. And I realized, the only way I was going to get that marriage is if I marry Clarke."

"Friendship is an important element," Claire agreed carefully. "But it's not the only element."

"Right. Sex," Naomi said again.

"Would you stop with that!" Audrey said, unable to keep the exasperation out of her tone as she turned to her friend. "I hear what you're saying. I do. I know that Clarke and I aren't going about this the normal way. But we're not looking for the normal kind of marriage. We're not looking for what you and Scott have," she said, looking at Claire, "or what you and Oliver have."

"But—"

"No," Audrey said firmly. "I'm allowed to do things differently than you two. You are doing it differently from each other!

Naomi, you've been living with Oliver since before Claire even met Scott, and Scott and Claire are married. So why can't I choose *my* own path? I love Clarke every bit as much as you two love Oliver and Scott. It's just different."

"And you want different?" Claire's voice was gentle.

It was something Audrey had asked herself constantly over the past few days, and she'd finally settled on the answer.

"I want safe," she said quietly. "I want someone who will never hurt me."

"The way Brayden did," Naomi said astutely.

Audrey gave a jerky nod.

"I can understand that. I *do* understand that," Claire amended. "But as special as what you and Clarke have, are you sure you want to give up on all hope of romance? You're so—"

Audrey lifted a finger in warning. "Do not say I'm so young."

Claire pursed her lips. "Okay. I won't. But plenty of people meet the love of their life in their thirties." She pointed between Naomi and herself. "What happens two years from now if you get swept off your feet in Food Emporium?"

Audrey's nose wrinkled. "Why would I be in Food Emporium?"

"Fine, then with the Citarella deliveryman," Claire said, referring to the fancy grocery store Audrey preferred. "You know exactly what I'm asking, and you're avoiding it."

Audrey sighed. "I know. And look, we talked about it. If one of us meets someone who we can't live without, we'll deal with it. But why would I just sit around lonely on the off chance that might happen, when I could have something really lovely and wonderful now?"

"Audrey." Naomi's face softened. "You're lonely?"

Audrey swirled the ice around in her glass. "A little, yeah. I mean, you have Oliver. Claire has Scott. We all get together plenty, but most of my nights are pretty solo. It's not like I have any prospects on the horizon, and my romantic history is dismal at best."

"And people do get married for worse reasons all the time," Naomi granted.

"Yes!" Audrey said excitedly. "See!"

"Okay, I can't believe I'm doing this," Claire said, "but I'm jumping on Naomi's bandwagon here for a second, and I'm going to ask the intrusive question. Is this a friends-with-benefits situation? Like, how does the living situation work?"

"We'll live together," Audrey said. "I don't know whose house yet. But separate bedrooms."

"So *no* on the benefits, then?"

"No. Clarke doesn't see me that way."

Naomi's blue eyes went wide. "Interesting choice of words."

"Yes," Claire murmured. "It *is* an interesting choice of words."

"How—"

"You said *he* doesn't see *you* that way. You made no mention of how you see him."

"Of course I don't—" Audrey broke off, thinking of Clarke's kisses, first at the engagement dinner, then at the cake shop. They'd thrown her off balance. The kiss at the ski lodge, though, had straight up knocked her off her feet.

If she were really honest with herself, could she say that she wasn't affected by him as a man? That she hadn't been thinking about him way too often, wondering what it would feel like if she and Clarke ever kissed for real? Could she deny that sometime in the past couple of weeks he'd gone from being *just Clarke* to the guy who gave her butterflies every time their hands brushed?

Putting her elbows on the table, Audrey frowned and dropped her face into her hands. "When did he get so hot?"

"He has always been hot," Naomi said, putting a sympathetic hand on Audrey's back. "You've just buffered yourself really well against it."

"Well, what changed?" Audrey wailed. "I want my buffer back."

Claire reached for her left hand, flicking the diamond engagement ring good-naturedly. "*This* has a way of changing things. It was bound to happen. By pretending to see Clarke in a different way, it forced you to actually see him that way."

"So how do I undo it?"

"Well, you don't *marry* him," Claire said in exasperation.

"No, no, hold on, I think this is workable," Naomi said. "I mean, what if you did propose the friends-with-benefits situation? Would it be so crazy? You're both beautiful. You trust each other. The sex could be epically fun."

"It could also be epically disastrous," Audrey said. "Claire, what do you think?"

Claire winced. "Um, do I have to answer? I'm still trying to wrap my head around the fact that in a month, you'll be Mrs. West. Or are you keeping your name?"

"I'll keep it," Audrey said. "Over a million people know me as @TheAudreyTate. It's *literally* my job to be her."

"And you don't think they'd follow @TheAudreyWest?"

"Huh," Audrey said, tilting her head. "I'd never thought of it, but that doesn't sound bad, does it?"

"It doesn't. But I think you have plenty of time to figure it out," Naomi said.

"Does she?" Claire asked doubtfully. "Her engagement's now moving at warp speed."

"Oh please," Audrey said. "You literally went to Paris as a single woman and came back married a week later."

Claire grinned. "That's true. Best decision of my life, too."

"Well, this is the best decision of my life," Audrey said. "So there."

She picked up her menu, wanting—*needing*—a break from the conversation, but she didn't miss the concerned look her friends exchanged.

She understood. The three of them had made a pact, and she knew they saw it as their duty to look out for her romantic interests, just as she'd looked out for theirs. Audrey just hoped they could understand that all situations were not created equally.

They'd made an agreement to help protect each other from scoundrels, yes. But there were different ways of doing that. With Naomi, it had been helping to expose one scoundrel so that she could see what was right in front of her—Oliver. With Claire, it had been helping her friend see that all men weren't like Brayden, and that some, like Scott, were pretty damn great. And absolutely perfect for her.

But Audrey didn't fit into either category. She hadn't given up on love. She didn't think *all* men were cheats. She just knew that with the big kind of love came big risks, and she didn't think she could survive another Brayden. Or at least her heart couldn't.

So, yes, she knew from the outside, she and Clarke sounded crazy. Even on the inside, it was a little bit nuts. But it was safe. *He* was safe.

Clarke was the only man who'd always been simply Audrey's, no one else's.

But now she just had to figure out how not to want him so that she didn't lose him.

Chapter Nineteen

"I'm still not understanding why I need to be here?" Clarke said, feeling uncomfortably large and, well, male, in the decidedly feminine space.

"It was part of the deal," Audrey said, picking up something that looked like a pile of hot-pink string and setting it back down again. "The store's giving me an entire trousseau on the house. In exchange, I document the shopping process. With my lover."

She blew him a kiss, and Clarke pretended to bat the kiss away. "What the hell is a trousseau?"

"It's an old-fashioned phrase," an approaching saleswoman said. "It refers to the articles of clothing that a woman would bring into her new marriage. Including, but not limited to, the unmentionables."

Clarke would love nothing more than to not mention the bras and thongs that were currently surrounding him. He'd love even more to not think about Audrey wearing any of them.

"So, where do we start?" Audrey asked cheerfully. "Bras? Panties? Teddies?"

Clarke's pulse raced in panic until he realized she was talking to the saleswoman, not him. Nope, cancel that. His pulse was racing regardless.

He looked around the store frantically. No windows. Why were there no windows?

"Why don't you two make yourselves at home back in the sitting area? My name's Michelle, and I'd love to bring out some things that you'll like. Both of you," she said with a playful wink toward Clarke.

He knew he was supposed to smile. Knew that he *should* smile. And though he was pretty sure he managed to show his teeth, the look she gave him was somewhat concerned.

Clarke refused to look at Audrey lest he give himself away, but it was probably too late for that. He was practically sweating.

"We've got a fridge in the back with some champagne, white wine, and beer. Can I bring you two anything?"

"Ooh, a glass of white sounds lovely. Is it too early?"

Clarke didn't care what the hell time it was. "Beer. Please."

He'd have preferred something stronger at the moment, but he'd take what he could get.

The saleswoman told them to take their time browsing, make note of anything they liked, and then head to the back and get comfortable.

His blood pressure slightly more under control, Clarke glanced over at Audrey only to have his pulse spike all over again. "What are you doing?" he said, putting a palm over her phone to block the lens pointed at him.

"Clarke! This is part of the deal! We have to take pictures of the whole experience." She gave him a bemused look. "What is with you?"

"What do you mean?"

"You know exactly what I mean. You look like you're about to be violently ill on that table of very expensive panties."

His eyes squeezed shut. "You know how when we started this, I banned you from using the word *vagina*?"

"Sure. Rather immature, but I've honored it."

"I'm adding *panties* to the list."

She rolled her eyes, unimpressed. "Don't be that guy. What else would you have me call them? Underwear? Wait, no. Are you an underpants guy? As in, 'Hey baby, let's get you out of those underpants.'"

Dear God.

"I don't know. I guess I don't . . . refer to them."

"So, what, we can discuss guys' boxers versus briefs, no big deal, but the women's equivalents are unmentionable? Hey! I bet that's where they got that name. I'm putting that in a story," she said, pulling her phone out of his grip and opening up Instagram.

She looked up from her phone when she was done, her expression softening slightly. "Okay, no joke, you're really not looking like yourself. What's wrong?"

"Nothing," he said, resisting the urge to run a hand over his forehead to check for sweat. "Just feeling a little out of my league."

"Out of your league?" she asked skeptically. "I was under the impression that you were rather proficient at this."

"Lingerie shopping? Hardly."

"Well, not the shopping part, but the product itself." She spread her hands wide and gestured around the swanky store. "You can't tell me you haven't seen plenty of the goods out in the wild. Don't underestimate how many mornings I've stopped by your place before we headed to brunch and found Saturday-night's companion lingering around wearing *very little*."

"Not my fault women never leave when you want them to leave," he muttered.

She tugged at the end of her ponytail, looking suddenly nervous as she studied him. "Are you going to say that about me?"

"What?"

"Well, I mean, we haven't really talked through any of the logistics of this. I was imagining we'd be living under the same roof—"

"Of course we will," he said, frowning. It was what he was most looking forward to, if he were being honest. His home always felt most *right* when Audrey was in it. More alive, somehow. And for that matter, it didn't have to be his house. He had the same sense of ease and rightness when he was at hers. Almost as though home was wherever Audrey was.

He promptly winced at the saccharine clichés of his own brain.

"Well, if you can't wait for those women to leave on Sunday mornings, how are we going to be any different?"

"Well, for starters, because it's us," he said, trying not to feel bothered by the fact that she'd put herself in the same category as his one-night stands, or even his five-night stands. Did she not realize that she was different?

"Hey." He moved slightly closer, not wanting to be overhead. "Are you having second thoughts? You know you can back out anytime, no hard feelings."

She let out a breathy laugh. "You realize how crazy that

sounds, right? A groom telling his bride there will be no hard feelings if she backs out of the wedding?"

"Which is what makes our situation so perfect," he said, reaching for her hands, almost without realizing he was doing so. "We care about each other's happiness. You being happy is what matters most to me."

"Same," she said, giving his fingers a quick squeeze. "But." She leaned in. "It doesn't explain why you're acting like a nervous virgin in here."

Clarke barked out a quick laugh. "I am, aren't I?"

She arched her eyebrows with a silent *mm-hmm* expression.

"Honestly?" he said, glancing around at the walls covered in tiny bits of lace and silk. "I haven't spent much time in lingerie stores. I'll confess I feel completely out of my element."

"I suppose," she said thoughtfully, pulling her hands away from his, picking up a peach-colored thong, and giving the elastic a very gentle tug, "that it must be different seeing all the unmentionables in their original habitat and not being peeled off some woman's naked body."

Clarke felt heat rush from his face to his groin, immensely grateful that Audrey was staring thoughtfully around the store and not at him, because his body's response to her words was immediate and unrestrained.

His brain's response was panicked.

Because the naked body that had flashed through his mind at her words wasn't some faceless woman of his past. It was Audrey.

Clarke dragged a palm over his face, grateful when Michelle returned with a beer and glass of wine in hand. "See anything you like?" she asked with a smile, handing Clarke the beer.

He managed an inarticulate grunt.

"You'll have to excuse my fiancé," Audrey said with a reassuring smile at the saleswoman. "His testosterone's flaring up."

Michelle laughed. "It's a very feminine space. We sometimes joke about putting a flat screen in the back just to make the guys feel more at ease."

Clarke didn't need a flat screen. He needed a cold shower.

He followed Audrey and Michelle to the back of the store. The two women were discussing panty lines, and before he could order his eyes to keep to themselves, his gaze dropped to the backside of the brunette he would be marrying in a month's time.

Interesting that after all these years being her friend, he'd never noticed how shapely her butt was, how perfectly—

"Clarke?"

He dragged his eyes back up, saw that she was looking over her shoulder at him with a puzzled look on her face. "Michelle asked if we had any plans for the honeymoon. I was telling her you'd insisted it be a surprise."

Clarke had insisted on no such thing. He and Audrey had never talked about a honeymoon, but he was sure as hell thinking about it now. Thinking about her in a tiny bikini or one of the skimpy white nightgowns in the front window of the store or wearing nothing at all . . .

He shook his head. This had to stop. It was Audrey, for God's sake.

Realizing both women were waiting for his response, he grinned, hoping it looked more normal than he felt. "Dree, if this is your way of snooping for details . . ."

"Told you," Audrey said with a dramatic sigh for Michelle. "He won't give me even a hint."

After Michelle had turned away, Audrey gave him a quick wink. She knew full well that he wasn't planning a honeymoon and was merely looking for him to play along to get out of the conversation.

But suddenly he *was* thinking about it. Why shouldn't they go on vacation together? Maybe Paris in April or some Greek villa.

The back area of the store was even more feminine than the front, if that was possible. A large, circular pale pink tufted couch was in the center of the room, beneath an enormous chandelier. Positioned around the seating area were dressing rooms, with heavy pink curtains that could be pulled for privacy.

"Okay, if you two want to have a seat here," Michelle was saying. "I'd already set a few things aside for you before you got here, but after seeing you in person, I've got a few more ideas. That long dark hair is going to look so fabulous against our white bridal line."

Clarke began shifting awkwardly in the chair, trying to get more comfortable.

"Give me just a minute," Michelle was saying. "Feel free to make yourselves at home, take pictures, whatever you want."

Audrey already had her phone out and was taking a video of the sitting area. He noted she was using the lens he'd gotten her for Valentine's Day and felt a surge of happiness around his increasing panic that he couldn't sort out his own emotions.

"Clarke, look like you want to be here," she instructed when the camera pointed at him. He lifted his beer and smiled dutifully.

"Perfect." She came toward him and, flopping on the couch beside him, held the camera out to take a selfie. "Smile! Oh wait, hold on. Shoot, this is why people have selfie sticks."

He sat patiently for about twenty seconds as she tried to find an angle that would capture both of them before setting his beer on a fussy-looking side table and taking the phone out of her hand. "Longer arms."

They'd taken selfies dozens of times over the years— hundreds—and he was used to her body pressed against his side, her cheek near his, but those were *friend* selfies. And though she was still his friend, and though their engagement was not a typical one, that pose didn't feel like enough.

Now, urged by some unidentifiable need, Clarke wanted something different. He craved something more. Not that he could tell her that. He glanced down at Audrey. "How's the Scandal Boy situation?"

She shrugged. "There've been a few subtext jabs about bets being placed on when a certain vain socialite and her BFF beard will back down and admit their 'wedding' is a joke, but nothing too nasty."

It was the only excuse he needed.

Reaching down, Clarke hooked his hand beneath her calves and scooped her legs up so they dangled over his. She yelped as she was thrown off balance and laughed as she looped an arm around his neck to balance herself. "Way to sell it, *honey*."

He grinned back. "Look in love, *pookie*."

She pressed her cheek to his as he snapped a couple of pictures of them hamming it up, surprised when he felt her head move, her lips press to his cheek.

He snapped the picture as she made a smacking noise, a playful kiss. A friend kiss. And again, Clarke was plagued with that pesky, inconvenient craving for *more*.

Before he could talk himself out of it, Clarke turned his face toward Audrey, his mouth capturing hers. She stilled in surprise but recovered more quickly than before, her lips parting beneath his almost immediately, allowing him to deepen the kiss.

So he did. Nudging her lips farther apart with his, Clarke let his tongue brush hers, playfully, experimentally, seeing how she'd react. How *he* would.

His own reaction was immediate. His body ached to do what his brain envisioned: lean her back on the cushion, discover what she was wearing under the pink sweater, learn the feel of her. The taste of her . . .

"Okay, so we— Whoopsie!" Michelle said with a laugh as she came back into the room.

Audrey pulled her mouth from Clarke's, and his fingers immediately pressed into her back, wanting to bring her back to him. Instead he slowly, reluctantly released her, letting her laugh and smooth over Michelle's interruption, not seeming the least bit embarrassed that they'd been caught making out in public.

And why should they be? Engaged couples were notorious for not being able to keep their hands off each other, and the entire nature of the store itself was a guarantee for a very naughty honeymoon.

A honeymoon that wouldn't happen. Or at least, wouldn't involve sexy delights like Audrey wearing tiny amounts of lace and nothing else.

Clarke reached for his beer and tried to pay attention to Michelle's rambling about the various cuts of their new Moulin Rouge line, when all he really wanted to do was hand the woman his credit card, tell her they'd take all of it, and drag Audrey home for a fashion show all their own.

Christ. Clarke tipped the beer back, wishing it were colder and stronger. *Get it together, man. It's Dree.*

"Well, I have my work cut out for me," Audrey said as she picked up her wineglass and headed back to the dressing room after Michelle had left them alone once again.

"Oh, phone," she said, coming back to him and holding out her hand.

He put it in her palm, and she began scrolling through as she headed into the dressing room.

She pulled the curtain closed, then popped her head out a second later.

"Clarke!" She held up the phone in exasperation. "You didn't get a single shot of us kissing! That would have knocked Scandal Boy down a peg or two."

"Sorry, babe," he said off-handedly, pulling out his own phone as though he hadn't a care in the world. As though he weren't shaken to his core that his reasons for kissing her had nothing to do with Scandal Boy and everything to do with the fact that he wanted her naked. And he wanted her to want him back.

Chapter Twenty

*A*udrey shut her laptop and stood, pressing her hands to the small of her back and arching backward, as she wondered if it would be a good idea to do some yoga to loosen up after a full day of sitting at the computer.

She'd just launched a new wedding resources section on her website, her brain already bursting with ideas for its future, even after her own wedding. She could interview other brides and keep in touch with the Wedding Belles to promote new venues and vendors. The Pinterest possibilities alone were mind blowing.

Someone knocked at her door, and she went to answer it, fully expecting it to be Clarke with takeout.

But it wasn't Clarke.

"Elizabeth," Audrey said, surprised by the sight of Clarke's ex-girlfriend standing on her front porch. "Come in."

"Thanks," Elizabeth said. "I'm really sorry to intrude like this. I got your address from Linda—"

"Clarke's mom gave you my address?" That couldn't be good.

Elizabeth nodded. "I should have called, but some things are best said in person. And I was afraid if I asked permission to come over, you'd tell me no, which would entirely be within your rights . . ."

Audrey's eyebrows lifted. Elizabeth was floundering, something she didn't imagine the cool, composed Elizabeth was accustomed to. "Here, let me get you a drink. Tea? Coffee? Wine?"

"No," Elizabeth said quickly as Audrey moved toward the kitchen. "This will be quick. I just need two minutes."

"All right." Audrey clasped her fingers loosely in front of her and waited.

Elizabeth exhaled. "I wanted to say that I'm sorry. Truly, very sorry."

"For . . ."

Audrey had a good idea what for, but she was curious about Elizabeth's take on the past couple months.

Elizabeth's smile was tight. "For trying to steal your fiancé."

"Ah," Audrey said lightly. "That."

"I know this is no excuse," Elizabeth said, rushing, "But to be honest, when I first moved back, when you and Clarke first announced you were engaged, I thought—"

"You thought it was a joke."

"I did," Elizabeth admitted. "Linda mentioned that you had had a couple of false engagements in the past, and I figured Clarke was just trying to make a point to Linda, or you were trying to do damage control on your reputation."

Audrey hid her wince. She had to give Elizabeth credit for hitting the nail right on the head.

"I figured I'd just wait it out, that you would tire of the

charade, that Clarke would have won the game he and his mother are playing constantly."

"And you figured you'd be there when it ended."

"Yes," Elizabeth admitted. "I was trying to prove to Clarke that I was in it to stay this time. Honestly, I'm a little embarrassed to admit I was even trying to prove that I could play along. I wanted him to see that I could fit into your weird friendship. I don't mean weird," she amended quickly.

"It's a little weird," Audrey admitted with a smile, throwing her a bone.

Elizabeth didn't smile back as she held Audrey's gaze. "But it's not just a friendship anymore, is it?"

A knot of dread formed in Audrey's stomach as she looked at the other woman. Elizabeth had never had soft features, and unsmiling as she was now, she looked as implacable as ever. Except the eyes. Her hazel eyes were unguarded, her pain unfiltered.

Instead of answering Liz's question, Audrey flipped it back around on her, wanting, or perhaps needing, to hear the full truth.

"You love him," Audrey said quietly. "It wasn't a game for you."

"No," Elizabeth admitted. "It wasn't. Clarke wasn't the primary reason I moved back to New York, but he was definitely a part of the decision. I didn't realize until I got to DC that I'd made a mistake by not appreciating him."

No, you didn't, Audrey couldn't help but think, even as she stopped herself from saying it aloud. *You didn't see that he tried to change for you, and he's the last person in the world who needs changing, because he's perfect, just the way he is.*

"Clarke brought out the best in me," Elizabeth continued.

"And I thought, hoped, I brought out the best in him, too. I asked Linda to just help get me some face time with him."

Audrey gritted her teeth to keep from pointing out that a grown man's mother had no place getting involved in her son's romantic relationships.

"But I was wrong," Elizabeth said with a sad smile. "Linda was wrong. Maybe we *did* balance each other out, but that's not what Clarke needs."

"No?" Audrey asked cautiously.

Elizabeth shook her head. "I didn't realize it until I saw the way he looked at you the day of the ski trip. Not until I accidentally stumbled upon you two kissing in the hallway."

"Wait," Audrey said, holding up a hand. "You walked in on us kissing?"

That wasn't right. Clarke had kissed Audrey because Elizabeth was already in his line of sight.

Elizabeth flushed slightly, clearly embarrassed. "I didn't mean to spy. I was going to head up to my room to get some ChapStick, and when I rounded the corner, you and he were . . . well, it's when I realized it wasn't a game. You weren't just pretending. And I wasn't what he needed. I probably never was. Clarke never kissed me like that."

"Like what?" Audrey couldn't help but ask.

"Like he'd die if he didn't kiss me. Like I was the only thing that mattered, the only thing he could see. I guess I always knew on some level that Clarke needed you. I just tried to convince myself when I came back that he needed me, too, but in a different way. I was wrong. I love him, but I love him enough to want him to be happy."

Audrey shifted uncomfortably, her conscience prickling at the fact that while she believed with her whole heart that Elizabeth and Clarke didn't belong together, it was also clear Elizabeth had the wrong idea about Audrey and Clarke. Which, when they'd started this, had been the point. But there was a difference between wanting to dodge a manipulative ex-girlfriend and standing in the way of another woman's happily ever after.

It's happening again, Audrey realized with a stab of horror. For the second time in her life, Audrey was ruining another woman's fairy tale. She'd first stolen Brayden from Claire. And now Clarke from Elizabeth.

Not that Clarke was in love with Elizabeth. Audrey would bet anything that he didn't feel the way about Liz that she did about him.

But what if he'd been given a chance to learn to love her again? What if Audrey hadn't been in the way?

All this time, Elizabeth hadn't been playing a game. It hadn't been about Clarke and Audrey versus Linda and Elizabeth. It had been Elizabeth fighting to win Clarke's heart, because she *loved* him. Like Claire had loved Brayden. *First*.

And once again, Audrey had been second, the other woman in the way.

"Elizabeth—"

"No." She quickly shook her head. "I don't want platitudes or sympathy. I just came here because I needed to apologize. And tell you how I never would have pursued Clarke like I did if I'd known how you really felt about him. So I'm sorry. Really sorry."

"But you've *always* known I've loved Clarke," Audrey said, even as Elizabeth was reaching for the doorknob. "We've been best friends forever."

"Oh, I know," Elizabeth agreed, stepping out onto Audrey's front porch. "I'm just sorry I didn't realize sooner that you were *in* love with him. But how could you not be. He's Clarke, right?"

She said this with a knowing smile, a shared understanding between two women who loved the same man.

Audrey hesitated as Elizabeth walked away, opening her mouth to tell Elizabeth she'd gotten it wrong, that her marriage with Clarke wouldn't be like that, that she wasn't in love with her best friend.

The words wouldn't come. Because her heart already knew they were a lie . . .

Chapter Twenty-One

*C*larke had just finished up an evening workout and didn't hear the knocking until he turned the water off in the shower.

He pulled a towel off the rack and ignored it. Not particularly in the mood for company following a tense dinner with his parents, he wasn't about to greet anyone unexpected while naked.

His mother had been entirely unreadable following his announcement that he'd be marrying Audrey for real, while his father was plainly pleased. And he was pissed at both of them for playing games that he suspected had more to do with irritating each other than they did with him.

Clarke dried off and, stepping out of the walk-in shower, knotted the towel around his waist and went to the vanity to shave, frowning when he realized the knocking at the front door hadn't stopped. If anything, it had gotten louder.

He checked his phone to see if he'd missed any urgent messages from Audrey or his family, but other than the usual slew of work emails, there was nothing to indicate that someone was that determined to get his attention.

Clarke reached for the shaving cream, then set it down again, curiosity winning out. He headed down the stairs.

He looked through the peephole and, with a frown, opened the door.

"Dree, what the hell?" he asked.

"Took you long enough," she said, brushing by him and stepping inside as he shut the door.

"You have a key."

"I forgot it."

"What about your cell phone?" he asked, arching an eyebrow.

"I forgot that, too."

"You—" Clarke broke off. Audrey's job was her cell phone. He couldn't remember the last time he'd known it to be more than an arm's length away.

"What's wrong?" he asked, giving her a quick scan for cuts and bruises, anything to indicate what she was doing here or why she was so out of sorts.

Other than the fact that she seemed a little frazzled and distracted, he couldn't see anything that would demand her urgently pounding on his front door. He also registered that he wasn't the only one doing a body scan. Her brown eyes skimmed over his bare shoulders and unclothed torso to the towel before they came back up to his, and she frowned.

"Do you always answer the door in a towel?" she asked, her voice testy.

"I wasn't planning to answer it at all, but I started to get curious about who in my social circle was part woodpecker." He smiled. She did not.

"Are you in love with Elizabeth?"

His smile dropped. "*What?* No. You know that."

She frowned and didn't look the least bit mollified. "I guess I do. But, Clarke, you can't just wander around in a towel after I move in here," she said. "There will be rules. You have to be fully dressed at all times. Same rules apply if you move into my place, if that's what we decide to do. And that's another thing, shouldn't we know by now? Whose house we're moving into? Shouldn't we know how we're going to deal with the fact that you apparently wander around in towels?"

His eyebrows lifted at her slightly incoherent babbling.

"I don't just wander around in towels, Audrey. I just happened to be wearing a towel when I opened the door for my best friend who's forgotten her key and her cell phone, *because I just took a shower*."

She continued as though he hadn't spoken. "And what about your women? What if *they* wander around in a towel, and you forget to mention that you've got a wife, except not a real one, just one who's there for companionship? Which, by the way, has gotten me thinking, do we even need to be married for that? If we're just doing this because we're lonely, because we enjoy spending time together, why don't we just move in together? We can be roommates without all the legal mess. Right?"

She finally paused to catch her breath, and as she looked up at him, it was the trust in her eyes that nearly undid him, the trust she'd always had in him to have all the answers, to do all the right things, to protect her.

He reached out and rubbed his hands reassuringly over her upper arms, giving her a quick grin. "Hey. What's bringing this on? If you're having second thoughts, you know you can just tell me, right? You don't have to worry about there being hurt feelings—"

"Shouldn't there be, though?" she burst out. "Shouldn't there be feelings in a marriage?"

"Of course there are feelings," he said, his hands stilling. "You know how much I care about you."

"I know," she whispered. "I care about you, too."

"Then what am I missing?" he asked, giving her the slightest shake in a desperate attempt to make it better. "What sent you running out of your house with no keys or phone and mismatched socks?"

She glanced down and winced. "I was in a hurry to talk to you."

"About?"

Slowly she dragged her gaze back up, but only as far as his Adam's apple. "About us getting married. Shouldn't there be . . . more?"

He swallowed, though it felt like a Herculean effort. "Do you want there to be more?" he asked roughly, needing to ask the question even if he wasn't at all sure that he wanted to know the answer.

Audrey was quiet for what felt like eons. She just stood there in her mismatched socks and messy ponytail, looking slightly bewildered but also strangely more determined with each passing moment.

Finally she looked up once more and took a deep breath. "I don't think I can do it."

Clarke let out a harsh breath, feeling as though his chest had just been shattered and the broken pieces were falling around his feet. "You don't think you can marry me?"

"Not the way we've talked about. I don't think I can have an open marriage. I guess I'm old-fashioned, but I can't be okay with calling you my husband, you calling me your wife, sharing meals and stories about our days, raising a kitten together, and spending Christmas together, but then also knowing some other woman is sharing your bed. I mean, what happens the morning after? The three of us have coffee together?"

She took a deep breath. "But I also realize I can't exactly ask you to be celibate for the rest of your life. *I* don't want to be celibate for the rest of *my* life."

Clarke's jaw tensed at the thought of Audrey being *non*-celibate with anyone but him.

"I have to ask you something," she blurted out.

"Sure," he replied cautiously.

"That day at the ski lodge," she said, her eyes locked once more on his throat. "When you kissed me . . ."

He voice was gravely. "Yeah?"

"Did you know Elizabeth was watching us? Did you kiss me *because* she was watching us?"

He knew what she was really asking. *Had he kissed her for show? Or had he kissed her for real?*

But he didn't know how to answer her. Play it safe and lie to keep them from going someplace that could destroy them? Or tell the truth and risk everything? It took him only a couple of seconds to realize there was only one answer. The truth. He owed his best friend the truth.

Clarke exhaled. "No."

"No, that kiss wasn't about Elizabeth?"

He shook his head and held his breath, feeling just about the most laid bare he had ever been in his entire life. "No. It was about you. Us."

Audrey took the slightest step forward and lifted her hand. It hovered for just a second before she slowly, purposefully set it on the center of his chest.

Clarke's breath whooshed out. "Dree."

Audrey didn't answer. Not with words. Instead she pressed her hand more firmly against him, laying her palm over his heart. Then she lifted her eyes to his, which held nothing but invitation and trust. She was too good for him. She was too good for everyone.

But Clarke was tired of fighting against what he wanted more than anything in his life. Tired of fighting something, he realized, he had wanted for far longer than he'd known.

He reached out and gently cupped Audrey's face, rubbing his thumbs over her familiar features, giving her plenty of time to step away, to change her mind.

When she didn't, he bent his head down and kissed his best friend. And this time, there was no doubt in either of their minds as to why he was kissing her. Or why she was kissing him back.

Breathless with wanting her, he tore his lips away from hers just long enough to nibble along her jawline, pressing his mouth to her exposed neck when her head fell back. "Be sure, Audrey. Be all the way sure."

Her hands found his waist, her fingers flirting across the knot of his towel.

"I'm sure."

Audrey didn't remember falling asleep. She definitely didn't remember making the decision to fall asleep at Clarke's place. But after she opened her eyes and registered the unfamiliar ceiling, the unfamiliar sheets, the unfamiliar alarm clock, she remembered everything else.

She remembered sleeping with Clarke.

With a quick glance to her left confirming that she was alone in the king-size bed, she lay on her back, and setting both palms against her stomach over the soft sheet, she drummed her fingers and waited for the crushing panic, the dread of having to look Clarke in the eyes now that she'd seen all of him and he'd seen all of her. Worst of all, she braced for the terror that nothing would ever be the same, that she'd ruined the best thing in her entire life.

She waited. And waited. But the emotions never came. Not the panic, not the dread, not the fear. Instead, she felt . . . good.

Audrey grinned. She felt great. The best she had felt in a really, *really* long time.

Ever? Nah. She was probably just extremely overdue for a little physical release.

She swung her legs over the side of the bed, deciding one of the benefits of sleeping with her best friend—no, her *fiancé*—was that she could use his shower without asking. She rummaged around until she found a fresh towel and helped herself to his shampoo and soap.

She drew the line at using his toothbrush, so she made do with her finger and his Colgate, then rummaged around in his dresser, coming up with a pair of sweatpants and a T-shirt that were way too big but more appealing than her clothes from the night before, which were . . . She scanned the room, saw her bra flung into the corner. She grinned at the memory.

Audrey skipped downstairs, still smiling, and it wasn't until she got closer to the kitchen and smelled coffee and breakfast that it hit her that she might be alone in this weird bubble of euphoria.

What if he didn't feel the same? What if he was thinking about how to give her the talk? To tell her that sex had been a mistake, that they should just pretend it never happened.

Or worse, what if he told her it had changed things irrevocably. *What if she lost him?*

Determined not to let herself go to the worst-case scenario without cause, she kept her smile firmly in place as she skipped into the kitchen. Or at least, as close to skipping as one could manage wearing a man's sweatpants, size large. Which was to say, she mostly shuffled.

Clarke glanced over from the stove and lifted his eyebrows. "Your followers are going to love this look. Does it have a name?"

"Walk of shame?" she supplied, going to the cupboard where he kept his mugs and taking down a navy-blue one that she'd picked out for him when he'd moved in.

"Shame, huh?" he asked, extending the coffeepot toward her outstretched arm and filling her mug.

His voice was casual and indifferent, but when he met her gaze, she knew he had the same reservations as she did. The same fear of rejection, the same worry that they'd made a mistake.

"Actually, scratch that," she said, cupping the coffee mug and smiling at him through the steam. She liked her coffee with a liberal dose of the chocolate syrup she ordered from a fancy French company. Clarke obviously didn't have any, but she could stomach it black when she had to. "No walk of shame here. Walk of satisfaction?"

His grin flashed in relief. "I was going to share the eggs regardless. No need to stroke the ego. Though if you wanted to stroke the—"

"No," she said, holding up a finger. "No sexual puns until I've had at least one cup of coffee."

"Fair enough," he said, picking up the spatula and stirring the mushrooms sautéing in a pan.

"Huh," she said, standing beside him and looking down. "It's weird to see you cook."

"I only do breakfast food. It's not a meal we've shared very often."

She leaned back against the counter and looked at him. His outfit matched hers, his sweatpants navy instead of gray, his shirt white instead of black. But of course they fit him a hell of a lot better.

A glimpse of her future, she realized. A lot of mornings just like this one lay ahead of her, and the thought made her almost unbearably happy, until something dark and worrisome began to lurk beneath the surface.

She looked down at her cup. "These are the cooking skills you picked up while with Elizabeth?"

He gave her a sideways glance. Curious, but not wary.

She shrugged in response. "You told me you learned to cook for her. To show off your husband potential."

"I didn't phrase it quite like that," he said, moving to the fridge and pulling out a carton of eggs. "But yeah. I used to cook breakfast for Elizabeth before she left for work."

Audrey felt an uncomfortable, unfamiliar stab of jealousy that she promptly shoved aside.

"Elizabeth came to see me."

Clarke's hand stilled for a moment, then he put the carton of eggs on the counter without opening it. "When?"

"Yesterday."

"Before you came over here?"

She shook her head. "No, Clarke. I had sex with you, waited until you fell asleep, got dressed, raced home, chatted with your ex-girlfriend, then raced back here."

He pointed a spatula at her. "Sarcasm in the mornings. This is my future?"

She smiled. "Having second thoughts?"

Clarke surprised her by reaching out and grabbing a handful of her T-shirt—well, his T-shirt—and hauling her toward him for a kiss. "Absolutely not. You?"

She smiled against his mouth. "Absolutely not. But about Elizabeth . . ."

He groaned and released her. "Fine. What about her?"

"I do think maybe I misjudged her—or we did. I thought she was just competitive, wanting what she couldn't have, wanting to prove that she could get you back . . . I dunno. I guess I turned her into a villain, and I don't think she was one."

She looked at her coffee mug once more, losing a little of her courage. "She's in love with you."

Clarke said nothing as he shoved the mushrooms around the pan, and Audrey looked up, watching him.

"You knew," she said quietly. "You knew that it wasn't just a game to her."

"I suspected," he said quietly. "Though I kept hoping it wasn't the case."

"Because you weren't in love with her."

Clarke set the spatula on the spoon rest without releasing it and stared down at the sizzling mushrooms. "No, I don't really do that kind of love."

The warmth of the kitchen seemed to escape the room. *There it was.* That was what had been lurking beneath their happiness all morning. She'd known when they'd started their game that he wasn't in love with her. And she'd known even when he suggested they marry for real that he hadn't been in love with her. She'd told herself it was fine, that she wasn't in love with him. That was the brilliance of this whole plan—they could love each other without being in love.

It had seemed so perfect, and now it just felt . . . hollow.

"Never?" she asked, keeping her voice light.

He turned to face her, his gaze curious. "The way I see it, if you're never in love with someone, you can never fall out of love with them. And if you don't fall out of love with someone, you can't hurt them. They can't hurt you."

She set a hand on his arm. "Clarke, you know I would never hurt you, right?"

"I know." He grinned. "Why do you think I want to marry you, woman? You know all my flaws and love me anyway, but you also know I'm no Prince Charming."

"Ah," she said, finally understanding him a little more clearly. "You can't fall off the horse if you're never the white knight in the first place."

"And you're smart, too," he said, leaning down and kissing her cheek. "Reason number 9,939 why I love you."

Love me. But not in love with me. Not now, not ever.

Which was what she'd signed up for. She knew the score. It's what she'd thought she'd wanted as well. To avoid being hurt like Brayden had hurt her. To remove herself from the dating pool before she could hurt someone else like she'd hurt Claire.

So why then did she so badly want to take Clarke's face in her hands and tell him that he deserved more? That he deserved to wait for a woman who did see him as the white knight, the Prince Charming, the hero of the fairy tale?

Because he was worth it, she realized. He was worth all the risk, all the pain. He was worth everything. He *was* everything.

She closed her eyes and let the realization that she'd been pushing back for weeks now roll over her. *Oh, Audrey. You are so in love, and so in trouble.*

Clarke grinned, oblivious to her thoughts. "So, bride, I've seen you naked, and it's an A+. The whole night was an A+, but don't think for one moment I didn't hear your slip of the tongue yesterday," he said, cracking eggs into a bowl and beginning to whisk them.

"What?" she asked, not following.

"When you showed up at my front door, you were babbling on about what married life would be like, and I definitely heard mention of a kitten, but now I'm thinking I heard that wrong. We're so clearly destined to be a dog family, right?"

She smiled at his use of the word *family*. Clarke would be her family. Her partner. They would have a cat, and sure, a dog, too, and every morning could be like this one.

It would be enough. It would have to be.

Chapter Twenty-Two

I'm not going to lie, I've been having regular nightmares that you were going to pick pink bridesmaid dresses," Naomi called from the other side of the dressing room. "I'm so relieved to be wrong."

"You look great in pink," Audrey protested.

"I look great in *some* pinks," Naomi said. "But there's a particular shade, not unlike the color of Claire's powder room, that makes me look like a sunset."

"Who wouldn't want to look like a sunset?" Claire asked indignantly, stepping out of her own dressing room. "They're everyone's favorite photo op."

"Not mine," Audrey said, already reaching for her phone. "*This* is my favorite, this moment. Oh, Claire, you look gorgeous."

"You get to take at least some credit," Claire said with a smile as she stepped in front of the mirror. "You picked the dress, and, well done you. It's beautiful."

"I know," Audrey said smugly. Despite her "wedding in a

hurry," Audrey had refused to rush any of the important decisions, taking her time to get her bridesmaid dresses exactly right. Whenever she'd planned her hypothetical wedding, she'd imagined her bridesmaids wearing something muted and soft to complement the whimsical fairy-tale version of her dream wedding. She'd toyed with the ideas of moss green, gentle lilac, glacier blue, a muted millennial pink that, for the record, would have looked lovely on Naomi, sunset and all.

Instead, she'd shocked herself by choosing . . . black. She wanted to be a princess, yes, but she was a Manhattan princess, and nothing said Manhattan like black. And nothing said Upper East Side like the ever-iconic little black dress.

She'd chosen a slightly different style for each woman. A daring V-neck for Naomi and a high-neck halter top for Claire that left her back sexily bare. Oliver and Scott could—and would—thank Audrey later.

She'd chosen a flattering one-shoulder cut for her maid-of-honor sister, who was still fretting about her post-baby body, and an assortment of sweetheart necks and edgy asymmetrical cuts for the childhood and college friends she'd asked to be in the wedding.

Naomi opened her dressing room, confirming what Audrey had already known. That, just as Claire's classic but surprisingly seductive dress suited her, the plunging neckline was the perfect fit for both Naomi's body and daring personality.

Audrey's wedding dress, though, was still under rush development with the designer, but if she'd gone a little unexpected with the bridesmaid dress, her own gown was almost an exact replica of her childhood dreams. Its bright white layers upon layers created an enormous ballroom skirt, and the fitted bodice was hand beaded with tiny pearls.

Audrey figured if she didn't get the fairy-tale marriage with a husband who was head-over-heels in love with her, she was at least having the fairy-tale dress.

Naomi and Claire obliged Audrey with photos for her Instagram Stories. Audrey was delighted that even with the artificial light of the dress shop, the photos turned out surprisingly well thanks to Clarke's thoughtful Valentine's Day gift.

"You look happy," Claire told Audrey.

"Hmm?" Audrey looked up. "Oh, I am. The photos turned out great."

Claire's smile was gentle. "I'm sure they are, but that's not what I meant. You look *happy* happy."

"She's right," Naomi said. "You've been glowing lately. This whole bride-to-be thing really suits you, even if your situation is a little atypical. And speaking of glow, is anyone as relieved as me that Scandal Boy's been keeping his mouth shut? I've been half expecting him to start whispering about this being a shotgun wedding, and I was ready to go Annie Oakley on his ass."

"Shotgun wedding?" Audrey said distractedly, sliding her phone back into her purse.

"You know." Naomi mimed a pregnant belly. "Old-fashioned cliché where the bride's dad gets the groom to the altar with a shotgun because the guy knocked up his daughter."

"Oh!" Audrey rested a hand to her stomach. "I didn't even think of that. Guess we're lucky Scandal Boy didn't, either."

She caught Claire watching her with a slightly narrowed gaze.

"What's that look?" she asked, giving Claire her own look.

Claire pointed at Audrey. "Your hand."

Audrey glanced down, lifting her hand and looking at it. "What about it?"

"When Naomi mentioned the rumor of you being pregnant, you put your hand on your stomach."

"So?" Audrey said with a laugh. "It's a rumor that doesn't even exist."

"Right, but . . ." Claire broke off. "Never mind."

"No, what?" Audrey asked curiously. "I was just surprised."

"Of course you were surprised," Naomi groused. "Since you're not having any damn sex."

"Except," Claire said slowly, "if she *weren't* having sex, she'd have merely laughed and rolled her eyes because the suggestion of being pregnant would have been *ludicrous*. Instead, she put her hand to her stomach, as though suddenly realizing it *were* possible."

Naomi's head whipped around to stare at Audrey, and she braced herself, knowing the gig was up.

Naomi gasped. "You *are* having sex!"

Audrey laughed and held up her hands. "Don't sound so accusatory, you've been the one ordering me to get laid for a year now."

"I know," Naomi said, looking alarmed. "But while I know your and Clarke's arrangement is very modern and all that, and I'm in full support, you can't possibly be okay marrying one man in a couple weeks while sleeping with another?"

"Um—"

Claire gave Naomi a good-natured swat on the back of the head. "Would you quit being so slow today?"

This time, Naomi caught on quicker and threw her arms around Audrey. "Oh my God. You boned Clarke. Finally!"

"She's so romantic," Claire said, even as she smiled at Audrey over Naomi's shoulder.

"We didn't bone. We just . . . okay fine, we boned." Audrey couldn't help the grin.

"How many times?" Naomi asked, pulling back and picking up her water bottle.

"Um." Audrey rolled her eyes toward the ceiling and tried to count. "Like nine times? Ten?"

"Damn, go you," Claire said. "Since when?"

"Tuesday."

Naomi spit out her water. "It's Friday."

"Yes, dear," Audrey said, unapologetically pulling Naomi's own scarf out of her purse and using it to mop water off the bridesmaid dress.

"You've had sex ten times since Tuesday?"

"Well, they *are* making up for lost time," Claire said. "But, Audrey, is this . . . are you guys . . ."

Audrey sucked in a breath, then let it out. "I don't know. I have no idea. It just sort of happened and it was good—"

"I bet it was *really* good."

"Okay, it was really good. And then it happened again. And then again."

"So now your marriage of convenience with your best friend to avoid the messy stuff involves sex. Isn't that sort of . . ."

"Messy?" Audrey finished for Claire. "Yes. Do I have any idea what I'm doing? Not really. Do I want to stop the sex? No. Do I want to stop the wedding? No. What does that mean? No idea."

"Oooh," Naomi said. "This is a doozy. Okay, Claire, babe, let's change out of these dresses. This conversation requires carbs. And possibly vodka."

Audrey sank onto a chair as she waited for her friends to undress and hand the bridesmaid dresses over, taking them up to the front of the store so they could be pressed and picked up on the wedding day.

"Where's Claire?" Audrey asked Naomi as her friend joined her.

"Bathroom," Naomi said distractedly as she wandered over to a dress in the window and tilted her head to study it. A wedding dress, Audrey noted. She'd never known Naomi to show the least bit of interest in anything that had to do with weddings, except as it pertained to Audrey's.

Interesting. And telling.

"It looks like you," Audrey said casually, going to stand beside her friend, testing her theory. "I could never rock that white leather accent at the hem, but you absolutely could."

"Do you think so?" Naomi murmured, shifting slightly to see it from another angle. "I've only been looking at ones with a narrow skirt, but I do love the way this one flairs without being goofy—"

Naomi broke off, catching herself but not fast enough. Eyes watering with happiness, Audrey pulled her friend around to face her. "You've *been looking at.* Naomi. Are you . . . are you and Oliver . . . are you engaged?!"

"Oh hell," Naomi grumbled, rubbing her forehead.

"What's wrong?" Claire asked, joining them.

Audrey looked at Naomi expectantly, since it wasn't her news to share.

Naomi dropped her arm, then gave a small smile that spread into a wide, glowing grin almost immediately. "Oliver and I are getting married."

Audrey made a squealing noise and pulled them both in for a hopping, awkward, three-way hug.

"How long? When did this happen? Why didn't you *say* anything?" Audrey demanded when a laughing Naomi extracted herself from the mauling.

"He proposed a couple weeks ago."

"Oh, Naomi. How'd he do it?" Claire asked, pressing her

hands together and resting her fingers to her lips, eyes watering like Audrey's were. "Sweet and romantic? Casual and cool? Huge spectacle?"

"The first one," Naomi said with a smile that softened her features. "It was . . . *perfect*."

"Details!" Claire pleaded as Audrey nodded in agreement.

"It was just a regular morning," Naomi said. "I'd gotten ready for work and come into the kitchen. Oliver was already there, already dressed. He handed me a cup of coffee, with just the right amount of creamer—"

"I love when they get that right," Claire said with an understanding smile. "It's such a small thing, but *so* romantic."

Audrey felt something tighten in her chest, realizing that she'd never had that kind of romance. Never had the chance to learn that sort of detail about someone. She and Brayden had rarely spent mornings together—he'd spent them with Claire, and she didn't think he had ever bothered to learn her coffee preferences.

She'd spent the night at Clarke's house twice now, making do with black coffee, no fancy chocolate syrup, and she was chagrined to realize that when Clarke had spent last night at her house, he'd had his coffee black that morning because it had never occurred to her to get milk for him. Because they didn't have that kind of relationship, the kind where you took care to make sure the other person had coffee just the way they liked it.

Not that either had complained—they'd both made do with black coffee, no big deal. But was that the future of their marriage? *Making do?*

"Anyway," Naomi was saying. "So Oliver hands me this cup of coffee, and out of nowhere he just says, 'I want to give you sunbursts and marble halls.' And I said yes."

Claire's arms dropped to her side in befuddlement. "Wait. What? What am I missing?"

"No, no, I know this," Audrey said, snapping her fingers, something tickling at the back of her brain. "It's familiar, it's familiar . . . Nope. I'm blanking."

Naomi merely smiled at their confusion. "It's from a scene out of the Anne of Green Gables series when Gilbert proposes to Anne. Sort of an inside joke, and honestly, it could not have been more perfect. It was a very *us* moment."

"Okay, well, I still don't get it, but I don't have to," Claire said, hugging Naomi again. "I am so happy for you."

"Me, too," Audrey said. "Though maybe *a little* mad that you didn't tell us!"

"I was going to tell you guys right away, I swear. But then you told me that you and Clarke were getting married for real, and Oliver and I agreed to wait until after to announce it. You two deserve to have your time in the spotlight."

"Yes, but—" Audrey broke off, not sure what to say.

"Don't be mad," Naomi pleaded. "You know I'd never intentionally keep anything from you two, but I really didn't want to steal your thunder. You've wanted to be a bride for so long. I wanted you to have your moment."

"No, it's not that," Audrey said, "I appreciate the sentiment. I'd like to think I'd have done the same if the situations were reversed. It's just . . ."

She felt her eyes welling and was embarrassed to realize that it was partially out of happiness for Naomi and Oliver, but also partially, shamefully, out of sadness for herself.

"Audrey," Claire said softly, putting an arm around her. "What's wrong?"

"Nothing," Audrey said, wiping her nose. "I'm so happy for

Naomi, but I'm just . . . she and Oliver! They're getting married for *real*, the fairy-tale love, like you and Scott have, and I thought I didn't want that. I thought I didn't deserve it—"

"Of course you deserve it," Claire said, sounding appalled. "You deserve it more than anyone I know!"

Naomi nodded in agreement, looking concerned.

"I don't," Audrey protested, looking at Claire. "I stole yours, Claire."

Claire frowned. "You stole my what?"

"Your fairy tale. You found your Prince Charming, and I took him, but he was *never* mine. I was so busy looking for the fairy tale, so selfish—"

"No," Claire said firmly. "I don't know why you've gotten this into your head, or how long you've been carrying it around, but I want you to listen very carefully. Brayden Hayes was *never* my Prince Charming. He was never any of ours. He was the witch, or the troll, or the monster in disguise, but never the prince. Scott is my prince. Oliver is Naomi's prince. And Clarke is yours," Claire finished gently.

Audrey wiped her eyes and looked between the two of them, admitting the truth she'd been running from for God knows how long.

She took a deep breath. "I think I'm in love with Clarke."

Naomi sighed and pulled her in for a hug, petting her head. "Oh, sweetheart. Of *course* you are."

Chapter Twenty-Three

*G*ood God, what is that?" Clarke asked, coming up to the kitchen table and looking over her shoulder.

She made a scoffing noise. "The seating arrangements. Obviously."

"It looks like you're planning a war," he said dubiously. "And that yellow is definitely going to annihilate pink."

"What?" she asked, writing a name onto a mini yellow Post-it note and tapping it against her lip, trying to figure out if she should place her cousin who couldn't go five minutes without mentioning the Yankees with Clarke's sports-loving colleagues, or with his own family who loved him but hated baseball.

"It just seems to me that the two lone pink guys don't stand a chance," Clarke said, pointing to the center of the poster board serving as her makeshift seating chart.

"That's *us*," she said. "See, we're at the center table, and everyone else—in yellow, just one color since I'm not differentiating our two sides—is at bigger tables situated around us. Honestly, you've been to like nine hundred weddings, how do you not know about the concept of the head table?"

"Huh. I guess I never really noticed the bride and groom."

"Wonderful," Audrey said sarcastically. "Your bride is such a lucky girl."

He planted an almost absent kiss on the top of her head. "As long as she knows it."

She knows it.

It was enough, Audrey reminded herself, the same way she had been for the past week and a half, ever since her breakdown in the dress shop. It was enough. It would have to be.

After a three-hour-long conversation with Naomi and Claire, she'd come to the decision that when you loved someone, you took them how you could get them. You loved them the way they deserved to be loved, even if they couldn't love you back in that same way.

Not yet, she reminded herself.

Guys can be dumb, Claire assured her. *Even the good ones. Give him time.*

Girls can be dumb, too, Naomi had added. *Oliver and I never would have gotten our fairy tale without a whole lot of patience on his part.*

Patience. She could do patience

Clarke was worth it. *They* were worth it.

"Dare I hope that the fact that the seating chart is in *my* kitchen means you're leaning toward living here after the big day?" he asked hopefully, wandering back into the kitchen for more coffee.

"Nope," Audrey said, resuming her sticky note planning. "But I needed a big table, and mine's currently covered in handwritten notes for the wedding favors."

"Right. Do you need help with that?"

She smiled. "Brownie points for asking. But you're off the hook, mainly because your handwriting is abysmal."

"Can you please write Mrs. Kerry and tell her that? She was always giving me crap about my penmanship, but I would like her to know that that particular lack of skill has served me well by getting me out of wedding tasks. I'd do it, but she wouldn't be able to read the note."

"Absolutely," Audrey agreed absently. "I'd love to! I don't have much else going on in the next couple of weeks. Just three dress fittings, figuring out my wedding makeup, finding a last-minute harpist since ours double-booked, finalizing the wedding programs, getting facials to try to ward off this pimple, and trying to convince my mom to go with the dress option that's not 100 percent glitter. I'm basically bored, so, yes, I'll make time to write your third-grade teacher and update her on your chicken scrawl."

"Yep. Sarcasm in the morning is *definitely* my future. More coffee?"

"Sure. Please," she said, distracted by trying to remember whether Clarke's friend Paul from college had neglected to call *Jess* Thomson after a one-night stand or *Jen* Thomson. Remembering incorrectly could lead to fireworks. She tapped her lip. She decided to put Paul between the two women and hope they'd all learned how to be grown-ups.

"All right," Clarke said, returning to the table, setting the coffee carafe next to her Post-it notes, and wrestling the plastic wrap off something. "Train me."

"Train you to do what?" she asked, not looking up. "I mean, I've got a list, starting with teaching you how to fold laundry in something other than a ball shape."

He shoved a small bottle in front of her face. "How much of this goop do you put in?"

Audrey glanced at it, then sat up straighter. "Where'd you get that?"

"Online," he said, lifting the bottle to his mouth and using his teeth to break the seal on the plastic wrap. The packaging was a bitch to open. Audrey knew from experience because she ordered it in bulk.

It was her favorite chocolate syrup. The kind she put in her coffee.

"Where online?" she demanded.

"From . . ." Clarke pulled the bottle away from his mouth and looked at the label. "However you pronounce this place. Their website."

Audrey's heart was pounding. "How'd you know the name?"

"Because I took a picture of the bottle last time I was at your house," he said, giving her an exasperated, puzzled look. "What's with the inquisition? Are you giving up chocolate or something?"

"No!" Audrey said, quickly swiping at her eyes. "No, it's just . . . I didn't realize you'd noticed how I drank my coffee."

"Of course I noticed," he said. "I mean, I don't support it. This stuff is so thick it looks like—well I won't mention what it looks like. But I figure since you've been at my place in the mornings a lot lately—Dree, why are you crying?"

"I'm not," she said, wiping at her eyes. "Just stress."

Stress. Love. Same thing.

He finally won his war against the plastic wrap. "Okay, you like a dollop, right? Like this?"

He dropped a small blob into her mug.

"More."

He added another blob.

"More," she said on a watery laugh.

"Seriously, Dree, this is disgusting. There, how's that?"

"Perfect. Absolutely perfect," she said. Then she leaned forward to kiss him. A distraction so that he didn't realize when she said *perfect*, she wasn't just talking about the coffee.

She was talking about the man.

Chapter Twenty-Four

*S*o nice of you to be able to squeeze me into the most momentous week of your life."

"Wow," Clarke said as he pecked his mom's cheek, then slid into the chair across from her at her favorite restaurant. "Passive-aggression before I've even put my napkin in my lap. A new record."

"Maybe if you'd learned to put your napkin in your lap promptly, the way I told you to every single night for eighteen years, you'd have beaten me to it."

"Eighteen years?" he mused. "Was that all? I seem to remember you nagging me about my table manners all throughout my twenties."

"And it looks like those lessons have finally paid off," she said with a serene smile. "After all, you're about to marry a lovely girl, take over the reins of an enormous company— Oh wait. Those two go hand in hand, don't they?"

"Huh?" Clarke asked, his attention on the menu, happy to

see they hadn't removed the cheeseburger. He set the menu aside and focused on his mother's words, then laughed as it clicked. "Ah. Dad finally let you in on his role in the game, did he?"

She sniffed. "Please. I've known for weeks now that your father tried to outplay me. I confess I'm a little surprised that he won."

Clarke took a breath out of habit to keep his temper under control. He started to go through the usual pep talk, reminding himself that it was rarely worth it to let his mom get under his skin, especially during his wedding week. But he was relieved to realize he wasn't even close to losing his temper. His mother aggravated him, certainly, but he found himself decidedly more amused and indulgent today. For that matter, he'd been practically walking on air for weeks now.

He didn't know if it was Audrey's infectious enthusiasm for all things wedding or because he was genuinely looking forward to Saturday or because he was regularly getting the best sex he'd ever had, with the best woman he'd ever known. Clarke had the distinct feeling that nothing could bring him down. Least of all his meddling mother.

Clarke grinned and helped himself to a sip of her wine, deeming it too oaky for his taste and picking up the menu to select a glass of red instead. "Dad didn't win shit," Clarke said.

"Lovely language, son," she said mildly. "And I'd say he most certainly did win. He got his way, didn't he? I bet on Elizabeth. He bet on Audrey, probably to spite me. And I confess, I didn't think he had it in him, to put his precious York on the line just to beat me. Nor did I think you'd go for it."

"Wait," Clarke said, laughing, and tossed the menu aside. "You honestly think I'm getting married on Saturday because I want the company?"

"Don't you?"

"Sure, of course, but not like that," Clarke said, a little offended by the notion that he'd get married simply to get a company or that he'd get a company simply because he got married.

"Then how do you want it?"

"Handed over because I've earned it," Clarke said. "I've worked my ass off for that company, Mom. I know you're pissed that I didn't become a lawyer, but surely even you can see that."

"I'm not *pissed* that you didn't become a lawyer," she said after a sip of wine. "I've only ever wanted you to apply yourself, to reach your potential."

"Sorry to disappoint you, as always," he muttered, picking up the wine menu once more.

"You haven't."

His head snapped up. "I'm sorry. That sounded suspiciously like a compliment."

Linda sighed. "You never make anything easy on me, do you?"

"Make what easy? You asked me to lunch. I said yes. So far I've gotten lectured about not putting my napkin in my lap fast enough and for marrying someone other than the woman you picked out for me, and *I'm* making things difficult for *you*?"

"I'm trying to apologize," Linda said stiffly.

Clarke sat back in his chair. "Wow. That's . . . new."

"Well, I haven't had much cause to in the past," she said, smoothing out the white tablecloth with her fingers. "But I can admit when I'm wrong, and I was wrong about Elizabeth."

"Wrong about her being the right woman for me or wrong about getting involved in my love life?"

"Both, I suppose."

"Wow," Clarke said again, genuinely at a loss for words. He

racked his brain, trying to remember his mother ever apologizing. He came up blank.

"Though I would like to state—"

"Ah, here we go," he said with a slight smile, surprised again when she smiled back.

"I would like to state that at the time, I really did believe Elizabeth was good for you. I knew that she hurt you when she left. I knew that you cared about her. You never got together, seriously, with anyone else after she moved. So when Elizabeth told me she was moving back, I wanted to be sure. I wanted to make sure you had a chance to decide what you wanted."

He shook his head, bemused. "Couldn't you have just *asked* if I wanted to get back together with Elizabeth?"

Linda gave him a droll look. "Clarke, I've known you for your entire life. When have you ever given me a straight answer?"

"True," he admitted with a boyish grin. "But then, when have I ever not done the exact opposite of what I thought you wanted me to do?"

"Very true," she said primly. "I made an error in judgment when I finagled you into lunch with Elizabeth, though I certainly didn't expect you countering quite so *robustly*."

"What, you didn't expect me to get engaged to my best friend?"

"I should have. It was what, the third time?"

He grinned, unabashed.

"I figured it would pass, the way it always does with you two. And then I realized I was wrong."

He smiled again, though this time it was genuine, one that came from deep inside, rather than the usual knee-jerk desire to provoke or charm. "Yeah. You were wrong."

"I'm glad."

Again with the surprises.

Clarke opened his mouth to ask for clarification but paused as the server came to take their orders. Clarke got the burger and a cab franc, his mom roasted salmon to go with her chardonnay.

"You're glad to be wrong?" he asked once the waitress had moved away. "Did I hear that right?"

"Well, I don't care to dwell on the sentiment," she said. "But as I said before, I want you to be happy. It was my initial goal in setting you up with Elizabeth, but I realized almost immediately that if you'd ever had feelings for her, they'd long since faded."

"When?" he asked curiously. "When did you know?"

"That night when we had you and Audrey over for your 'engagement dinner.'"

He snorted in disbelief. "Sure. If you knew that early, why'd you try to call our bluff with the engagement party?"

His mom merely smiled and sipped her wine.

Clarke's eyes narrowed. Then he sat up straighter. "You weren't trying to call our bluff?"

She met his eyes steadily, and Clarke's heart pounded.

"And with the wedding planner? When you set up that appointment, it wasn't to try to force our hand and get us to back out?"

"No," she said. "And when Gail Marea's daughter's engagement fell through, I offered to pay half of the Plaza's cancellation fee if she called and gave Alexis Morgan first dibs on the vacancy."

"*Why?*"

"You know that I've never really understood Audrey. She's always been a lovely girl, and I've appreciated her being such a good friend to you. But I guess, if I'm being honest, I never let myself acknowledge that she's no longer a flighty fifteen-year-old whose main preoccupation was how shiny her hair was. Just like I never let myself acknowledge that you'd grown well beyond your wild years."

"So you had an epiphany?"

Linda nodded. "That night at dinner. You were pretending to be engaged, I knew that. But then I saw you look at each other, just for a second. A casual thing, the way that couples do, and I realized. You were pretending to be engaged. But you weren't pretending to be in love. That part was real."

"No," Clarke said automatically. "It was for show. She was just trying to preserve her reputation, and I was trying to . . ." He trailed off, realizing how pathetic the reasons sounded, even to his own ears, how pathetic they'd always sounded. And all of a sudden, he realized just why he'd been in such a good mood the past few weeks. It wasn't just Audrey's enthusiasm for the wedding rubbing off on him or the fact that work had been going well. It wasn't even that he was getting regular epic sex. It was Audrey. It had always been Audrey.

"How did you know?" he asked, stunned. "How did you know before I knew?"

"That you're in love with her?"

He nodded. *He was in love with Audrey.* It was both the most momentous and yet somehow the most blindly *obvious* realization of his life.

She leaned forward and patted his hand. "Oh, Clarke. A mother always knows."

Chapter Twenty-Five

*Y*ou are the most amazing sister in the whole world," Audrey said as she undid the ankle strap of her busted sandal.

"Not even close," Adele said cheerfully, pulling off her own stilettos. "I've been feeling so bad that I've missed all your wedding festivities. I hope this will at least restore your faith in me as matron of honor."

"You flew in to be here, and you'll be standing by my side tomorrow," Audrey said. "That's all I need. Well, that and your shoes."

"I still can't believe your strap just snapped like that," Adele said, picking up the discarded stiletto sandal. "You're going to get a refund, right? They look brand-new."

"They *are* brand-new," Audrey said, glaring at the pretty but faulty shoe. "I'm just glad I chose them for the rehearsal dinner instead of the wedding. Can you imagine if I'd worn them tomorrow?"

"They'd have made a pretty crappy something new," her sister agreed, pulling a pair of flats out of her bag.

"Thank God you brought backup shoes," Audrey said as she slipped on her sister's stilettos.

"A habit I picked up during my swollen-feet-during-pregnancy phase, and I can't bring myself to break it. Blisters just aren't worth it."

"Oh, they so are," Audrey said, extending her feet and wiggling her toes, delighting in her sister's light pink satin pumps. They weren't quite as perfect of a match with the white Stella McCartney cocktail dress Audrey had chosen for the rehearsal dinner, but they had the distinct edge of not being broken.

"I owe you big," Audrey said as Adele picked up the broken shoes and stuffed them into her huge, but stylish, diaper bag.

"I'm just glad we have the same size foot," Adele said.

"Really? I remember you being not so thrilled about that in high school."

"Because my pesky younger sister stole my shoes without asking."

"Borrowed. I *borrowed* them," Audrey clarified, opening the bathroom door so they could head back to the party.

As was tradition, the groom's parents had hosted the rehearsal dinner, and Clarke's parents had gone above and beyond, renting out the entire rooftop bar of a brand-new hotel not even open to the public yet. Audrey had been pleasantly surprised that instead of a formal sit-down dinner, the Wests had opted for a buffet, allowing groups to mingle among all the elaborately decorated indoor and outdoor spaces of the rooftop. A different cuisine and band played in each room, creating a lavish around-the-world experience.

"You seem happy," Adele said with a knowing look as she and Audrey moved back toward the music and laughter.

"I am happy."

"You should be. Clarke keeps getting hotter each year. How is that even possible?"

"Hard to say," Audrey said. "We could ask Joel. He's a doctor."

"Hmm." Adele pursed her lips. "Let's leave my hubby out of this particular debate. If he asks, I don't even remember what Clarke looks like."

Audrey heard a familiar laugh and paused outside a partially open door to one of the private rooms. Seeing Clarke chatting with someone, she waved her sister on. "I'll find you later. I need Clarke to remind me of his old boss's name so Alton doesn't chew me out for not memorizing the company org chart he sent over."

Adele waved in acknowledgment, heading back to the party, and a smiling Audrey headed toward her fiancé.

Her future husband.

The love of her life.

She smiled. She may not be able to tell him yet, but she would someday. And someday, she felt in her heart, he would tell her, too.

Patience. Love is patient. Love is Clarke, however I can have him.

She stepped up to the door, listening for the other voice, wanting to make sure it wouldn't be an unwelcome interruption.

There was a quick barking laugh that she recognized as Alton's. Clarke's father didn't laugh often, but when he did, it was distinctive. She knew Alton wouldn't mind the interruption, since Clarke's old boss was one of Alton's employees.

"I *still* can't believe she one-upped me," Clarke was saying, and she heard the smile in his voice. "I was so sure I'd beat her at her own game."

Audrey reached out a hand to push open the door.

"You get used to it," Alton said. "And let's not forget, she beat me, too. I thought I was damned clever, coaxing you to choose Audrey over Elizabeth by offering you the company. That was supposed to be *my* checkmate move, damn it."

Audrey's hand froze, thinking—hoping—she was mishearing, even as she knew there was no way to misunderstand what she'd just heard. Alton had offered Clarke the company—something Clarke had been fighting for, for *years*—if he married her.

"In your defense, the company was a good bargaining card," Clarke said, taking a sip of his cocktail, and Audrey stepped to the side, not wanting to be seen through the open doorway. "Damn impossible to resist . . ."

Audrey pressed a hand to her mouth just in time to stifle the sob. She leaned against the door, trying to catch her hiccuping breath.

That's why Clarke was marrying her. Not because he was in love with her, though she'd known that. But she'd believed him when he'd said that he cared about her. That he wanted to spend his life with her. That they were good together.

It was a marriage of convenience. *His* convenience.

Don't cry, don't cry, don't cry.

But Audrey was a crier. She'd always been a crier. While plenty of women had stoically watched *The Notebook* and *Titanic* with proud proclamations that they "weren't criers," Audrey started blubbering in the opening credits, just knowing what was to come.

Tonight, however, she somehow managed to hold it together. For once, her body listened to her command not to cry. Her wobbling chin stabilized, the ache in her throat eased. The blur of the tears disappeared.

It was as though she shut down, from the inside out.

She calmly returned to the party, playing the part of happy bride even as she studiously avoided the groom.

It didn't hit her until much later as she lay alone in her bed, staring at the ceiling, her phone stubbornly turned to off, *why* the tears hadn't come. There was no point in crying over something that wasn't real.

Her Prince Charming was never coming. He had never even existed.

Chapter Twenty-Six

*A*nd that, my little man, is how you properly tie a bow tie," Clarke said to the ring bearer, sitting back fully on his haunches and admiring his handiwork.

The adult-size bow tie was far too large for Audrey's four-year-old nephew, but it had stopped the tantrum in its tracks, so Clarke was counting it as a win.

"You know that tinier members of the wedding party usually get the clip-on variety," Alexis Morgan said as she watched Stevie dash off to show his parents his new accessory.

"I do," Clarke said, standing and grinning at the wedding planner. "But his had an unfortunate run-in with the men's urinal."

"Ah." She gestured at his neck. "And so now the ring bearer has a bow tie, and the groom does not."

Clarke shrugged. "Stevie wanted it more than I did."

Alexis lifted her eyebrow. "That, and you knew I'd have a spare?"

He grinned. "I knew you would."

He expected her to smile back, or at least to talk into her fancy headset thing and have the assistant he'd seen running all over the place bring in the replacement bow tie.

Alexis didn't smile. And she didn't speak into her headset. In fact, looking at her more closely, Clarke realized for the first time since he'd known her that Alexis Morgan was uncertain and seemed to be trying to figure out the best way to deliver bad news.

Clarke's stomach dropped, his world tilting sideways. *Audrey.* He knew with complete certainty that whatever was wrong had to do with her.

An accident. There'd been an accident. An illness. Some freak sickness.

His words came out in a frantic rush. "What is it? Is she okay? She hasn't been answering my texts, but I figured she was just taking the don't-see-the-bride-before-the-ceremony thing to a whole new level . . ."

Before Alexis could answer, the door to the small room on the side of the church deemed "the groom's room" opened, and Scott and Oliver stepped in, looking even more grim than Alexis. The three of them exchanged a look that Clarke didn't understand, and Alexis quietly left the room without a word.

He didn't waste any time, his heart clawing at his throat. "What's happened? Is she okay?"

"Audrey's fine," Oliver said, holding up a hand.

"Well, not *fine*," Scott muttered.

"She's not hurt," Oliver amended. "Physically."

Clarke's breath came out in a whoosh of relief as he felt his world turn right side up once again, even as Oliver's clarification set off a slight warning bell. "Thank God."

"She's not injured," Oliver said again, "but she's also not here."

Clarke frowned. "What do you mean? Was there traffic? Do we need to delay? Is there some sort of wardrobe malfunction? Someone tell her she can get married in a garbage bag, for all I care."

"I bet you don't care," Scott muttered.

Clarke narrowed his eyes at Scott. Scott was rough around the edges, but he seemed downright antagonistic at the moment, and for that matter, Oliver didn't seem particularly happy with Clarke, either. Clarke frowned in confusion.

"She *was* here," Oliver explained, a distinct edge in his voice. "She did the whole bride-prep thing. Got her hair done, makeup done. She put on the dress, arrived at the church in a limo with the bridesmaids."

"And then?"

"She made it as far as the steps," Scott cut in. "And then she bolted."

The world tilted again, and Clarke stumbled back to a chair. "What do you mean she *bolted*?"

Audrey had left him? Didn't want to marry him? Forget Clarke's world tilting. That didn't even matter when it felt like his heart had been ripped out.

He shook his head. "I don't understand. She wouldn't have just bailed without telling me. We had a deal. Either of us could back out at any time, no hard feelings."

Hurt feelings, he realized. Very hurt. But not hard feelings. They'd have gotten through it, and eventually, he'd have been able to bury his feelings and pretend everything was the same as it had always been.

"You had a *deal*?" Scott repeated angrily, stepping forward. "Is that anything like the deal with your father?"

"Scott," Oliver murmured in warning.

"What?" Clarke looked between the two men, bewildered. "What deal with my father?"

"The one where you get a billion-dollar company if you marry Audrey," Oliver said, his eyes as hard as Scott's voice had been.

"What the hell—" He groaned. "Oh, *Jesus*. Audrey found out about that?"

His brain tried to sort out how, but then he realized it didn't matter. It only mattered that he find her, that he explain.

"Where is she?"

"We told you, she bolted."

"Where?"

Scott shrugged, and Clarke lurched across the room, catching his groomsman by the front of the shirt. "Where?"

"I don't know!" Scott shouted back, shoving at Clarke's shoulders. "But don't think for a second—"

Clarke didn't wait to hear his friend's lecture. He had no time for anyone or anything but finding his bride. He tore out of the suffocating room, ignoring the startled looks of the guests being escorted in by the ushers, and raced to the back of the church, scanning the crowds for Audrey, before charging outside.

There. Naomi and Claire looked unsurprised and decidedly displeased to see him. Naomi's blue eyes were spewing venom. Claire's gaze was ice-cold.

"Where is she?"

Neither woman said anything. Clarke took a step forward, but someone caught him by the arm. "Don't touch my wife," Scott snarled.

Clarke shrugged him free. "I wasn't going to touch your wife. I was going to *beg*." He turned back toward the women. "Please. If anyone knows where she's gone, it's you two."

"You used her," Naomi said, stepping forward and giving

Clarke an ungentle shove in the center of his chest. "She is the best person any of us know, and you used her. You let her think she was getting a happy ending, and all you wanted was a damn job?"

"Screw the job," Clarke shouted, not caring who heard him. "It was never about the job."

"Really?" Claire asked sarcastically. "Your dad didn't offer you the company if you married Audrey?"

Clarke ran a hand through his hair. "No, he did, but I didn't even . . . that's not what this is," he said, gesturing down at his tux, their formal wear, then back at the church. "That's never what this was. I honest to God didn't even think about it after he offered it. I should have told Audrey, obviously, but it was just so stupid, just some stupid game my messed-up parents played. You know what, I don't have to explain to you. I'll explain to her. Now, where is she?"

No one said a word, and Clarke fought the urge to roar at the entire lot of them, to tell him that the longer they stayed silent, the smaller his window to win her back became.

"What do you want?" he asked. "You want to punch me? Punch me. You want to kick my balls? Do it. But for the love of God, please just give me a chance to talk to her. *Please*." His voice broke. "I love her."

He was watching Claire as he said it, sensing she had the softest heart of the group, praying she'd understand. Her eyes widened infinitesimally, then narrowed. "Do you love her? Or are you *in* love with her?"

"Both. *Both*."

Naomi and Claire exchanged a glance, but they still didn't give him the answer he wanted. Needed. Out of the corner of his eye, Clarke saw his cousin and his wife getting out of a car, two daughters in frilly pink dresses in tow. His cousin, who was a jackass, was staring, and his wife, who was a snobby gossip, had her mouth gaping open at what he could only assume was his feral appearance, but he didn't care about either of them.

His eyes fell on the younger of their two daughters, a small blonde with twin ponytails at her ears. She was clutching a coloring book with a kitten on the cover.

Clarke moved quickly but gentled his motions as he approached the girl, lowering slightly so he was closer to her height. "Hi. Melissa, right?"

"Marisa," she said in a tiny voice.

Crap. Rough start.

"Hi, Marisa. I'm your dad's cousin. You remember me from the big boat party last summer? I snuck you a Coke? We promised not to tell your mom?"

She gave him an unimpressed look. Perhaps a lot of people snuck her Coke.

"Look, Marisa, I know this is a big request, but do you think I could have a page from your book there?" he asked, pointing at her coloring book.

She clutched the book closer to her chest and scowled.

"Clarke, what the hell, man?" his cousin muttered.

"Shut up, James," he snapped.

He saw the little girl's eyes go wide. "You're not supposed to say 'shut up.'"

He closed his eyes. "I know. I'm sorry. I shouldn't have said it, but I'm in a very big hurry to find someone."

"Who?"

"My—"

There were no words to describe what Audrey was to him. His world. His everything. His best friend. His love.

"His princess," Naomi said, stepping forward. "He needs to find his princess."

The word worked like magic on the little girl, and after only a moment's hesitation, she messily ripped a page out of the very center of her coloring book, and then, out of the tiny little purse draped over her shoulder, she fished out a handful of crayons. "What color?"

"Surprise me," he managed on a laugh.

"Pink. Perfect," he said, accepting the crayon and the torn piece of paper, and kissed the little girl on the cheek.

Then he kissed Naomi's cheek. "Thank you."

He reached out and spun Oliver around, setting the coloring book page against his suit jacket for a firm surface to write on.

Oliver, thankfully, stayed still, but Clarke didn't need long. A few words to get the point across and a messy scrawl of his signature in pink crayon. "Here," he said, thrusting the paper at Scott's chest, because he was closest. "Give this to my father."

Scott looked at the wrinkled, illegible piece of paper. "Does it come with a translator?"

"It's my letter of resignation," Clarke said, hearing Naomi's sharp intake of breath as he said it. "I don't want the company. Not like I want her."

Need her.

He turned back to the two women who had made a pact to protect Audrey from Brayden Hayeses.

"Please," he said quietly. "I'm not like him. I'm not Brayden."

I was never a Brayden. I want to be the damned prince.

Clarke thought the prolonged silence would kill him, until finally Claire spoke.

"I think I know where she might be."

Chapter Twenty-Seven

f Audrey could have managed a smile, she would have. Not a happy smile—she was fresh out of those—but a smile at the cruel little jab of irony.

Nearly two years ago she'd walked up to a church to say goodbye to a man she'd thought she loved and ended up here instead.

Today, she'd walked up to a church to say yes to a man she *did* love. Yet somehow, she'd ended up, once again, on a park bench in Central Park. The *same* park bench.

Audrey tipped her head back up to the sky, wishing for the sun to warm the chill coming from within her body. But her wedding day was cloudy, and there was no sun to take away the ache.

She couldn't do it. She'd thought she could, and sometime in the middle of a sleepless night, she'd even convinced herself that marrying a man for reasons that had nothing to do with love was tolerable. She'd convinced herself as she'd put on the dress, as she'd had her highlighter and lash extensions applied, as she'd sat and watched as a manicurist fixed the chip on her index finger-nail. It would be enough. Even being married to a man she loved who didn't love her back was more than she deserved.

But when she'd stepped out of that limo, it had hit her. She couldn't get married.

Not because she didn't deserve marriage. But because she deserved *more* than the marriage being offered. Audrey had been so focused on the damage she'd done to Claire and Brayden's relationship, and to a lesser extent to Brayden and Naomi's, that she hadn't realized until today that none of the past two years was about Brayden.

It may have been their simmering resentment and borderline hate for Brayden that had brought Naomi, Claire, and Audrey together, but it wasn't what had kept them together.

It had been love. Love had kept them together. Not love for Brayden, but for one another, three women who'd become like sisters.

And although Audrey cherished the love she had with her friends, she wanted real love, fairy-tale love. She was worthy of it. And she would wait for it.

Audrey exhaled and opened her eyes, taking in the fresh blooms of spring, the damp dirt from last night's rain, even the openly curious stares from people trying to ascertain why a woman in an enormous white wedding dress was sitting alone on a park bench and not crying. She was too numb for that.

She knew that Claire and Naomi would figure out where she had gone and come for her eventually, but for now, she was glad they'd given her space to think. Or rather space to try *not* to think about what Clarke must be thinking right now, if he was pan-icked about his father backing out of the deal or wondering . . .

Audrey had been so studiously ignoring the people trying to

pretend that they weren't staring at her that it took her a moment to register that one person wasn't pretending at all. He was staring right at her and began walking toward her with purpose until he loomed over her. She didn't move, not even when he slowly lowered himself onto the bench beside her.

Audrey turned her head and met the gaze of her best friend. "Where's your bow tie?"

He let out a harsh laugh. "I lost it. Only one of a couple of things I lost today."

"Oh yeah?" she asked casually, proud of how cool her voice sounded and the way it didn't waver, not once.

"Yeah."

She lifted her eyebrows. "Let me guess. You're missing a bride?"

"No," he said, his eyes locking on hers. "I'm missing my best friend. My soul mate. The woman I want very much to make my wife."

Her heart twisted traitorously in her chest at words a part of her was still thrilled to hear.

She looked away. "Right. So you can get your company?"

Clarke reached out and gently hooked a finger on the side of her jaw, drawing her face back around to his.

"No," he said, his voice tender. "Because I love her."

Audrey let out a small exhale.

Not enough, she reminded herself. Clarke had always loved her with the strong, everlasting love of a lifelong friend. She'd never doubted it, and she didn't doubt it now. But she wanted more. She wanted the wild, take-your-breath-away, risk-every-thing love.

She knew how she felt about him, and she knew she deserved nothing less in return.

"I was looking for you last night, at the party," she said quietly. "You were talking to your dad."

He closed his eyes, and when they opened, they silently begged her to understand. "I know what you heard, Dree. And I'm not going to tell you that my dad didn't offer me the job if I married you. I'm not going to pretend that my parents aren't completely messed up or that my mom didn't have one up on all of us the entire time, but that's not important right now. What is important is that the damned company had nothing to do with why I proposed to you that day in the Plaza. And it has nothing to do with the reasons I'm proposing to you right now."

Audrey's lips parted in shock as Clarke slowly lowered to one knee in front of her and clasped his hands around hers, his eyes gleaming with unshed tears.

"Marry me, Audrey. Marry me today, marry me next week, a year from now, ten years from now. I don't care, just promise me someday. *I need you,* Dree. I need you with every fiber of my being. I've needed you from that very first day on the playground. I know the way you tell the story is that I saved you from a bully, but the truth is you save me from myself every damn day. Marry me because I love you, not in the way a boy loves a girl, not in the way a friend loves his friend, but the way a man loves a woman. *Forever.* Marry me because I just quit my job, and now I need a beautiful Instagram influencer to support my unemployed ass—"

It was a good speech. A fairy-tale speech. Too bad she had to cut it off with a fairy-tale kiss.

Clarke's fingers plowed through her hair the second her lips pressed to his, and he kissed her like he'd never kissed her before. She kissed him back, pouring in not hours, not days, but *years* of love for the man who'd been her Prince Charming the whole damn time.

When she pulled back, she was a little surprised to find her cheeks wet, and she couldn't stop herself from laughing as he brushed away the proof that she wasn't numb inside after all.

"I love you, too," she whispered, in case her kiss hadn't been abundantly clear.

He let out a harsh exhale of relief.

"Marry me," he begged, kissing her again. "Will you marry me, Audrey?"

"Yes," she whispered against his mouth. "And if you don't mind a tearstained bride, I've got just the place in mind, right around the corner."

He smiled his familiar grin and got to his feet. She accepted his hand, letting him help her up, not caring in the least that her dream grown was rumpled and dirty.

All that mattered was that she'd found her dream man.

Epilogue

*L*ater that day, after a father walked his daughter down the aisle and a mother in sequins bawled through the entire ceremony . . .

After another mother dabbed furiously at tears that wouldn't seem to stop and another father tried to make sense of a scribbled pink note written atop a cartoon kitten that he would throw away and insist he never saw . . .

After a bride with a dirty hem and a groom with a missing bow tie said their vows and stole a few minutes just for themselves before joining friends and family at a picture-perfect reception at the Plaza . . .

After the cake was cut, the toasts delivered, the dancing begun, and the groom and two of his groomsmen stepped out into the night air . . .

Those three men smoked cigars and watched as the three women they loved snuck a few bottles of champagne into Central Park, sat on a bench, and made a pact.

To friendship.
To new beginnings.
And to the healing power of love.

Acknowledgments

*I*t's always a little bittersweet to come to the end of a series, but I couldn't ask for a better way to say goodbye to the Central Park Pact crew than with Clarke and Audrey's book. I know a lot of you were anxiously waiting for their love story from the very first time they appeared on the page together, and I was right there with you, anxiously awaiting the moment I could help them realize what I'd always known: they were perfect for each other.

This book was fun and easy to write, I suspect because I had an amazing support team. Editors are always an important part of the book process, which is why I was extra lucky to have the help of three on *Marriage on Madison Avenue*: Marla Daniels, who has been this series' biggest champion from the very beginning; Sara Quaranta, who seemed to have a sixth sense in helping me bring out Clarke's romantic side; and of course, Kristi Yanta, my editor for twenty-plus books now, who helped me develop this one into what she dubbed "the most Lauren Layne" of the series—and she's absolutely right. Thanks to all the help I got on this one,

Marriage on Madison Avenue is one of those books that captures all of the reasons I set out to write romance in the first place.

As always, the rest of the team at Gallery Books shows flawless expertise in taking my word jumble and making it comprehensible and pretty, as well as making sure it gets into the hands of as many readers as possible.

Lastly, to the rest of my "crew," my amazing agent Nicole Resciniti, fabulous assistant Lisa Filipe, my author friends, my nonauthor friends, my family, and of course, you, lovely readers, for making it possible for me to continue doing what I love.

Don't miss the rest of
The Central Park Pact series!

Available from

Don't miss Lauren Layne's hilarious and romantic standalone novel

The Prenup

Available from

HEADLINE
ETERNAL

Meet *The Wedding Belles*.
They can make any bride's dream come true.
And now it's their turn.

Available from

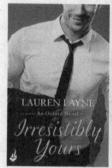

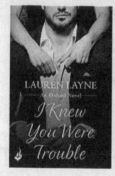

HEADLINE
ETERNAL

FIND YOUR HEART'S DESIRE...

VISIT OUR WEBSITE: www.headlineeternal.com
FIND US ON FACEBOOK: facebook.com/eternalromance
CONNECT WITH US ON TWITTER: @eternal_books
FOLLOW US ON INSTAGRAM: @headlineeternal
EMAIL US: eternalromance@headline.co.uk